Usta, the Sultan's favorite, led Jessica into the luxurious pink and green marble baths. She clapped her hands and two slave girls reached to remove Jessica's robe.

Jessica pulled back. "What are they going to do?"

"They will massage you . . . perfume you. Pamper you in every way."

"No! Tell them to leave me alone."

"This is a matter of manners—not morals," Usta said gently, gesturing for the slaves to continue. "The problem is in the way you've been raised. It's said the English have the finest women in Europe and least know how to use them. Perhaps that is why they choose to keep you so ignorant."

"But I'm not going to be the Sultan's toy."

"Oh, my dear, you are not here to dance or sing. You are here to learn the art of making love to a man . . ."

HAREM

HAREM

Diane Carey

Based on the screenplay by Karol Ann Hoeffner

with 8 pages of photos

A SIGNET BOOK

NEW AMERICAN LIBRARY

NAL BOOKS ARE AVAILABLE AT QUANTITY DISCOUNTS WHEN
USED TO PROMOTE PRODUCTS OR SERVICES. FOR INFORMATION
PLEASE WRITE TO PREMIUM MARKETING DIVISION, NEW AMERI-
CAN LIBRARY, 1633 BROADWAY, NEW YORK, NEW YORK 10019.

PUBLISHER'S NOTE

This novel is a work of fiction. Names, characters, places, and inci-
dents either are the product of the author's imagination or are used
fictitiously, and any resemblance to actual persons, living or dead,
events, or locales is entirely coincidental.

Copyright © 1986 by Highgate Pictures Inc.

SIGNET TRADEMARK REG. U.S. PAT. OFF. AND FOREIGN COUNTRIES
REGISTERED TRADEMARK—MARCA REGISTRADA
HECHO EN CHICAGO, U.S.A.

SIGNET, SIGNET CLASSIC, MENTOR, PLUME, MERIDIAN AND NAL BOOKS
are published by New American Library,
1633 Broadway, New York, New York 10019

First Printing, February, 1986

1 2 3 4 5 6 7 8 9

PRINTED IN THE UNITED STATES OF AMERICA

PART ONE

CHAPTER ONE

It was an American day. There was an English mist and English wildflowers in the English countryside, but it was an entirely American day. The doves and the horses in the stables knew the subtle difference. Even the pebbles bouncing off the window glass at Greyhurst Mansion chimed with a special bell tone today. As the sun reached up over the soft green hills of England, the pebbles continued to clink against the glass, one at a time, until the frilled curtains stirred and a face appeared.

A young woman shook out her blond hair and pushed the window open, already smiling. Her smile had not lost the feisty qualities of her teens, nor her eyes their glimmer of mischief as she peered down at the prim young man in riding clothes who stood beneath her window.

"Would Madame care for a ride before breakfast?" he called up to her, as properly as if he had met her at the door downstairs.

"Charles Wyndon," the girl accused, using his name as an epithet, "what are you doing up so early? I thought diplomats stayed in bed until teatime."

Charles grinned even wider at the sound of her voice, that clear, unaccented American delivery so unlike his own upper-class English twitter. He loved the melodic differences between their voices. He loved to talk to her just so he could hear her speak. Her complexion was the rosy pink of an English face, her eyes the blue of that sky just over the trees, but the sound of her voice was completely American, as wild and independent as America itself. There weren't many special things he held dear, but Jessica Grey was the most precious part of his life. He had to shake himself before he could respond—she looked like Juliet up in that window in her lace-cuffed nightgown, her hair all undone . . . "Only old diplomats," he told her. "The young ones with beautiful fiancées are up before dawn."

Jessica leaned her chin on her hand. "I'll go with you if I can have the sorrel."

He laughed. "I'll race you to the stable. Whoever wins gets the sorrel."

"Be right down!"

She disappeared from the window, and Charles knew he'd played his hand well. Jessica couldn't resist a challenge—but how far would she go to win? In desperate afterthought he called up, "Better get dressed first!"

The grass was bright green and dancing with

early-morning dew. The young man and woman celebrated their youth with each stride as they ran in abandon of spirit across the grounds, laughing themselves breathless. Charles really had to run just to keep up with her. Jessica's figure shone like a chiseled emerald in the tailored green riding habit. He stole a glance at her in time to notice her hair slip from the pins and bounce on her shoulders. It cost him a stride or two. He plunged forward to gain on her again. Jessica shot a look back at him as he came up behind her, then caught at his coat as he passed her. He dodged to his left, but they were already at the stables. The big fieldstone building smelled of fresh manure and horseflesh, stimulating to the senses of anyone with English blood.

"I won!" Jessica trumpeted as she caught herself on the wide doorway.

"You didn't," Charles gasped, breathless. "I took you by a nose."

Not to be outdone, Jessica cornered the nearest stable hand and demanded, "Tommy! You saw, didn't you?"

The boy nodded and raised both bushy eyebrows. "Looked like a draw, miss," he said cautiously, guarding his grin.

"Tommy, you're blind!" Charles accused. "I won by a length."

Jessica stooped to pick up a hairpin that had shaken loose at the last minute. "A moment ago it was by a nose. Now it's a length. Whew! If Aunt Lily could see me now, she'd faint."

She turned to Tommy and admonished him, "Don't you tell."

Tommy grinned. "No, miss."

Jessica piled her hair into an echo of the neat bun she'd coiled this morning and spoke to Charles with two hairpins in her mouth. "She says diplomats' wives have to cultivate dignity."

Charles handed her another pin. "She's right."

"I'm not a diplomat's wife yet," she said airily. She said to Tommy as she nodded toward the stables, "Would you bring Mr. Wyndon the new mare? I'll take the sorrel."

"Sure, miss."

Tommy disappeared into the darkness of the stable.

Charles cornered Jessica immediately. "*You* get the sorrel? And why is that, might I inquire?"

A twisted little grin appeared on her lips. God, it was wonderful to be twenty-three and have the upper hand. "Because you're an English gentleman," she told him. "Because you're chivalrous. Because you love me . . . and I love you. And I wish we were getting married tomorrow instead of three long months from now."

The giddiness flowed away into her eyes as Charles enveloped himself there. He raised his hand, fingers hot from the morning run, and touched her face lightly. He bent slightly over her. Jessica waited, never flinching.

The clopping of a horse's hooves made them abruptly step apart. Charles tried to regain his composure, tried to come up with something socially acceptable to say to her in front of

Tommy, but her eyes took his breath away. At moments like this he felt unequal to her. In silence he led her to the massive sorrel hunting horse as the boy handed him the reins.

The meadow was sparkling with sunlit dew on this blue morning in the summer of 1909. The sedate mare and the big sorrel moved along trimmed hawthorn hedges in a lazy canter, glad of the easy hands on their bridles. Good riders were precious to horses who still had tender mouths, and the animals loped along placidly without resistance, insensible to the conversation going on above them.

"But I want to know."

"You will, eventually."

"But I want to know *now*. Tell me more about Constantinople. Tell me everything." She leaned forward in the saddle, trying to draw his full attention. She ached to know, to see the wonderful things of the world without the spine of a book holding them down to the pages. They were out there, waiting for her, and here she was, lucky enough to have fallen in love with a man who was destined to travel the farthest reaches of the world, and all she'd seen so far was a corner of America and a corner of England. It wasn't enough. She wanted more. She wanted the *flavor* of the world to be hot upon her tongue like wild mountain wine.

Charles drew his horse down into a walk, wishing there was a way to draw Jessica's enthusiasm down a notch or two. "Well . . . it's hard to describe. Nothing like this, of course. Very hot, very dry."

Jessica shook her head in frustration. She didn't want a weather report. How could she make Charles understand the visions she saw, the hopes and images she cultivated about the stirring life before them? Why didn't he see any of the exciting possibilities? They seemed so clear. "I mean the people," she explained carefully. "Tell me what they're like."

"The women are always veiled," he said hesitantly, not knowing what she wanted. "The men go about in—"

"Not what they wear. What they're *like*. Is everything very exotic? Are there really dervishes? Do the women dance in costumes made only of beads?"

Charles laughed to cover his discomfort. "I never knew a girl who asked so many questions. Now I've lost track."

"Dervishes."

"Oh. I suppose they exist. I've never met one." He sighed. "I do hope you'll be happy there."

She smiled assuringly. "As long as I'm with you, I can be happy anywhere."

Charles surprised her with an unexpected frown. "I'm glad to hear that. I didn't know how to tell you before."

"Tell me? Tell me what?"

"My tour of duty. It's been changed to Antarctica."

"What? But there's nothing there!"

"They want to establish a British embassy, begin building relations with the penguins. We're very keen on learning where they buy their dinner jackets—"

"Oooooh, I'll strangle you! Charles, you come back here and let me strangle you!"

But he was gone, galloping off at a right angle, straight across the meadow grass. Jessica immediately twisted the reins around her hands, neck-reined the horse in a most improper American fashion, and wheeled the sorrel into a wild run.

"A wedding in three months. It's simply not possible to do properly."

Lily Grey sipped her tea as though it might save her from the encroaching American wilderness. The list sitting before her on the table had gotten three times longer just in the past twenty minutes. She leaned back and stared down her robust bosom at the slip of notepaper, then scratched out two items. There simply would be no time.

"His leave is up in three months," her brother uttered sedately, in a tone that made no commitments. Arthur Grey gazed at his newspaper and nibbled on his second muffin, refusing to meet his sister's stern disapproval. His silver mustache caught a smudge of peach marmalade as the muffin went by. "After all, they've been engaged for a year."

"You know what I mean." Lily tapped the quill pen against her ear, only to grumble in frustration when it caught in her hairnet. She worked to free it. "The invitations, the parties, the dresses, the guest list . . . it's endless."

"Keep it simple, then, Lil."

"She's your only daughter. Don't you want her married properly?"

At this Arthur did look away from his paper, his ruddy cheeks turning to chubby balls as he grinned over reading spectacles at his sister. "Just happily."

Deflated by his honesty, Lily inhaled deeply and gazed out at the lush garden that sprawled below Greyhurst's glowering stone facade. "It's a pity her mother, God rest her soul, isn't here to see Jessica married. It's just not right, don't you think, for a mother to miss her daughter's wedding. . . ."

Arthur stared at the paper but saw something else entirely. "Yes," he murmured. "You know, I don't have to tell you what a help you've been. Jessica's needed a woman's influence."

The mood broke instantly as Lily eagerly agreed. "There's no denying she lacks self-discipline. It's not your fault, Arthur. It's in her blood. You know I loved Katherine, God rest her, but why you had to go and marry an American—" She let her words drop off into their proper oblivion, her point made. It couldn't be undone. Arthur's wry smile told her there would be no satisfaction in her twenty-five-year-old disgruntlement. He had stopped arguing the point with her years ago, and the satisfaction had since gone out of it.

"Who's coming to the party tonight?" he asked, smoothing the linen cloth tucked at his chin to clear the way for another biscuit.

Lily sifted through her papers and came up with a list. "I've invited our cousins from Manchester. Jane has three girls—one Jessie's age—and I thought they'd spend the weekend. Of course, they'll—"

"Good morning, Daddy!"

They turned as Jessica breezed in from the corridor, still wearing her riding habit.

"Morning, Aunt Lily," the girl chimed after pecking her father affectionately on one of his red cheeks. She approached Aunt Lily, who offered her own cheek.

"For heaven's sake, Jessica, go up and change," Lily scolded. "You smell like a stable hand. You're wet! What happened?"

Jessica stood back and clasped her hands behind her, taking refuge in her father's sudden disinterest as he looked away with a roll of his eyes. "Charles and I took the water jump," she admitted.

Aunt Lily's chin pressed into her chest with staunch disapproval. "You and Charles were out riding? Alone?"

Arthur cleared his throat. "Lily . . ."

"It's not proper!"

Arthur turned to Jessica. "Did you fall?"

Jessica's blue eyes widened as she spied a fresh piece of toast spread with marmalade and stole it from her father's plate. "No. Charles did. I had to help him out. He's upstairs changing. You know, I never realized a diplomat knew so many swear words."

"Jessica." Lily huffed.

Pleased with herself—she loved to see how far she could push Aunt Lily—Jessica murmured, "Sorry. I don't want to disappoint you, Daddy."

"You never disappoint me," Arthur admitted in spite of Lily's deprecating expression. "Charles is going to have his hands full when I give you to him in marriage, and then it will become his duty to explain you to all of England."

"I love England, Daddy," Jessica said. "You're free to stop worrying about it. I'm not sorry you decided to bring me here."

Arthur moaned and gazed at the grass. "I brought you here because of my weaknesses, not because of yours."

"Because your past is here. You're comfortable here. Tallahassee just reminded you of Mama. Do you think I don't understand?"

Charles emerged from Jessica's other side. "There, Arthur. And you're worried about this girl? It's natural. We all have a bit of the homing pigeon in us, after all. You return to England, and someday perhaps Jessica and I will return to Tallahassee . . . for a while."

Jessica poked him playfully. "For a while?"

Charles laughed. "Well, my dear love, I might be able to explain you to all of England, but I'm not at all sure I could explain Tallahassee."

She looked at his clean clothes and caught another whiff of Aunt Lily's disapproval. There was, however, time to steal another piece of toast before she said, "I'll go change. Have fun talking about me while I'm gone!"

She disappeared into the generations-old halls of Greyhurst, leaving a spangling trail of memory behind.

They watched her go.

"Well," Aunt Lily decided, "if she keeps on this way, she'll never fit into proper English society."

Charles sat down beside Arthur as the two men caught the last glimpse of Jessica's mud-caked riding skirt before it whipped up the ancient stairway. "God," he muttered, "let's hope not."

"Really, miss, you shouldn't be doing that."

"Oh, Mary, don't be so stiff. This is fun. If I don't learn how to do it myself, how will I ever be able to supervise the staff once I'm married?" Jessica licked a smudge of icing from the back of her hand and went on decorating the tray of tarts while the pastry cook looked on dubiously. Behind the cook, two of Jessica's visiting cousins crowded in, fascinated by their unruly American relative. The kitchen was a maze of activity. Servants flowed in and out and the cooks went about their business, all a little nervous because of her presence. Wasn't she supposed to be out in the main hall, greeting her guests? After all, this was her engagement party.

Jessica felt their confused stares and knew they were trying to read her thoughts from the back of her ruffled party frock, but she didn't care. In fact, she rather liked throwing an apple into their proper cherry pie. She'd heard all the mutterings and whispers a hundred times since she and her father had arrived in England. Yes, her mother was American. Yes, she tended to act on impulse. So when had "American" and "impulse" become foul language? Jessica knew the implications of being half American. Everyone in Merrie Olde Englande expected her to spring into tea wearing moccasins and buckskin, gnawing raw meat, and spouting trapping stories. What could be the harm in living up to just a little of that image? And she did enjoy being the one who was about to embark into the great dark adventure of marriage to an actual, living, breathing man. It gave her an advantage over her cousins, the girls who would be her bridesmaids, as they crowded around her—not to watch her decorate tarts but to hear the story she started about meeting Charles.

Cousin Charlotte nudged her way past the pastry cook and urged, "Go on, Jessica. The whole story."

"It was at the British embassy in Washington," Jessica continued. "There was a big party for Lord Something of Somewhere—"

"Take care, miss—" the cook urged, pointing out a tart with too much icing.

"What did you wear?" Charlotte interrupted.

Jessica looked up for a moment. "I don't remember."

"Not too much, miss," the cook tried again.

Charlotte's sister, Victoria, shoved the cook even farther back. "You don't remember what you were wearing when you first met Charles?"

Jessica responded with a saucy grin. "I remember what he wore."

Victoria scoffed. "That's easy. A dinner jacket."

Jessica started to answer, but the youngest cousin, Emily, popped in the kitchen doorway, blustering, "Jessica! Aunt Lily's looking for you and she's ready to *pop*!"

The cook stumbled back a step as Jessica shoved the pastry decorator back into her hands. The cook then collected herself in time to shout, "Miss, the apron!"

Jessica whirled once, and a white pouf of floury fabric landed square on the cook's head.

The party was eternally English. A proper dinner, followed by a proper toast to the engaged couple, during which Jessica plied poor Charles with an intentionally improper kiss right on the mouth in front of everyone. Then the men lumbered quite properly into the library for brandy and cigars, and the women twittered off to gossip over crumpets and tea. Jessica was fawned over until she thought she might die of it and was eventually driven to sneak off to the library door where she could eavesdrop on the men's conversation. She relished their conversation and inhaled the heady aroma of cigar and pipe smoke, reflecting how comfortable it made her feel. It reminded her of home, of her father when her mother was alive, of days when

Jessica was small enough to go to bed just after sunset and her parents would retire to the veranda to rock together on the lovely old porch swing. There were so many memories . . . and she knew she now stood on the threshold of making memories of her own husband and family. If only there was a way to get on with things. Everything in England seemed to take forever.

She approached them quietly, delighting in the chance to eavesdrop. Charles was listening to old Lord Henredon's fatigued voice as the country gentleman said, "The Ottoman Empire used to be so exotic. The air of mystery—turbans and all—but now all you read, it seems, is one bloody massacre after another."

Jessica stepped aside, cloaking herself with the archway curtain as the butler strode through, giving her only a brief look before moving into the library.

Concentrating on the men's voices, Jessica ignored the butler's disapproving glare as Charles spoke up from the other side of a massive leather couch. "Believe me, I have no intention of defending what Sultan Hasam has been doing, only England's diplomatic position. You see, it's very difficult to judge a culture so very different from our own."

Dear Charles, always so generous and malleable. Jessica smiled affectionately and listened, though what she heard wasn't Charles's even tone but Aunt Lily's cackle from behind her.

"Jessica, dear! Time for all you young—Jessica, what are you doing here?"

"Oh . . . nothing, really. I was just rearranging my petticoat."

"Well, it's time for bed. Charlotte and Victoria and Emily are already upstairs, and so should you be. Run along now!"

Charlotte, Victoria, and Emily were indeed already upstairs, but they had no more intention of going to sleep than Jessica did. By the time she got to her room her cousins were in their nightgowns and had opened the wardrobe that held Jessica's wedding trousseau. They were stuffing themselves with leftover hors d'oeuvres they'd smuggled up, and Emily was smelling each bottle of perfume on Jessica's dresser as though to discover which of them turned her into an engaged woman.

"And they call me undisciplined," she teased as she stood at the door.

"Oooh, Jessica!" Victoria rolled off the bed, snatched up a hanger from which a fluttering cloud of silk wafted, and ran to her as Jessica stripped out of her party dress. "Look at this! Jessica, it's beautiful. Where will you wear it?"

Charlotte, with a mouthful of kippers, informed, "To bed. It's a nightgown, you goose."

"All this embroidery," Victoria crooned. "And no one will see it."

Charlotte rolled her eyes. "Charles will."

Jessica nodded toward Emily and hushed the older girl.

Immediately Emily retaliated. "I know about married people. You don't have to hush."

"You don't know anything," Victoria said, pretending that she did.

"I know more than you."

After sticking out a practiced tongue at her sister, Victoria turned to Jessica. "Are you in love, Jessica?"

Charlotte forced the kippers down for the privilege of answering this one. "Of course she is. And put that nightgown away."

"When did you know?" Victoria prodded. "That you were in love, I mean. When he kissed you?"

Jessica strolled to the bed, brushing her hair out with very adult strokes—everything she did from now on would be grown-up—and lowered herself onto the thick quilts. Her cousins eagerly gathered around. "I can tell you the exact minute. We were playing bridge—me, Charles, my father, and someone from the French embassy. It's silly, really, but I just happened to look up. Charles was frowning at his cards because he's a terrible player, really, and I looked at him . . . and I knew."

Victoria frowned. "That's all?"

Jessica smiled, remembering. "He must have felt me looking because he looked up. And he smiled, as if he could read my thoughts."

"That's not very romantic."

Charlotte softly disagreed. "Yes, it is."

"With Uncle Arthur there and some old Frenchman?"

Emily shoved her way into the circle of older girls. "Charlotte has a beau. Andrew. I've seen them kissing."

Victoria added her opinion. "Andrew's too short. I don't intend to marry a man who's not incredibly tall. He has to be able to ride, fence, dance like an angel . . ." She jumped off the bed and demonstrated her list of requirements with wild antics. The girls were laughing at her when the door opened and Aunt Lily came in. Victoria stopped her gyrations, and for an instant—if that long—the four young women saw a flicker of a distant time on Aunt Lily's gray-framed features, a time when she, too, was young and dreaming of loves that might be, staying up too late and conspiring for paradise with other girls of her age. The moment faded, replaced by the carefully cultivated propriety. "Emily! What are you doing up? Bed, all of you. And food in the bedroom! You'll all have nightmares, eating this late. Go on, out! To your own rooms."

Jessica's cousins each threw her a guilty grin as they filed past Aunt Lily and offered contrite good nights while Aunt Lily continued to deride Jessica. "It's after midnight and you have to be up early for a fitting. Do you want Charles to see you with dark circles under your eyes? And what's this doing hanging on a chair?" She retrieved the silk nightie and tapped Jessica's hand away when it strayed toward the luscious embroidery.

"Aunt Lily," Jessica began, "may I ask you something?"

"You can't leave silk heaped over a chair like this, dear."

"What's it like?"

"What's what like, dear?"

"Being married. You know."

Aunt Lily hesitated, stopped moving entirely, and paused with her face turned toward the closet so Jessica couldn't see her discomfort. She'd never been anyone's mother and knew that Arthur had returned to England so Jessica would have some feminine framework in which to be married and to find some influence besides that of an aging English gentleman who'd broken protocol himself by marrying an American, but Lily had never had to face a moment like this one. Could she find the answers? No one had ever explained anything to her . . . she didn't know the right words. Oh, as time passed, of course, she had discovered the gnarled truths of what went on between men and women in the privacy of marriage, but as for words . . . there really weren't any. She had learned to suffice with fairy tales and leave out the physical realities, to deal in dreams as she'd heard the girls doing just now, to find things out in their own ways, in their own time. A motherless girl now turned to her and asked the one question for which there were no proper words. Lily struggled to avoid betraying herself while she also fulfilled Arthur's trust in her.

She opened her mouth to speak and tried to

make herself turn to face the eager young face behind her, but something froze her to the base of her being. She swept the nightgown smooth and forced a place for it in the crowded wardrobe. "You have . . . a duty to your husband, Jessica," she said. But then she withered internally and stiffened. "We'll talk about it another time. Good night, dear. Sleep well."

Aunt Lily turned out the light and hurried from the room, closing the door behind her and escaping from the words she could not find.

"Good night," Jessica murmured far too faintly for anyone to hear. She turned the light back on. The warm yellow glow fell across the ocean of organza ruffles and taffeta skirts and frilled sleeves that would flutter free on her wedding day. She rose from the bed and moved to the full-length mirror on its gold-framed stand near the wardrobe. She gazed at herself, at the heavy cotton nightgown she now wore, wondering how her body would look in the filmy silk she wasn't allowed to wear until she became Mrs. Wyndon. Would she be so different on that night? Would things change so utterly that she might not see Charles in the same light that shined upon him now when she looked into his studious expression and saw the pride he had in her? She was twenty-three years old, yet she hardly knew what lay beneath those cotton folds she saw in the mirror now. Proper young ladies were discouraged from examining themselves, or even from looking in mirrors until they were fully dressed. Silly, of course, but she'd never given it much thought until now. And Aunt Lily hadn't wanted to talk about what would change after marriage. Oh, Jessica knew about love and lovemaking. Girls much younger than herself learned from other girls, who learned from boys they weren't supposed to be seeing. Nothing ever went quite as smoothly as the upper-class matrons would have preferred. Girls still had ways of finding these things out.

She continued to look at herself in the mirror for a long time and never found the answers.

As it had for a century, morning came quietly over the countryside around Greyhurst. The estate seemed to have found the spell that made magical dawns appear over its horizon of hawthorns and cherry trees. The only disturbance was the delivery boy and his bicycle peddling down the road. He pedaled into the broad gates and up to the old oak door, then hammered upon the wood until the butler appeared and relieved him of a telegram from the British embassy. The butler continued the perfect order of events by delivering the message to Mr. Wyndon, who was breakfasting with the master of the house in the west wing.

Charles took the telegram and dismissed the butler, waiting for the man to leave before he opened it. In fact, he waited quite a long time before opening it. He had a feeling.

"I wonder what's taking Jessica so long to

come down," he murmured, distractedly parting the envelope.

"She's having a dress fitted," Arthur told him while lathering a biscuit with the real reason he'd come back to England—peach marmalade. "Is something wrong?"

Charles read the telegram, then dropped it into his lap. "My leave's been canceled. I bloody well felt something was up. They want me back in Damascus right away."

"More riots?"

"Ambassador Grant wants a firsthand report. I don't see why. These insurrections have been going on for years."

Arthur shook his gray head. "And we continue to support the Sultan."

"The embassy can't pass judgment, Arthur, you know that."

"When do you leave?"

"Godawful tomorrow morning."

"Leave for where?" Jessica's clear voice rang against the morning quietude.

Charles glanced at Arthur, but there was no way out. "It's not very good news, darling."

"Go ahead. I can probably take it, darling."

"I received a wire from the diplomatic corps today," Charles said quickly, watching Jessica's face. "They want me to tour the Ottoman Empire before reporting to Constantinople. Sort of a visual geography lesson, I gathered. How do they put it? Ah, yes . . . to better understand the diversity of Sultan Hasam's subjects."

Arthur Grey tediously refilled Charles's teacup, but for himself he poured a dose of medicine from a hand-size vial and downed it in a sticky gulp. "You should be very pleased," he said, then finished swallowing. "To take such great pains they must have very big plans for your career." Jessica knew why her father said this. He thought she would need placating.

"I'm delighted," Charles said, but he sounded doubtful. "And flattered, of course, except . . ."

At this Arthur took over, knowing his daughter loved to dote on him and that he had the best chance of the two of them to keep her under control. "You see, pumpkin, it would mean postponing the wedding."

"I don't see why," Jessica said with unnerving determination. "I'm coming with you."

"Jessica, his ship leaves tomorrow," her father said.

She draped her arm around his shoulders. "You'll come too. We'll all go. The three of us. Charles and I can be married in Constantinople. Before you say anything, just consider the possibilities. Daddy, you need the diversion. And if I'm going to be an ambassador's wife, I need to be familiar with the Orient."

"Out of the question," Charles said. "It's much too dangerous."

"But it's not as if Damascus were in flames," Jessica insisted. "I mean, it's just a bit of rioting. You said so yourself."

"I will not risk exposing you to political upheaval."

"Though you'd leave me here to be smothered by little pink bridesmaids."

"Now, Jessica," Charles tried, weakening, "you must realize that I have no choice. I have to go."

"Of course you must. And as the future wife of an ambassador, I should go along."

Weakly Charles protested, "I'm hardly an ambassador."

"But you will be someday," Jessica said, radiating a calculated confidence in him. "What if things get worse? What if they won't let you come back for months and months and months? Oh, Charles," she pleaded, kneeling at his knees in a pose she knew would melt him, "I simply can't bear to think of our being apart for so very long."

"If it weren't for the risk . . ." He groaned.

"You can't frighten me out of wanting to be with you." She made her eyes as big as they could get.

He gazed down at her, newly amazed. "You're really not scared, are you?"

"You told me there will always be an element of risk in the Ottoman Empire. So what difference will it really make if I join you now or in six months or in a year? The danger won't have changed. All we will have lost is precious time together. And what could be more appropriate than a wedding at the embassy? The perfect finale to our travels!"

Charles's brow furrowed, then smoothed, and

his brows went up as he mused, "A wedding at the embassy . . ."

"Just a small affair," Jessica went on, looking into her father's eyes. "Please, Daddy . . . I can't bear to have him leave now, not knowing when he'll be back." She beamed at her resigned father, realizing he hadn't said a word in several minutes.

Arthur tipped his head. "I've never been to Constantinople," he mused.

Jessica sprang up, settled on the arm of his chair, and squeezed his slumped shoulders. "You'll have to admit, it's a brilliant idea!"

CHAPTER TWO

"To the beginning. To Syria."

"And to a grand adventure," Jessica added to Charles's toast. Champagne glasses clinked. Against the crystal-blue night sky and the apricot-colored coastline of Syria, the ship was barely visible in the last fading glow of sunset. The great steam whistle hooted its own long, howling celebration. A few feet away, the ship's ballroom fluttered with gowns and tails and whirling couples. It wasn't really appropriate for a woman to take part in a political discussion, protocol and Aunt Lily had always told her, but Jessica found herself listening rather intently to the men's conversation as she pretended to gaze out to sea. These young diplomats were on their way to taking a hand in history, and Jessica was soon hanging on every word. After all, it was going to be her life as well as theirs. The subject, of course: Turkey. Sultan Hasam. Syria. Sultan Hasam. Bulgaria. Sultan Hasam. She leaned on the rail and continued to wait.

The French diplomat—Jessica couldn't remember his name. She had a mental block with French names—was commenting, or rather baiting, "How can it possibly be serious? There's always trouble of one sort or another in the desert."

Sitting to the Frenchman's right, the Russian representative said, "Two thousand lives have been lost in four days." He leaned to Charles and added, "The French always refuse to see the obvious." Of course, he said it loud enough for the Frenchman to hear. That was part of the game. "I think that in these insurrections lies the possibility for revolution. What do you think, Mr. Wyndon?"

Charles puffed up noticeably. "A revolution takes a united front—a united effort. I see no evidence of that in the Ottoman Empire."

"What about the revolutionary movement? Can you deny that it exists?" the Russian asked.

"You don't overturn hundreds of years of a dynasty with a paltry group of young Turkish dissidents," Charles said.

Jessica nearly spoke up. Though she parted her lips, she ultimately opted to remain silent rather than point out so blatant a difference between herself and Charles. He spoke from a totally English point of view. He could not conceive of an established dynastic system being overthrown, or thrown out, by a handful of upstarts. But as an American, Jessica knew better and believed differently. The simple truth of her right to call herself American instead of a British subject stood as living proof. She closed her mouth as Charles went on, but the obvious difference did not soon leave her thoughts.

"They could never unify the Empire's different nationalities," Charles continued, "the Kurds, the Greeks, Albanians, Armenians, Bulgars—they all speak different languages, they worship different gods, they have virtually nothing in common. They are nationals first, Ottomans second."

"But they are developing a common bond," argued the Russian. "A desire to see the Sultan overthrown."

"Even that is not enough to unite such disparate groups," Charles said. "No, I believe, and more importantly, England believes, that Sultan Hasam will squelch these insurrections."

The Russian huffed. "England wants to preserve her passage to India, therefore she chooses to believe that the status quo will be preserved."

Charles leaned forward slightly, countering, "And perhaps Russia chooses to believe in revolution because such actions could realize her historical ambitions in Constantinople."

Touché, dear. Jessica swung around and took Charles by the arm. Here was the perfect opportunity to make sure Charles walked away with the upper hand. "And I can see that I've lost all my charm. Over an hour and not one invitation to dance."

The diplomats bowed briefly to her as she

tugged on Charles. Then Charles smiled proudly and said, "Excuse me, gentlemen."

Once inside, whirling gracefully around the dance floor, Charles paused before saying, "I'm sorry, dear, if you were bored."

"Not bored, really," Jessica admitted, "but diplomats always seem to think international problems can be solved with a lot of talk and cigar smoke. I'd rather see you out in the field tackling those difficulties and doing something about them. You will be the kind of diplomat who takes action into his own hands, won't you? Stir things up a bit?"

"Well . . . well, of course I will. But don't forget, I'm a long way from that kind of power, darling. I've got a lot of acclimating to do before I can make any waves. And it's not as easy for one person to make a dent as you seem to think."

"Excuses," she teased. "History is full of stories about individuals making dents."

"Perhaps. We'll see." Charles would never have admitted how grateful he was when Arthur Grey appeared beside him and tapped his shoulder.

"Might I cut in?" the older man asked.

"Certainly. I'll find the deck-master and check on our reservations for the train ride tomorrow."

Jessica flowed into her father's arms without missing a beat. Her father, after all, had been the one who taught her to dance in the first place. "I thought you were resting," she said.

"I kept thinking of how much you look like your mother when she and I attended our first ball together, and I had to get out of that cabin and get up here to see it."

"Charmer."

"And . . . an ulterior motive."

"I thought so. What is it?"

"I've been thinking about how I should've asked your Aunt Lily to come along with us."

Jessica stood back. "What on earth for?"

"To finish your education, tell you what you need to know . . . help you learn all the things a woman and a wife should know and, well, you understand."

"Ridiculous, Daddy."

"Oh, I don't know that it's so ridiculous. I did, after all, take a peek at that book you've been so involved with during our transatlantic voyage."

Jessica felt a twinge of guilt. But what was so bad about being more interested in your future husband's career than in French fitters and bridesmaids? "It's just a book."

"And what is the subject of this just-a-book?"

"What difference does it make?"

"I want to hear you say it, Jessica."

"It's a treatise on the effects of nationalism on global politics."

Arthur chuckled. "Who's going to be the diplomat? You or Charles?"

"But I thought you'd be pleased."

"I am. It's just that . . . sometimes I worry that I've done you a disservice, preparing you for life with books and travel. I'm afraid I've done little to prepare you for being a wife."

Jessica gazed out over the glowing, exotic coastline of Syria. Distractedly she said, "What can there possibly be to being a wife? I've seen the most stupid girls do it with so little effort."

Helpless to change the past, Arthur shook his head and remembered his wife. He hadn't exaggerated when he said Jessica made him think of the lovely American woman he'd married. He'd discovered an unlikely spark of defiance in himself then too. Proper English gentlemen just didn't pop off to America and come home wed to commoners. But Katherine had been nothing common, just as Jessica could not be classified. Arthur lived a charmed life with his wife and his sparkling little daughter, never quite sure what either of them would do next. He began to believe that impetuousness kept him alive, kept him looking forward to the next day, the next hour. Only when death stole his wife from him did he realize his own mortality.

He was saved by that thought when the ship's whistle blew again and made him wince.

Seven hours later, a different pitch of whistle sang across the endless stretch of desert, percussioned by the hum of the train wheels against the endless track laid by nameless people on this endless desert. Jessica stared out the window at the barren beauty, a desolation that had nothing to call its own but the promise of something beyond it. Charles broke her concentration when he returned, opening the door to the compartment in which she and her father sat, and ushered in a charming, perpetually elegant woman in her late forties. The woman's smile held both grace and mystery as lithely as her body wore Paris fashions. In fact, the two Rhesus monkeys that followed her were almost as finely dressed in their little red jackets and turbans. Behind her, or rather, behind the monkeys, stood an entourage of servants.

"Mr. Arthur Grey, Miss Jessica Grey," Charles began, "I'm pleased to introduce you to Lady Ashley. I've asked her to join us. We can have no better friend in the Orient."

Arthur struggled to stand up in the rhythmically rolling cabin. "Absolutely. We're . . . we're very . . ." He did his utmost to be social above and beyond being climbed upon by one of the monkeys.

Lady Ashley rescued him. "Come here, darlings," she said to the monkeys. "You have to go with Paulie. Paulie, please take them." A black servant stepped into the cabin, corraled one of the animals, then went for the second.

Lady Ashley took the place next to Jessica and surveyed her generously. "Your young man so graciously offered me refuge. It seems there's not room enough for all of us in my compartment." Jessica smiled back instinctively. Lady Ashley seemed far different from other English-women, although she was quite English, judging from her accent and her manner. "Are you a fellow traveler, then?" Jessica asked hopefully.

"Always, my dear. But I keep a house in

Damascus. Even in the desert one needs roots."
The lady accepted a goblet of wine from Arthur
and arranged her skirt for comfort instead of
appearance. Jessica got a second surge of liking.
She was about to say something when one of
the monkeys slipped out of Paulie's grip as the
servant tried to get out the narrow cabin door.
It headed for Charles.

"Don't let him get on your leg," Lady Ashley
warned. "It can be rather embarrassing." A moment later she had rounded the beast up and
put him on Paulie's shoulder. This time it looked
permanent.

Charles ignored the near disaster and noted,
"Some say it's easier to get an audience with
Sultan Hasam himself than an invitation to
one of your rooftop soirees."

"There you have him," Arthur huffed, smiling beneath his mustache. "Subtlety on the
hoof."

Charles ignored him. "Lady Ashley is probably the most famous Englishwoman in all of
Syria."

Lady Ashley turned to Jessica. "He's much
too polite. 'Infamous' is a more apt description.
And I shall be happy to see you all at my very
next rooftop affair."

"I can hardly wait," Jessica admitted, the excitement of youth getting the best of her. She
started to say something else, something very
American because it wasn't the least bit restrained, but a commotion outside the train in-

terrupted her. She blinked. Outside the train? How could anything be—

Nearest the window, she looked out. "My God . . ."

Horses. Desert horses, thin and strong, fast as the harmattan that blew overhead. And desert riders, robed and savage. How nice of them to welcome the train.

"Bedouin," Lady Ashley supplied. "Riding *djerid*."

She was referring to the way they rode and not the horses, as Jessica first thought. The Bedouin rode violently, more insanely than any Wild West show, hanging over their stirrups with the bridles in their mouths. How could they stay on the animals that way and at that pace?

Breathless, Jessica stared, her cheek pressed against the glass, mesmerized.

Arthur closed the blinds on his side of the window. "Jessica, draw the curtain."

But Jessica was on a charging horse with a Bedouin. Discreetly Lady Ashley reached past her and drew the curtain. The train jolted, shaking them all nearly out of their seats.

Arthur grunted, "What in the name of civilization . . ."

"Debris on the tracks," Lady Ashley explained calmly. "They're trying to stop the train."

"Good God."

Jessica inhaled. Adventure suddenly lost a measure of its intrigue.

*   *   *

Tarik Pasha had sensed himself being watched. His horse had a bad gait at high speed, but he had urged it on, knowing that a desert stallion had the heart to race until it dropped—nothing at all like the placid thoroughbreds he'd ridden in Cambridge. Of course, he'd left everything of Cambridge behind. In fact, nothing in the desert even faintly resembled the orderly rows of university buildings. Riding through the land of his youth, Tarik knew he was Turkish in everything but his education and the neat British cut of his hair. Soon that, too, would be gone. He would keep the education, and the haircut would naturally disappear.

Someone was still watching him. He looked up over the flying white mane of his struggling horse, still gripping the bridle in his teeth, and tried to find the eyes he felt. All he saw was a hand closing the blinds on one of the train compartments. Ah. Curious tourists, or perhaps . . . his very goal.

Tarik quickly forgot the train compartment. It would be Radik's duty to search them, for now, he was approaching the engine. He swung back into his saddle, his teeth aching from gripping the coral-and-silver bridle, and elbowed back the edge of his flying blue Bedouin cape. He felt the sun on his deep bronze complexion even through the chapping wind. With a whoop he forced his foaming horse flush alongside the locomotive.

"Stop the train," he shouted in Arabic.

The engineer, a small man in a turban, stared

in terror but lay hard on the throttle in defiance. Tarik hadn't the time to put up with that, though he did respect it. He would do the same, after all. He threw himself under his horse's belly for the sake of looking horrific, and brandished a fierce feathered lance. The engineer's eyes bulged, but he shook his head and leaned harder on the throttle.

"Brave man," Tarik muttered to himself. "Not a bad way to die." But he spared him. The lance flew home straight through the man's turban, baring his head but leaving him alive. Tarik had made his point. The train shrieked to a halt.

Tarik smiled.

The Bedouin boarded the train instantly, without celebration or apology. In their compartment Arthur Grey and his party awaited any unexpected fate to be allotted them. The door clicked and slid open.

Lady Ashley urgently whispered, "Keep silent . . . and absolutely still."

The Bedouin pushed their way through, examining their faces, and one grizzled old man, whose lewd eyes shone from a robed face, muttered something to the other Bedouin. He clenched a foot-long dagger in one gnarled brown hand and glared at Jessica, his ancient eyes wrinkling up in delight. The other Bedouin moved on, but this artifact remained and continued glaring obscenely at Jessica. She started to squirm.

Charles shifted. Jessica instinctively knew he

had had enough and was thinking about going for the dagger. But she was frozen. Fear, curiosity, primal response—whatever it was, it held her rivoted. Luckily Lady Ashley also sensed Charles's thoughts and interceded.

"Nahnu milihin!" she said sharply to the old man.

At first Jessica thought the words meant as little to the old man as they did to her, but after a moment the smile under the robes grew wider and he nodded and bowed his way out of the compartment.

"Thank God," Arthur gushed, mopping his brow.

"What should we do?" Charles considered, getting to his feet.

"Nothing," Lady Ashley admonished strongly. "It's obvious they're looking for someone or something specific. Relax. We are quite safe."

The door clicked shut.

Jessica parted the blinds. "Oh, look. Turks." She watched as a group of Turkish soldiers, identified by their red fezzes and frock coats, were led to horses by the Bedouin.

"Sultan Hasam's men," Lady Ashley explained.

Jessica peered through the blinds. "I don't understand. What would they want with Turkish soldiers?"

"I would imagine," Charles interceded, "that it's a retaliation for the burning of a Bedouin camp."

"Mustapha's army burned a camp?" Arthur's voice cracked. "For what reason?"

Lady Ashley said, "Some say the Sultan is making an example of the Bedouin, punishing them for a rash of insurrections."

"The Bedouin revolt against everyone who tries to rule them," Charles added. "It's practically part of their tradition."

"But there must be some explanation," Jessica decided.

"Of course." Lady Ashley comforted her. "Some say that Sultan Hasam is making an example of the Bedouin in an attempt to return to the old ways when the Ottoman Empire was feared and great. And I'm not so sure the Bedouin are behind the retaliations."

Sensing something Jessica missed, Charles pressed, "What are you saying?"

Lady Ashley looked at him. "What if I were to tell you that some of the men we just saw were not Bedouin but a group of young Turkish rebels. Turkish, mind you."

"Impossible," Charles said, but the hint of belief was there.

"It's only a theory," Lady Ashley said, "but there are those who think these young rebels have been behind every insurrection in the past three years."

"Revolutionaries, then," Arthur suggested.

She smiled at him. "Of course. Impossible to have a revolution without them, isn't it?"

Jessica turned to Charles automatically, giving in to a tendency to trust him that had lately become quite natural for her. She loved his ease, his confidence in matters of political import, loved his interest in what would become his life's work. He would have an answer, an explanation, and he would say it with polish.

Charles did not disappoint her. "For six hundred years no one has been able to unite the Ottoman Empire's mixed peoples enough to incite a revolution against Sultan Hasam."

"Ah, but these rebels are different," the older woman told him. "They've been abroad, been influenced by Western ideas. They've seen another way of life, and they want to bring it home—"

"Is it really so bad here?" Jessica interrupted.

"The people are subject to the whims of a single man who has the right to determine life or death. People have starved because their crops have gone to the Sultan. Whole villages have been destroyed, hundreds massacred, because one refused to join the army." Lady Ashley paused to pat Jessica's hand. "Yes, it is hard for us to understand. We have a system that guarantees basic human rights. But the people here have no recourse, no rights. No hope."

Lady Ashley's sympathies were clear, as clear as the determination and comprehension in her eyes.

They were interrupted momentarily as the train jolted and began to move again. A united sigh of relief purged the tension they had been covering with their conversation.

Thriving on the debate, Charles plunged in

again with, "And you would have me believe
that for the last three years they've been assuming the identities of Bulgars and Greeks and now
Bedouin?"

"Absolutely." Lady Ashley didn't seem to see
the improbability in that. "They're quite brilliant, these revolutionaries. Chameleons. Mas-
ters of disguise. Surprisingly cunning, actually,
for men so young."

Arthur Grey cleared his throat and glared at
Charles, awaiting his response and deliberately
saying nothing.

Feeling the eyes upon him, Charles also felt
an unaccustomed moral weight. Carefully he
said, "Of course, I have no intention of justify-
ing what Sultan Hasam has done. Only England's diplomatic position . . ."

"Which is," Arthur prodded.

"That the revolutionaries have neither the
strength nor the support to overthrow the Sultan." He turned to Lady Ashley. "You realize,
Lady Ashley, that this theory of yours would be
laughed right out of the embassy."

Lady Ashley grinned, thriving on such noto-
riety. "A fate, I can assure you, to which I am
well accustomed. Between you and me, I do
know for a fact that the revolutionaries fought
side by side with the Bulgars three months ago."

Arthur leaned toward her flirtatiously. "It
sounds as if you know more than you're telling
us."

"Oh, I learn things." Lady Ashley smiled

again. "You see, sooner or later everyone comes to Damascus."

Tarik had only just now begun to relax. The camp fires had a distinct Bedouin glow tonight, a deliberate reminder of nomadism. He had missed it while in Europe and now savored its freedom. These were camp fires meant to spark in the night and be gone by morning. The fires of perpetual movement. They crackled like red stars in the desert night.

He was looking for Salim but only halfheartedly. After today's raid on the train, he thought about not disturbing his friend at all. But there were still things to plan. So . . . find Kala and he would automatically find Salim.

Salim had had his eye on Kala ever since he and Tarik had returned from Britain. And, yes, there they were. Kala was preparing dinner over one of the camp fires while Salim twittered away at her in Arabic, obviously being somewhat salacious. Even veiled and robed, Kala was beautiful. She moved fluidly beneath the blue Bedouin livery, making the robes flow, and her elegant black eyes danced in the fire at Salim's words. Tarik considered, then made his decision and moved up behind his friend, remembering how it had been the same at Cambridge. Find the women, find Salim. Handsome Salim. Smooth Salim.

"Ah, to be twenty-two again," Tarik muttered.

Salim looked around. "Oh, and you're so old. So much older than I am, eh? A year? Maybe two?"

"So, Salim"—Tarik brushed over the comment, nodding toward Kala—"you embrace this way of life. Or is it just the woman you want to embrace?"

Salim smiled, cocked his hat in a most emblematic way, and punched lightly at Tarik's middle. "Better a woman than a camel, eh, friend? Or does your revolutionary rhetoric keep you warm at night?"

"In all your books you have never written of love," Tarik said. "Is that to be your next subject?"

Salim grinned self-consciously. "A writer must take inspiration where he finds it."

Then, unexpectedly, horses whinnied on the horizon. In a breath Tarik and Salim spun, standing back to back, each holding a weapon that moments ago had been invisible. Tarik grabbed two Bedouin robes and tossed one to Salim. Instantly they pulled the robes over their frock coats and once again bared their weapons toward the sounds at the camp's perimeter. But they had only blades, useless against the rifles now lining the horizon.

"Damn—" Tarik choked on disgust with himself. The Empire's men were getting better at this game.

There was no escape.

In moments the entire tribe—men, women, children, babies—had been rounded up, the hub of a great wheel of armed soldiers of the Empire. The Turkish commander turned to his second in command, a tall man with a mustache—

Murat, who could speak Arabic to these barbaric Bedouin. He stoically instructed, "Tell them Sultan Hasam wishes no harm to his Bedouin subjects. That he respects their desert. Tell them that the Sultan has no battle to fight with the Bedouin." He paused, studying people he obviously regarded as savages while the interpreter translated his words. Then he resumed. "All the Sultan wants are the revolutionaries who are among you. Give us their names and nothing will happen to your people." Again he waited for the interpreter to complete the passage, then waited longer for a response. The faces of the Bedouin, even the children, remained like stone. "Surely someone has the information." He began to pace along the line of dusty faces.

Salim flinched as he saw the Turkish commander hesitate beside Kala. This time the girl's beauty would betray her, and he was too far away to do anything about it.

"Stay still," Tarik warned under his breath, feeling Salim tense beside him.

Sure enough, the Turk took Kala by the shoulders. "Tell me where the revolutionaries are hiding." When she said nothing, he ripped the veil from her face and turned her toward her tribe in humiliation. "Such a beautiful face. See what a beautiful face—" The commander wrenched Kala's hands away when she tried to cover her face, forcing her to display herself before her people. "A face this beautiful should not be disfigured." There was no viscious teasing in his voice. He was quite serious. To the interpreter he said, "Tell them what I said. Tell them what will happen to her if she refuses me what I want."

Murat buried a shudder and protested, "But, sir—"

"Tell them."

Murat sighed and told the grisly story. The girl's black eyes flashed with panic. The commander saw it and spoke to her firmly. "I am not asking you to betray your own people. Just give me the names of the revolutionaries among you."

Kala struggled, then gave in to the iron grip. "I give you nothing!" she cried in Arabic. The meaning required no translation.

The Turkish commander let go of her, and for a moment Salim breathed more easily. Perhaps the bastard had tired of Kala and would move on. . . .

The big Turk gritted his teeth and scraped his sword from its scabbard in a great swooping motion. It arched powerfully toward Kala's neck and did not stop.

The interpreter blinked into a splatter of blood. The girl's head tumbled into his shin.

Before Kala's body knew enough to collapse, Salim's raging cry of agony became a cry of battle. Enraged beyond sanity, the Bedouin bloomed outward against their oppressors.

Surprise was their only weapon. The Turks were not used to rebellion after capture, but they had misjudged the fury of Bedouin loyalty.

In the midst of the midnight fray Tarik fired a pistol from one hand and swung a sword from the other. He was clumsy this way, but there were so many Turks that hitting one from time to time was inevitable. He kept shooting and swinging. Only when he saw two small children about to be dismembered did his shooting and swinging gain direction. He plunged through a camp fire, a phoenix of sparks and flame as his robe caught fire and scattered bits of burning wood. The offending Turk released the children, gawking at the incredible sight, but before he could react, Tarik had grabbed him and skewered him onto an upright lance buried in the ground. The Turk shrieked, clutching at the spear where it emerged from his body and trying to reach around to the place where it parted his spine, but in seconds he was mercifully dead. Tarik ground his teeth bitterly. He hadn't intended to be merciful. He gathered the tiny children close to his smoking robes. "Quickly, come here—Radik! Radik!"

Radik appeared from under one of the tents, eyes wide.

"Come here," Tarik ordered. "Take the children. Take them to the ridge. Those over there too. Go!"

Scared into silence, Radik herded half a dozen Bedouin children away from the core of the battle. Tarik formed a one-man line between the Turks and the children. He burned with a thousand emotions. Isolated, each of those feelings would have been impotent. Together, they rang.

High on a ridge the next morning, Tarik lowered his binoculars and handed them to Radik, who looked out over the dunes.

"Where will they take them?" the old man wondered, scanning the long line of captured revolutionaries being threaded along the sandy floor of the Earth. Twenty of them. And on either side a long column of Turkish soldiers walked their horses, taking no chances. The prisoners were chained and shackled, dressed in Bedouin rags. Salim was in the lead, holding his head up.

Tarik raged with himself. "To Sultan Hasam." He resisted the desire to look through the binoculars again. Salim's stoic pride would only have been painful. And the blood on Salim's ankles from the shackles might as well have been Tarik's own.

"There are too many soldiers." Radik lowered the scopes. "We cannot fight them."

"I can't just let them go to their deaths!" Tarik struck his thigh in frustration, hating the Bedouin robes he wore; an irrational feeling but potent.

"There is nothing we can do," Radik said. "Not . . . until they reach Constantinople."

Tarik wheeled toward him, hearing the idea glimmering behind the old man's tone of voice. "What are you saying, old man? Do you have some kind of plan?"

"We cannot fight for their lives," Radik said. "But we can bargain for their release."

"With what?"

The toothless smile spread before Tarik. Radik delighted in his ingenuity. "You tell me. What does Hasam value most? Where does he spend most of his time?"

Tarik shrugged. "In the Imperial Harem."

"Exactly! He has an insatiable appetite, and since the slave markets have closed, he has a very limited supply." Tarik scowled at him, and Radik rushed to defend himself. "It's true. I know a man who says that the Kislar Agha is having great trouble finding new girls for the harem. They say that Sultan Hasam grows bored and that the Kislar is losing power. For the right kind of girl—something special—for a girl like that the Kislar would be willing to pay any amount. If you want . . . I can make arrangements."

Tarik had turned back to the heart-sinking sight on the desert below him. His heart buried itself in helpless misery. In Syria, in Greece, in Turkey, women were basically the same. "What kind of arrangements?" he muttered.

"A trade," Radik explained. "One girl for twenty prisoners."

"But where are we going to find a woman who would give us that much bargaining power?"

A thrilling dream to bring such a plan to life, but Sultan Hasam already possessed the finest, most erotic, most divine women in thousands of miles. Thus Tarik hardly believed it when Radik's spindly finger tapped his shoulder and the gummy grin appeared in the periphery of his vision.

"I," Radik informed, "have seen such a woman."

CHAPTER THREE

Radik moved through the crowded streets of Damascus, simply another form amid the hundreds of monochromatic Arab robes, robes designed less for fashion than for fending off the scorching Syrian sun. His anonymity was pleasing to him, perfect for his task. At such an age he felt great pride in Tarik's trust, revitalized by the opportunity to be an important link in this political chain. Allah had surely smiled upon him to give him league with a man like Tarik Pasha. Radik would polish that trust until it shined.

The train had just pulled into the station. Damascus immediately turned into a dazzling bazaar of bangly Eastern music, filling the air with distinctively erotic sounds: chimes; percussion beats as sensual as a woman's rotating hips; twanging strings, and the bone-penetrating blend of tambourine, zither, cymbal, mandolin, and clarinet. On the platform a very young girl, teetering on the edge of womanhood, danced to the music and hoped the tourists would drop a few coins into her folded veil as she held it out to them. Radik noticed a stout, tired-looking Englishman favor the girl with a handful of coins—too much, Radik could tell, for a dance so amateurish—but an instant later his attention had left the Englishman. The girl's brown wrists and bony hands swirled nearer the man's face, embarrassing him, and a spangle of brass bracelets rolled on the girl's arms as she thanked him with her entire body. The man blinked and looked away, unable to take the erotic motions as casually as the rest of the crowd. Radik thought this was funny. The girl had learned those movements at her mother's knee, and all Eastern women had an inborn knowledge of them, a natural response to the cadences of Eastern music. Eastern men would not look away but knew how to appreciate these things. The Englishman was wasting a perfectly good dance by not looking at it.

A vision appeared on the platform, brilliantly white, ribboned in blue, and belted by a golden cord. The young woman's alabaster face shone like a diamond among all the dark, veiled faces of the Syrian crowd, her clothing alone setting her apart, but her face caught the sunlight and made the clothing seem dull. Her bullion-yellow hair fell long and free, as no Arab woman could ever possess or would ever have the courage to display.

Radik smiled his toothless smile. Surely he

gazed upon a prize well worth the lives of twenty men.

He watched from his place within the crowd as the Englishman and the young woman joined another man and woman—the second couple was just as mismatched as the first, but this time the woman was too old for the man. Perhaps they were all one family, Radik thought as he watched them climb into a coach after their luggage was mounted securely on top. As the coachman snapped the reins and the horses jolted into a slow trot through the crowd, Radik smiled and hurried in the same direction.

"I'm so glad you could come to my party," Lady Ashley said as she greeted Jessica and Charles at the edge of her palatial home in the center of Damascus. "I really did mean the invitation sincerely, and not just because you cornered me into it." She smiled teasingly at Charles.

But Charles and Jessica were still staring at her.

Lady Ashley was utterly transformed. No longer primly English in her European fashions, she now wore the traditional blue robes of the Bedouin. Her huge blue eyes were counterpoised by thick outlines of black kohl in the Eastern fashion, and her light hair was plaited down the back of her head. Her feet were actually bare. Bare feet!

Jessica shook herself. "My . . . my father sends

his regrets. I'm afraid he was quite exhausted from the train ride."

"Is he feeling ill?" Lady Ashley asked.

"He won't say, but then he never does." She gazed at Charles, secretly wondering if her father had ever confided in his future son-in-law about his health. Though she had questioned her father about his mysterious fatigues and the medicine he took, she hadn't been able to pry any real answers from him. He would only say that the doctor was unhappy with the way his blood flowed these days. Too thick, he said. Nothing serious, he insisted.

Charles interceded. "He has assured us that a few days of absolute quiet should help him recover completely. He lamented the fact that men with daggers take it out of him."

Lady Ashley laughed and looped an arm in each of theirs. "Rightfully so. Come along now. I want to show you my gardens."

She led them through a portal in space. They were suddenly transported from Damascus in 1909 to Shakespearean England. Fruit trees lined the cobbled path they walked, nesting in candy tuft and sweet william, bordered by thyme, Canterbury bells, lavender, chamomile, Johnny-jump-up, sweet woodruff, and lily of the valley. Lady Ashley named the floral bunches as they passed, and for a moment Jessica felt as if she were truly back in England. A cold shudder passed through her. Regret? Foreboding? She felt a strange urge to break away from Lady

Ashley and peek just beyond the hollyhocks, for certainly Greyhurst would be there.

They walked around a corner, past clutches of violets and damask roses, and ran squarely into contradiction. Jessica stopped short, staring.

Before them sprawled a camp of Bedouin reposing right in the middle of the otherwise English garden. The Bedouin gazed unaffectedly at her. She gaped back, wondering what these savages were doing here.

Lady Ashley touched Jessica's arm. "I should have warned you. After yesterday I don't wonder that you're startled."

"Do you know these men?" Jessica narrowed her eyes.

"Oh, they stop in from time to time. They're relatives."

"Relatives?"

"On my husband's side, of course."

"Your husband?" Jessica shifted her stare from the Bedouin to Lady Ashley. "That awful man on the train—the one you spoke to—was he a relative too? Is that why he left us alone?"

"Jessica, you're being impolite," Charles warned.

"It's quite all right," Lady Ashley told him, and turned back to Jessica. "He left us alone because of what I said." She paused and diplomatically turned Jessica and Charles back toward the house. "*Nahnu malihin.* It means, 'We are salt fellows.' It refers to the sacred ceremony of breaking salt together. It renders travelers safe among all the tribes. You see, even among awful old men there is still a kind of chivalry left among the Bedouin." She looked ahead, then said, "Oh, good. There he is."

At the top of a spreading staircase stood an amazing man. Jessica was stunned stiff by his visceral sexuality as he stood above them—literally above, and figuratively, too—a Bedouin prince straight out of legend. He made not a move until they had gained the top step and stood with him. Lady Ashley made a social bridge between this legend and her two guests.

"Jessica, Charles," she began, "I'd like you to meet my husband, Sheikh Medjuel."

The Sheikh bowed his staglike head. His eyes never left Jessica. Charles hardly existed at all. "I am honored."

Jessica never for a moment doubted it.

She and Charles followed as the legend and his smoothly dichotomous wife led them into a splendid octagonal drawing room. They gawked unashamedly at a majestic collection of memorabilia that reflected years of travel, mixing European and Oriental tastes. Never had Jessica seen two cultures so effectively merged. Brass samovars lived quite happily beside Dresden china and an elegant silver tea set. Louis XIV tables reposed upon Byzantine prayer rugs. A portrait of Queen Victoria seemed natural hanging against a tiled, mosquelike wall.

The guests milling in the room were just as mixed. The only common elements were the fluted glasses from which they sipped champagne. Bedouin, Greeks, Arabs, Britons, and

unidentifiable others chatted casually as Lady
Ashley surrendered her husband to a business
associate and turned to Jessica and Charles.
"There's Mrs. Pendleton sitting with her husband," she said, nodding discreetly toward a
small woman with uncombed wisps of graying
hair seated on a Turkish divan. "They're archaeologists. Fascinating people. You must talk
to them, both of you. But don't say anything
about her sensible shoes." With a devilish grin
she nudged Jessica in the Pendletons' direction
and excused herself to tend to other guests.

True to Lady Ashley's word—Jessica was beginning to believe Lady Ashley could be nothing but right—the Pendletons were indeed
fascinating folk. Mrs. Pendleton stubbornly drank
tea instead of champagne, while Mr. Pendleton
happily downed his own share of champagne,
then went back for his wife's share.

"Yes, tomorrow we begin our caravan to the
ruins of Palmyra," Mrs. Pendleton was saying.
"This part of the world has always held my
heart . . . an empire built upon the ruins of
other empires. One peels off the layers of the
past—the Christian, the Muslim, the Roman.
It's a place of constant change. Even now the
West begins creeping in."

Charles typically observed, "But you must be
aware of the danger of going anywhere. Just
yesterday we were assaulted on the train."

Jessica leaned forward. "We were not assaulted. The Turkish soldiers were assaulted,"

she said, keenly aware of the inconsistency. "We were simply inconvenienced." She carefully downplayed the danger, sensing an advantage in it.

Mrs. Pendleton seemed neither surprised nor put off by Charles's announcement. "I would gladly risk inconvenience and assaults to see the pink columns of Palmyra rising out of the desert stillness. There is no other sight in the world like it."

Jessica inhaled, breathing not the air of Damascus but the air of Palmyra. "It sounds glorious . . ."

Mr. Pendleton took a sip of his third—fourth? —glass of champagne and commented, "What it is . . . is tedious." He turned to Charles, hoping to find refuge with another male. "Classifying remains and all, you know."

The elder woman leaned toward Jessica. "He's a good man, but he has no sense of romance. So I make my own. It's the only sensible thing to do, don't you agree?"

Jessica nodded, but the nod never even came close to conveying the depth of her agreement. "You know, I never expected to meet anyone like you here. . . ."

"You mean at Lady Ashley's?"

Not knowing any polite way to answer, Jessica nodded discreetly.

Mrs. Pendleton nodded back. "Well, granted, in England she would be far less than acceptable. But here in the East much is overlooked. It is enough to be English."

Four hours later Jessica and Charles sat together on a brocade mattress, one of many mattresses and divan cushions thrown casually around the rooftop for the few remaining guests. They were utterly mesmerized. Before them, Sheikh Medjuel sat kinglike, smoking his *narghilye*. Below him, Lady Ashley was washing her husband's feet. Incredible.

Only her words mellowed the alienness of her actions for Jessica and Charles.

"The Arab object in life," she explained, "is to be. To be free, to be brave, or simply to be. It's in opposition to the way I was brought up, which was to have. Wealth . . . knowledge . . . whatever. And it's different from others, like our young revolutionaries, who believe it is simply enough to do. Movement, action for its own sake."

Mistily Jessica weighed her ladyship's words. "To be, to have, to do . . . which do you embrace?"

Lady Ashley smiled as she dipped the cloth she was using to wash the Sheikh's feet into a ceramic bowl filled with spiced water. "Only when you have savored the desert stillness can you know what it is to be. And once you understand that, life's poetry can never sink to prose."

Jessica tightened her shoulders thoughtfully and stared up into the starry sky over the desert city. Deeply affected, she stood up and walked to the edge of the rooftop, taking in the sprawling panorama of night over Damascus. An unexpected hunger rose within her to see things that waited over that distant horizon, to touch and experience the wonders facing people like the Pendletons every day, until they were almost in danger of being taken for granted. The low-pitched conversations from other parts of the rooftop became vehicles for her imagination. Suddenly she was in a thousand places at once.

"Are you all right?" Charles's voice lanced from her left ear. She hadn't been aware that he'd followed her.

Half teasing, she wondered, "Why is it that men worry whenever women become reflective?"

"I don't know," Charles admitted, not ready to hold the male cross too high. "What are you reflecting about?"

Not knowing how to tell him the truth, not sure he would understand, Jessica said, "I can't help wondering what Aunt Lily would make of our ladyship."

Charles leaned on the balcony rim of the rooftop. "Not much," he said drolly.

Jessica mused, "I think I prefer places where things are overlooked." That cold feeling came back. The one she'd felt in the garden. Desperately she swept toward Charles, disturbed by how surprised he was to find her in his arms. "I love you, Charles," she said, "for bringing me here, for sharing this with me."

He wrapped his arms around her waist, thinking they were alone in the world, just two lovers framed by the minarets of Damascus.

But he didn't fully understand when Jessica murmured, "It's a perfect time for beginnings, don't you think?"

And he sensed that he was being left behind.

Arthur Grey awakened from a restful sleep, his first in weeks, and tried to ignore the tightness in his chest. He sat up, stretched, and reoriented himself to the sounds of the bazaar below his window. Hardly the twittering of Greyhurst's sparrows. It was getting harder and harder to remember that he wasn't in England any longer, that Jessica's mother had been dead quite a long time now, and that he would soon be alone. Had he been a more selfish man, he would have found some socially acceptable reason to decline Charles Wyndon's request for Jessica's hand in marriage, but Jessica was hardly cut out to be a nursemaid to her father, which she didn't deserve, anyway. Nursemaids could be bought. Daughters couldn't. Neither could decent sons-in-law.

Arthur ran a hand through his hair while sitting on the edge of his bed, then took a swig of his medicine. Only when he put the vial back on the dressing table did he notice the note. He knew what it said—in essence—even before reading it. Jessica's handwriting was easy to spot even in the dimness of early-morning light. His chest constricted with foreboding. Jessica only wrote notes when she knew he would disapprove. He also knew she wouldn't stay around to be scolded.

Struggling out of the bed, Arthur blinked at the note.

"Dear Daddy . . . Please don't be angry with me, but I simply had to see the pink columns of Palmyra."

Lady Ashley was drinking aromatic Turkish coffee when Charles, quite flushed, burst through her doors unannounced. He was covered with Syrian dust from head to foot. Evidently he had gone into the streets and none too carefully. He was uncombed, unshaven, and exhausted.

"Please excuse this uninvited interruption, Lady Ashley, but this is urgent. Do you know anything about this?" He flagged the good-bye note in her face.

She knew he wasn't meaning to be accusative. "First sit down and compose yourself. Then we shall see about what I know." She waited until he was safely seated, then read the note. Charles frowned when Lady Ashley showed no form of surprise. "I see," she murmured. "Jessica said nothing to me about a trip to Palmyra, but perhaps you've gotten lucky."

Charles vaulted to his feet again, quite agitated. "How can you say lucky? She's gone on that fool trip and she's my responsibility. I'm worried sick. And her father's beside himself."

"There's no real cause to worry, Charles. Palmyra is an ancient city just northeast of Damascus, a day or so by caravan. It's on the edge of the Syrian desert—not hard traveling by Eastern standards. She'll stay until she's tired of the drudgery of archaeology, then she'll come back. Give her a week. She needs it."

Charles pressed his lips together. "A week . . . I just don't understand her sometimes."

"This much I do know," her ladyship explained, compensating for his nervousness. "Jessica needs an adventure. Perhaps this will be it. And if you're lucky . . . the end of it."

"I just wish I understood why she had to go."

"You're not listening. All young girls need to strike out on their own for a bit. When I was Jessica's age, I left a proper English gentleman with a perfectly proper English fortune to run away with a Russian count who was sailing for Tahiti. So you see, you are lucky. After all, Charles . . . what could be tamer than an adventure supervised by a middle-aged woman wearing sensible shoes?"

"Most good, lady. She look good on you." The barterer stood back and surveyed the long waistline before him, nodding at the particularly snug fit. The silver-bangled, hand-twisted metal belt, with its tiny pictures of animals on ceramic buttons, looked out of place against the British twilled cotton walking skirt. But the woman liked it, judging by the smile on her pale face, and had actually paid him full price for it. The barterer resisted a victorious giggle at the woman's haughty expression. These Britishers. They looked down their noses at his people, yet they didn't even know how to haggle.

His eyes gleamed as he collected the belt's full price of coins in his dirty palm. "Most nice," he said, and reached for a bracelet made of penny-size silver domes held together by intricately meshed threads of silver and copper. "I *dash* you this."

"*Dash?*" The woman seemed puzzled as the barterer attached the bangle around her narrow wrist.

He was trying to find the English words to explain it to her when a stooped, white-haired lady dressed in khaki stepped toward them. Behind her was a little man wearing a Bombay pith helmet and Gurkha shorts.

"He's giving you a gift," Mrs. Pendleton explained. "For making the purchase of the belt. Take it. If you refuse, you'll insult him."

Jessica murmured, "Oh. Well, thank you very much."

The barterer bowed and uttered, "*Allah minakh.*"

"Yes . . . you too." She turned to the Pendletons and showed off her new belt. "Isn't it exotic? I feel like a belly dancer or something. Look at the craftsmanship. How could anyone work with such thin threads? Have you ever seen such fine filigree? And look . . . they've actually made little beads out of silver. I'm so glad I came." She walked with the archaeologists through the central bazaar of Damascus, past the honey seller and the prayer rugs and the ceramic pottery and brightly-painted urns, through a world of tiles and mosaics, domes and arches. She had never imagined that a foreign place could be so foreign. Could England exist on the same world as this place? "Are all these sellers Syrians?" she asked.

Mrs. Pendleton gasped, "Oh, no, my dear, no. These bazaars are made up of people from all over the Middle East. Syrians, Assyrians, Hausa traders, Turks, Arabs, Bulgarians, Armenians . . . you may hear them talking in a dozen different languages and never be sure which language or which dialect you're listening to."

"You'll never get used to it," Mr. Pendleton admonished. "Don't try."

Jessica smiled at him. For all the cynicism Mr. Pendleton tried to put across, he certainly enjoyed talking with these people, she'd noticed, and he hadn't at all minded getting "dashed" a beautiful, though useless, brass censer after buying a leather bandolier this morning. Now he wore the bandolier, and the censer hung from it, looking rather silly dangling against his regimental belt and Gurkhas.

Mrs. Pendleton cuffed her husband lightly and scolded, "Don't discourage her. An extra language or two wouldn't hurt you any." She turned back to Jessica. "These people wander all over the East, buying and selling. Damask, spices, sugar, lemons, brassware, handcrafts, muslin, amber and ivory, jewelry made of every imaginable medium, as you can see. Now, Jessica, we have to buy some water bags from that merchant over there. Don't wander too far—we'll be right back. This fellow always wants twice what his water bags are worth, and he loves a good fight."

If there is one thing a well-to-do American woman with a well-to-do English father loves to do and does well, it's shop. Jessica thrived on the bazaar, even though she bought nothing more than the belt she was wearing. It was enough to smell the new smells, feel the exotic textures, imagine herself in the mist-thin silks with their shimmering gold borders, and examine the metal bowls and vases so heavily painted with intricate scenes that they seemed at first to be porcelain.

She moved past a fruit stand, aiming for a fascinating wagonload of ready-made skirts of every color in the universe, and found herself face-to-face with a snarly old man with no teeth. He grinned obscenely at her. She shook herself and stepped to one side, but he stepped that way also, refusing to let her pass. Something about him, about the way he looked at her, was too imposing to tolerate. She tried stepping the other way, and still he moved to block her way.

"Get away from me," she said firmly.

The gaping grin widened. The man stayed where he was. Jessica was nearly a head taller, but the sturdy little man looked quite unmovable. There would be no graceful way to get past him. Not quite ready for confrontation, she turned around. The wagonload of skirts could wait. She could live without fringed hems for the moment.

She heard him following her, perhaps more by instinct than by actually hearing his footsteps in the loud bazaar. She knew he was there and forced herself to walk slowly and deliberately. Some unused international instinct told her that running would only deepen her predicament by showing fear and weakness. But the sigh of relief when she saw Mr. and Mrs. Pendleton heading her way with armloads of goatskin water bags belied her near panic. She headed straight toward them.

"Ah, Jessica," Mrs. Pendleton said in greeting. "I see you've met Radik."

Jessica whirled around, less surprised that the old fossil was still there than by the fact that Mrs. Pendleton knew his name.

The elder woman went on, "We've been told he's a most expert guide."

The old man continued to leer at her with that empty grin. "I best," he acknowledged. "I make all the right bribes. I keep you safe."

Jessica inhaled, squared her shoulders, and turned to follow Mrs. Pendleton to their waiting caravan. "You just keep away."

Because she had turned her back, she did not see the toothless grin widen behind her.

By evening she was drenched in dust. The belt at her waist, once the shining white of unrefined silver, was now dull with dirt. She had endured the day-long trek in staunch fashion, and had grown gladder by the moment that she had trained her body with long walks and grueling horseback rides. It all came in handy now as she trudged beside her camel—disgusting beasts, ornery as unmilked cows—but she put her mind to sleep and continued trudging. Anything Mrs. Pendleton could do, she could do too. It was all right—this mindless walking prevented her from thinking about Charles or her father. They'd get over their anger. They'd understand eventually. She wasn't yet sure what she needed, why she felt compelled to strike out on her own, or even what she expected to find and feel. She only knew that Charles deserved a wife who knew how to handle herself in this savage world and that her father should know that his daughter was capable of dealing with the change in cultures. Well, all right, perhaps she *was* disguising her impulsiveness with concern for the two men in her life, but she knew they didn't have what she needed right now. The Pendletons just might, though. All Jessica knew right now was that she felt abundantly alive, as though she were teetering on the verge of something unknown and thrilling. Even her aching muscles sang with anticipation as she kept up the dogged pace beside her camel.

"Missy . . . missy . . . you want water?"

Radik. Jessica's skin prickled. Over her shoulder she said, "I'll wait for the well."

"Why you don't ride?" the old man asked, but she knew he was taunting her.

"I don't want to tire the animal," she answered flatly.

He jogged up in front of her, laughing in ridicule. "And what tires you?" he asked rudely.

She pushed past him and aimed for the horizon.

They walked all night. Travel in the desert made more sense at night than under the grueling midday sun. Now that the rose-yellow dawn glowed on the eastern horizon behind distant mountains, the team of archaeologists, their young American guest, and their only hired man began setting up camp. Jessica watched with a mixture of curiosity, admiration, and distaste as Mrs. Pendleton cooed into a stupid, lateral face and patted the camel's neck. "There, there, baby. Let's put her down."

The huge beast dropped to the ground and groaned.

Jessica shook her head. Camels. No matter how many beads and tassles and pretty rugs they were decorated with, they still looked stupid.

She took a moment to gaze out over the serene desert, an expanse of barren beauty. The pale sunrise, showing nothing of the glaring, deadly brightness to come, colored the desert a mystic amber. It would feel good to sleep. Today she felt satisfied. Today . . .

She squinted. Was that a dust cloud? Yes, but it was moving too fast to be a natural phenomenon. And it was coming toward camp. She waited until it began to take shape. Men, horses, all at full gallop. Mrs. Pendleton had been, it seemed, in the desert too many years not to sense something amiss before it was pointed out to her. She appeared beside Jessica and watched as the dust cloud took shape.

"What is it?" Jessica asked.

"Nothing to be alarmed about, I'm sure," Mrs. Pendleton said, but only a child would have missed the concern in her tone. "We're quite safe." Apparently she thought of Jessica as a child. "Radik has made all the right bribes. . . . Still, it might not hurt to consult him." She moved away.

Jessica continued to watch the riders as they drew nearer. Behind her, the English camp erupted into confusion. She looked around, spied Mrs. Pendleton going from tent to tent, and called, "Mrs. P.! What's wrong?"

Mrs. Pendleton's round face looked ashen in the dawn light. "He's gone . . . vanished. I don't understand it."

Jessica's heart shriveled. She stared at the approaching riders. There was no mistaking them now—a band of Bedouin marauders riding *djerid*. An instant later she put her panic to good use and ran through the camp to her camel. Tearing through the supplies, she dug until she found the eating utensils, which included a good sharp knife for cutting the dried meat that would be— would have been—a staple meal on this quest. She armed herself with it, stood, and turned, frozen in place.

At the camp's center reared a bone-lean white

desert horse, bridled with coral and silver, draped in boldly striped cloths. Astride this wild bit of wind sat a disturbing man, stunning in his savagery and elegance. He was wrapped in traditional blue Bedouin robes, yet these hid none of his unpredictability. Beneath him the foaming horse bucked and reared, but this did nothing to alter the posture of the rider as he stared unblinkingly—at Jessica.

Around him the camp roiled. People and camels and Bedouin and horses and panic. He was a rock in its mist. Jessica could not move. She felt the knife in her hand, tucked between folds of her skirt.

With a glimmer of triumph in his eyes the Bedouin raider pulled the elaborate reins high and brought his knees in on his horse's shoulders. The beast sprang forward, toward Jessica.

Shaken from her trance, she dodged to her left, heading for an open space between two tents.

She felt the earth throb as the horse drove down upon her, and a great blue shape sailed past her, right through the tent at her right. The tent collapsed in a heap. Jessica dipped down, doubled back, and dodged in another direction. She heard the horse scream as its rider forced it to wrench around, and the horrible truth rammed home: He was after her, her in particular.

The earth drummed again.

She ran.

A force crushed the air from her, tightening

around her waist. The ground fell out from beneath her feet, and she smelled sweat and foam. She saw hooves beneath her now. He had her.

She forced herself to think clearly. She took the knife in both hands and twisted around in the Bedouin's grip, swiping upward. He flinched. Blood drained down his face, soaking into the cloths that covered his mouth. The horse sensed his rider's shift in weight and ran even faster. The camp disappeared and the desert spilled out before them.

Jessica's heart sank now, a hard, thudding ball within her chest, too crushed to sustain her life. He hadn't let go of her. He still had her. And she would never again break this grip. The knife, she realized, was gone. Had he knocked it out of her hand? Yes, she remembered that. She had only her fists now, and they were pinned down by what seemed to be one of his legs. In all these folds of fabric Jessica felt lost. But, even beneath the fabric, she felt the strength of muscle and bone. He had her. And he wasn't letting go. She could only cling to the raging horse and think about escape.

The remaining Bedouin raiders trampled every tent in the camp to discourage anyone from trying to follow them. Just a polite warning, one might say. Once the tall rider on the white Arabian swirled away with Jessica scooped up in his grip, the others shrieked in triumph, too, and rode away in streaks of rising dust.

Mrs. Pendleton stood on the head of the precipice where they had set up camp, watching helplessly as Jessica and her captors dissolved into silt.

"Jessica . . ."

CHAPTER FOUR

The tent smelled like her father's cigars mixed with the strange aromas in the bazaar. Jessica's body ached from the long ride at full gallop. Only a desert horse would have such endurance. Without shame she admitted to herself that she didn't. Not yet, at least. She tried not to think of how humiliating it was to be so dazed that her captor had to carry her into the tent. But now her head was cleared. She had been shaken back to reality when he dumped her in this pile of carpeted cushions. She stared up into his coal-black eyes as he leaned perilously over her, a much more dangerous closeness than the ride they had just shared. She had tried to prepare herself. She had known this moment would come.

He was going to rape her. A desert mongrel would have nothing better to do with a white woman. She knew that. She'd prepared herself for it from the moment she first realized she could not break away from him. She would have to endure it. Get it over with, survive it.

He glared down at her. His face had stopped bleeding, but his entire left cheek was a paste of blood. She inhaled and smelled his sweat effusing from the thick robes. Above her his eyes flickered.

He backed away.

Jessica slumped. Backed away? That was even more frightening than the idea of being raped. It meant he had something else in store. If she didn't know what it was, she couldn't prepare for it.

She struggled to sit up in the smothering pile of cushions. He was across the tent now. He was washing the blood off his face, dipping a gold-threaded cloth into a brass urn, and using the water sparingly—a giveaway desert habit. Charles had told her about that . . . how some people who had grown up in the desert never quite got used to the availability of water, even after they'd lived in England for years.

Jessica composed herself, accepting the fact that, for the moment at least, she was safe. She got to her feet, forcing shaky knees to support her, and moved to him, but not too close. Pantomiming her words, she asked slowly, "What . . . is . . . going to happen . . . to . . . me?"

The man glanced at her and continued to wash his face, tugging away the wrap of cloth around his mouth. He said nothing.

"*Nahnu malihin,*" she tried. "*Nahnu malihin.*"

Nothing. Not a blink.

Jessica narrowed her eyes. "*Nahnu malihin*, I said. *NAHNU MALIHIN.*"

The man dried his face and straightened up, wiping off the last cakes of dirt and blood. He was darkly handsome, exotic in a most masculine way, wild as the desert horse he rode, and she hated him for it. And hated him that much more when he said, "Sorry, but my Arabic is a bit rusty."

She backed away, stunned. "How dare you let me make a fool of myself!"

Tarik moved toward the girl, doing his best imitation of a cobra on the prowl. Best to keep her in her place. "Believe me, pride is the least of your worries," he said. "You see, first of all, I'm not a Bedouin. And secondly, I'm not very chivalrous. Keeping those things in mind, I strongly suggest you do exactly as I say." He scooped up an armful of Bedouin robes and illustrated his point by saying, "Put these on. We leave within the hour."

The clothes landed in her arms and did a perfect about-face onto the carpet between them. She glared at him in abject defiance.

Patiently Tarik retrieved them and stepped dangerously near her. "You have a choice," he told her. "Either you put these robes on or I'll put them on for you."

He would. She could tell by his expression. Here was a man who cared nothing for decorum. He would use her genteel upbringing against her, and she knew it could be a formidable weapon. Better not to give him the option. She took the robes from his arms. "You'd like that," she said, "and I won't do anything you like."

Half a victory seemed plenty for him. He nodded in satisfaction and murmured, "I thought so." He left her alone to figure out what he meant.

Ten minutes later the tent parted and Jessica emerged, wearing the traditional blue robes and hood of the Bedouin. Over her shoulders hung a flowing white cape. The point was obvious: If anyone was looking for her, as she was sure they would be, they would look for a woman in English clothes, not in Bedouin robes. In a few days her face would be tanned and she would be just another Bedouin in the tribe.

She blinked in the bright sunlight and stared at the two forms before her, caught in their conspiracy. There, before her, was the man who had snatched her, handing over a purseful of coins to—damn him—Radik.

Of course. It seemed so obvious now.

"So it was you," Jessica accused, striding toward them boldly. "You made a mistake, Radik. My father would have paid you more."

Radik humiliated her with another of his back-bending laughs, his insolent, toothless mouth gaping roundly as he sauntered away. Two other Arabs came to lead her toward a pair of heavily decorated desert horses—her captor's white, and a thick-boned bay mare. Radik turned around and called back to her kidnapper, "Fair hair is unlucky, my friend. Watch out for that one."

Jessica sneered as Radik faded away in a round of laughter.

The kidnapper appeared beside her and sedately asked, "You know how to ride?"

"Well enough." If she'd thought fast enough, she would have denied it.

"Then the bay is yours."

One of the other Arabs was binding her wrists with rough cord. When he finished, Jessica held her wrists up to the man who had arranged this picnic for her. "There's no point to this. Why would I try to escape? I don't know how to survive on the desert . . . where the wells are . . . even the direction toward a town eludes me. Without you I most certainly would die."

He gazed casually into her eyes, and she felt the heat of his thoughts. He only half believed her, no matter how true her words. A tiny grin tipped the corner of his lip upward. Whether or not he accepted her logic remained to be seen. She waited, and held her breath.

With a swaggering motion he presented a curved dagger. The ropes fell at her feet.

Jessica swallowed tightly. "Thank you."

Demurely she swung up into the saddle on the bay mare and gave her captor an upper-class nod as he stood below her with a smug look on his face. Too bad. He made her curious. She would've liked to get to know him better—under entirely different circumstances.

With a wild shout she spurred her horse violently. The beast responded with a startled bolt and bounded to a full gallop. Arab robes filed past in a single blur as Jessica leaned down into the animal's withers and gave the mare her head. The white cape flowed behind her. Jessica adjusted her legs on the saddle and prepared herself for a ride such as she had never before experienced. She knew well enough how to ride across Florida's flat sands or the rolling greenery of England, but the dunes rising and falling before her would be something entirely different, not something a rider could learn on the run. She would have to trust the horse. She made no attempt to coach the mare as the dunes and valleys surged up and plunged down beneath the horse's hooves. Each dune was a fight upward. Jessica felt the strain in the horse's body, but the animal deftly shifted her weight to her hindquarters and lowered her head for leverage against the moving sand. Each crest was like falling over a waterfall. Jessica clung to the saddle and put her mind forward, refusing to think of being caught again. The ride was exhausting. Everything happened at an angle. The mare nearly had to sit down in order to slide down the steep dunes without falling forward. Jessica had to stand up in the stirrups to keep her own weight from throwing the mare off. She had never had to fight so hard to stay in a saddle.

But she was free. Free.

The dunes became broader and steeper. Jessica concentrated on learning to ride this way, on improving her horse's efficiency with each climb and each drop. Just when she got good at it, a whirl of sand and robes appeared at her side. She turned her head to look and got a faceful of sand flayed from the hooves of the familiar white horse. And that man's face, those eyes, held steady beside her own. His hand flashed toward her.

She struck out before he was able to grasp her reins, catching him a glancing blow across the cut on his face. He gasped in pain and lost ground. She pushed her horse harder still. But now she knew why he had given her the bay. A fine mare, to be sure, but the white was the swifter of the two and the man soon caught up again. This time he let go of his own reins and caught her around the waist with both arms. At this speed she could do nothing to break the grip and stay on her horse at the same time. Instinct made her pull away. Gravity and centrifugal force betrayed her.

She toppled off the other side of her horse, bringing her kidnapper with her. In a vertigo of Bedouin robes they rolled down a sheer cleft, struck the sand, and tumbled to the foot of the dune.

Jessica heard the sound of her own breathless panting and knew she had been working harder than she realized and fighting harder than she knew she could. She felt the electric grip of her kidnapper, felt his eyes, and tasted sand. She blinked the sand out of her eyes and found herself looking squarely into his face. Was he amused? Or was his fury real?

"You've made a fool of yourself," he growled, yanking her against him as some form of crude punishment, "and now you've made one of me. That makes us even." He pitched her away and stood up. A rope came out of his sleeve. Evidently he'd expected to need it. He retied her hands and enjoyed giving the rope an extra twist, then tied it with a knot that looked like something one of the crewmen on the ship had shown her.

And her hands stayed bound throughout the long day's journey to come. Unlike the archaeologists, this man and his marauders thought nothing of traveling under the scorching desert sun. Jessica soon became dazed and flushed, weakened by the tedious plodding of the horse beneath her and the white heat above. The cord lacerated her wrists. She refused to express her pain, and it eventually dulled her senses beyond care. All she could do was try to sway with the horse instead of against her and endure the torture. By the movement of the sun Jessica guessed that they were moving northward, but after so many hours she lost track of the direction, the turns and twists through endless dunes and barren crags. Her head lolled. Her eyes closed, and she slumped in her saddle, insensible to the passing hours.

Ages later, the cool arms of desert night wrapped around her shoulders and supported her as she slipped from the saddle. The ground felt strange, alien beneath her feet, but the change of position roused her senses, and she blinked her eyes open. Something with water in it touched her lips, and she drank greedily until it was taken away.

"Too much water will make you ill," his voice said. Yes, she knew his voice already, recognized it quite clearly among all the other voices now chattering around her.

"Will food make me ill too?" she countered, less interested in food than in stalling any effort to walk yet. She was sure, from the way her knees and thighs felt, that she would fall flat on her face if she tried to move. She'd never allow him to see that. "Do you have a name?" she asked in a deliberately condescending tone.

"You don't need to know my name," he said flatly.

"At least loosen these ropes. I've no skin left on my wrists."

He looked at her bleeding arms and breathed deeply. "I had no idea. They'll be taken off immediately, of course—"

"Thank you."

"And replaced with muslin ties," he added firmly.

Jessica leered at him. *Thank* you."

"Quite welcome. But I must protect my investment."

"Meaning me."

"Meaning you."

An hour later she was gnawing indelicately at a chunk of dried meat, preserved by heavy spices that burned her lips and gums. She forced herself to choke down as much as possible, knowing that sustenance in the desert was sparse, and she would need her strength when the time came to attempt an escape. Before her crackled a Bedouin fire. On the opposite side sat the man who said he was not a Bedouin.

"You haven't sent a ransom note, have you?" she asked, speaking slowly through swollen lips. Her tongue felt twice its normal size, and it tingled. The man stoked the fire and refused to answer. After a moment Jessica decided that it must be because she knew the answer already. They might kidnap her for ransom, but they would never bother taking her so far away. The landscape had changed drastically; they were nowhere near Damascus anymore. "You're taking me far from Damascus, aren't you?" Still nothing from him. She shrugged and choked down another bite of the red-hot meat. "Maybe you don't have a master plan," she suggested. "Maybe you just operate on a day-to-day basis."

The man glanced at her, stone-silent.

"Did anyone ever tell you you're a fascinating conversationalist?" she said. "You surprise me. I thought the Young Turks were an intellectual sort."

This got his attention and won her a victory for her guess. It all added up, after all.

He demanded, "What do you know about the Young Turks?"

"I know they want to overthrow Sultan Hasam."

"They want to see the Ottoman Empire enter the twentieth century," he responded defensively.

She straightened up, her gaze telling him quite clearly that he had given himself away and was enjoying it. "So you are one of them. A revolutionary."

He sank back onto his cushion. "I never said that."

"You didn't have to."

He hid his disgust behind a match, which he touched to the tip of a hand-rolled Tuareg cigarette. "I have no intention of discussing my politics with you."

"Why not?" she countered. "I'm evidently their victim."

"Because most Europeans don't understand our complicated heritage. We're made up of dozens of nationalities that constantly intermix. We are Jews, Muslims, Christians, statesmen, tribesmen, traders . . . there is hardly an end to the list of differences. Our Empire is not just a land or a people. It is the quality of an idea. And that means we don't have to fester with the nationalism that plagues Europe."

Jessica sifted through her exhausted mind to find the things Charles had told her about these people. "But there is nationalism here," she argued, "even among the revolutionaries. 'In all things, Turkish,' right?"

Embarrassed, he folded his legs beneath him and half nodded. "There are some who think that way. But they are wrong."

Oh, a sore spot—good. Just what Jessica was prodding for. "If they're part of the Young Turks, then you're bound to them. That puts you in an ethical dilemma, doesn't it?"

"Yes, but after—what do you know about ethical dilemmas?"

"I know they can be unfair," she said. "At least you know what your dilemma is. Mine evades me."

The man's black eyes softened, even in the camp fire's harsh yellow-orange light. The sky had darkened a shade before he spoke again.

"Go to sleep, Jessica."

It was the first time he'd called her by her name. The shock numbed her. To think that he understood her identity—thought of her as a person—stunned her, and she was stricken by the tenderness in his voice. Was this the way a captor speaks the name of his prisoner? If only she could read the message behind his eyes now, a message clouded by the camp fire's smoke and the unexplained sadness she saw in him. He wasn't telling her anything . . . but he *wished* he could tell her. That much was plain. Jessica knew regret when she saw it, when she heard it—and she heard it in the gentle brush of her name as it fell from his lips.

I'll find out, she promised herself. *Before this is over, I'll know what he feels when he speaks my name. I'll know . . . because he'll tell me.*

She watched as her captor rolled over and curled up with his back to her. For a long time she merely gazed at him. When sleep finally touched her with its soft fingers and pressed her down into the sand, Jessica's promise had grown into a vow.

A day later the wristbands came off entirely. Jessica knew now beyond all doubt that any attempt at escape would mean a dusty, prolonged, agonized death at the hands of the desert. The man who walked with her now as they led their horses across the desertscape knew it also. They stopped at a baobab oasis under the blazing afternoon sun. Tarik hardly knew himself anymore.

He scooped water from the tiny, struggling pool beneath the clutch of baobab trees and went beyond any principle he knew by holding the cup to Jessica's parched lips. His gentility belied his sorrow, the regret of having to do this to her. She had talked about ethical dilemmas. He pressed his mouth into a tight line and tried to forget that she was an intelligent, courageous person. He tried to think of her bargaining power. Tried to think of Salim and the others. One in exchange for twenty. He had to think of that.

Anger raged in him toward the primitive bargaining traditions that forced him to do this to a civilized woman. She hadn't cried, not once. Not a whimper. Not even a complaint. She would be the victim of these pathetic, antiquated vogues that he himself was trying to stamp out, and he was not only letting it happen to her, but also perpetuating it with his own hands.

Was this all he could give back to the civilized European culture that had educated him? Could he only spit in its face by condemning this brave girl to his culture's unforgivable vogues? For now there could be only one answer. Tarik knew it, knew and hated it.

He tried not to look into the reddened face and blue eyes. But he looked, anyway.

Her voice withered him.

"I need to know what is going to happen to me," Jessica said. "I'm not afraid of you, but . . . I'm afraid of what you're going to do with me. I need to know. I need to prepare." She paused, composing herself, and asked the hardest question of all. "Will I ever see my father again?"

Tarik felt his heart dry up. He thought of Salim . . . of all the others who depended upon him, and the pain of separation redoubled. His only consolation was to tell himself that this girl's father was not in danger but that his friends definitely were.

He looked at her and clamped his lips together. His silence was her answer. Tears welled up in Jessica's eyes. Tarik saw them and had to turn away.

Charles felt cleaner but not better. Quite worse, in fact. At his right on the divan Arthur Grey seemed ten years older. Across from him Lady

Ashley sat, playing the part of a much-needed anchor in the midst of their maelstrom while Mrs. Pendleton held a cup of cold tea from which she had yet to take a sip. The archaeologist's wispy hair looked even wilder than the last time Charles had seen her. Her eyes were dim, without light.

"We were released after we paid a small ransom," Mrs. Pendleton explained after telling how the Bedouin had trampled their camp and ridden away in a swarm, only to return the next morning and take their food and water, thereby forcing them to return to Damascus. "But they would tell us nothing of Jessica."

Charles rasped, "And you never saw her again?"

Mrs. Pendleton sank every heart in the room when she shook her head. "I feel desperately responsible. I'm so sorry . . . so dreadfully sorry."

Lady Ashley used the ensuing silence to pour brandy into two snifters, sensing the two men needed strong drinks to help them through this helpless moment. "I respect the two of you far too much to lie. I'm terribly concerned because this fits no pattern. I can't explain what happened to Jessica, but I'm afraid she may be far away from us and in great danger."

Arthur slumped visibly. Charles tried to take control by saying something . . . anything. "I've tried to get help from the authorities here in Damascus, but they're totally unwilling to provide any help whatsoever."

Handing him his brandy, Lady Ashley waited until he looked up at her, until she had his gaze firmly in her own. "I'm afraid you'll find that's the rule rather than the exception. The authorities are useless here, but there is one thing in your favor."

He perked up. "What? Tell me."

"Quite simply this: There is nothing in the Ottoman Empire," she said, "that cannot be bought. And no secret that cannot be sold."

Nothing more was said. But Arthur and Charles completely understood Lady Ashley's meaning and took it to their hearts as a singular hope in favor of the girl whose life they mutually cherished. Arthur had bade Lady Ashley and the distraught Mrs. Pendleton a quick goodbye and dragged Charles back to their hotel. Without a pause he opened a drawer and violated a trust as old as love itself. Against a blood-red sunset that streamed in the hotel window, he opened a wooden chest the size of a loaf of bread and showed its contents to Charles.

"She thought it was terribly old-fashioned," he said, "but this was to be her dowry. Most of the jewelry belonged to her mother, of course."

"There's a fortune here," Charles breathed, entranced by the mismatched treasury of ruby necklaces, sapphires set in platinum and gold, a brooch heavy with diamonds, a chiseled emerald in its center, and strand upon strand of pearls.

"It's enough to buy every spy in the Empire."

Conquering hesitation, Charles carefully and slowly took possession of the chest. "If that's what it takes," he murmured, "then that's what we'll do." His voice grew stronger now that he held Jessica's salvation in his own hands. "We'll find her. I promise."

CHAPTER FIVE

Constantinople. A city of spires. Once called Byzantium, a vast empire had pulsed around it in ages gone by. All across the city rose the domes and pointed arches of its past greatness, the buildings made of priceless ceramic tiles and carved with runic inscriptions, miles upon miles of mosaics, minarets, friezes, and Oriental motifs. And higher than the highest building vaulted the Great Mosque of Suleiman the Magnificent, its needle spires, turnip-shaped towers, and *mihrab* prayer niches all pointing the way to Mecca, reminding all who passed that this was the hub of the Earth, where culture met culture. Where the Black Sea met the Sea of Marmara. Where mankind realized its own grandeur.

Here the world had come to trade and buy in centuries past, to gaze in awe at the splendid glazed tiles and arcades, and to sense the wonder of an ancient empire that had plaited together a scattering of nomadic tribes and given them identity as a single people. Here was the focus of the Ottoman lust for power, and even now, as the gleam faded, the beauty remained.

High above the strait between the Black Sea and the Marmara, the strait called Bosporus, loomed a vast palace, ornate enough to have turned the head of Suleiman himself. Within the great spired walls, between the walls and the palace itself, was a veritable forest of exotic gardens. To one side was an aviary, enclosed in latticework, almost as big as a palace itself. Over the next wall a trainer cracked a whip at a defiant Bengal tiger, obtained at great price from India. The tiger was frightened by the shrieking of the parrots from the aviary.

Outside the cage, on a pathway of mother-of-pearl, a lone man walked. He watched the tiger and its trainer impassively. He wore a plain frock coat and a fez, set apart from all the other fezzes in the palace only by a diamond clasp holding an egret feather. Though he was over fifty years old, his years gave him a patina of sorrow rather than a grayness of age, and he had not forgotten youth. His face was regal and bored. The tiger stared at him. The trainer began to sweat and cracked the whip louder, but the tiger refused to move, continuing to stare at the observer as though meeting one of its own kind.

The observer clasped his hands behind his back, nodded to the trainer, and walked on. He passed beneath arched doorways and over parquet floors and priceless Smyrnan and Persian carpets and tapestries that craftsmen had spent decades creating. Chairs covered in red damask garishly bordered walls made of pastel mosaic scenes, battling the decor in a struggle between East and West. Sultan Hasam felt that the New World encroached upon him as he walked across the grand reception room, through flanks of men awaiting audiences with him: court moderates led by the Grand Vizer Bey, advisers of his unofficial cabinet, reactionaries led by the court astrologer, and the large Black eunuch, Agha, who was the Kislar—chief eunuch and keeper of the Imperial Harem. Behind them gyrated a veritable circus of clowns, jugglers, and dervishes, each doing what he did best— clowning, juggling, or spinning.

With a fatigued sigh Hasam reclined on his divan and gestured to Murat, whose big mustached face he picked out from the gaggle of attendants. "So have you learned anything more?"

Murat stepped forward uneasily and performed a ceremonial salaam before speaking. "We have been suggesting to the prisoners that they give us the name of their leader." Both Murat and the Sultan thought of the shrieking of the parrots and the noise they were meant to cover up—the noise coming from the palace torture chambers . . . another brand of shrieking.

"And—?" Hasam prodded.

"The prisoners have confirmed our suspicions. The same group of young rebels that has been behind the scattered uprisings in the Empire were also behind the Bedouin raid on the train in Syria."

"And how is this information going to help the army deal with the problem," the Sultan went on, "considering how ineffectively they've dealt with the rebels so far?"

The barb was undisguised. Murat took it with a deep breath and went on. "This morning one of the men elected to share the name with us. The leader of the revolutionaries is Tarik Pasha. He led the raid in Damascus."

"Very good. And is this Pasha among the prisoners?"

"No, Your Imperial Majesty. We suppose he escaped during the last battle." Murat winced against his will as he said it.

Calmly Hasam said, "The Empire's entire army can only produce twenty prisoners. And the leader is not even among them. Perhaps the problem is not the revolutionaries but the army itself."

"All respects, Majesty," Murat dared to say, "but armies fight better when they are paid."

Sultan Hasam raised up on his arm, his eyes ablaze.

Murat opted to change the direction of the conversation, and quickly. "It is difficult to control a group that moves from place to place in disguise . . . a group that is upredictable, that does not operate in any military fashion."

Grand Adviser Bey stepped forward, sensing an opportunity to look worthwhile. "With all respect, I don't think there is a military solution to this problem."

"And what would you suggest?"

"Perhaps if the rebels were allowed a chance to speak . . ."

The ruler studied Bey with his hematite-black eyes.

The Kislar stepped forward, but only one step. "Your Imperial Majesty might be interested in hearing what they have to say."

Sultan Hasam snapped a harsh glare at him. "And what do you know about what interests me?"

The Kislar was silenced. The entire court felt his humiliation.

"Your suggestion," the Sultan said to Bey, "as reasonable as it is, poses a difficult problem. One should surely listen to all who have something to say . . . *if* their words can have effect. But these men, with their 'vision' of the changes they would bring—" He cut himself off with a shake of his head.

Hasam leaned back on his divan, already bored again, and pointed to the papers Bey carried under his arm. "What is that?"

"Writings of one of the prisoners. A man named Salim. In them he explains the political purposes of the revolutionaries." He gave the papers to Hasam, unable to hide his disappointment that he hadn't been the first to read them.

"Go on," Hasam instructed after placing

the papers beside him on the divan—a clear gesture of possession. "What is your solution?"

Bey licked his lips. "Reason. I believe these revolutionaries would be satisfied if Your Majesty were to agree to a constitution guaranteeing basic rights to all citizens of the Empire."

The Kislar Agha leaned forward, adding, "Such a constitution would appease our European critics as well."

The Sultan struck him with a scolding glare. The rest of the court did not fail to take note of it. Kislar Agha and everyone around him, from the Imperial ruler to the lowliest juggler, felt the tug and strain of palace politics in full operation. It remained to be seen who would leave this audience in Sultan Hasam's best favor, and who would fall out of favor today on His Majesty's whim.

Bey went on, taking advantage. "The revolutionaries are growing in strength. They will have to be dealt with one way or another."

Sultan Hasam stretched his left leg. "Kill them? Reason with them? Or perhaps ignore them?" In a rush of frustration he swept the prisoner's writings off the divan. The papers twisted in the air, scattered, and drifted lazily to several places on the floor. The court held a collective breath. "It seems," Hasam went on after a strained pause, "that most of you are in favor of this constitution. Most of you feel it is appropriate." The sensation was not one of favor. To agree with that statement was to invite death itself. He scanned his court with an ironlike dare in his eyes. Then he turned to the astrologer. "Tell them."

The astrologer, a small, wry man with a twitch in his right eye, nodded and carefully stated, "There can be no law but the Sultan's will."

Hasam looked around at the expanse of faces and gave them a ludicrous shrug. "So how can we have a constitution?".

Pleased with himself for solving so complex a problem, he reached for a bowl of figs.

The court dispersed.

Adviser Bey and the Kislar separated from the flood of attendants as they spilled out of the reception room. "We are losing influence with Sultan Hasam," Bey commented. "He hears only what he wants to hear. The army hasn't been paid in three months. The soldiers grow more discontent with each passing day and less willing to fight for a ruler who rewards them only with hunger. Loyalty isn't enough anymore, and with the rebel strikes increasing every week, he needs his soldiers now more than ever."

Agha's large ebony face remained unchanged. "He spends his money only on pleasure. He indulges his harem with jewels and extravagances that exceed all bounds. He never sees the soldiers, so they do not interest him. But he visits the harem every day."

"Is he blind to the danger? Blind to what is happening around him?"

"He was raised to believe himself invincible. There was a time when he listened to me."

"There was a time," reminded Bey, "when you provided him with the most wonderful women in this world. I understand his wife does that now."

"That is going to change."

Other things, too, were changing in the palace that day. Fates were being decided and sealed. Among them, Murat's. He stood before his Sultan while Hasam sat at a low Chinese table and stuffed himself with pilaf.

"I believe," Sultan Hasam said between swallows, "that the Imperial Army should be led by men who fight from conviction and not for how much they're paid. That is why I've decided to give you a promotion." He waited for Murat to look pleased, then said, "You will be the commander of the Third Corps in Macedonia."

Murat's eyes widened in astonishment. "Macedonia? Some would say that this is more of an exile than a promotion."

The Sultan shrugged. "Some would say that you overestimate the strength of the revolutionaries to protect your own incompetence." He took another bite of pilaf and waved his hand in dismissal. "That will be all."

"Arthur!" Charles ran into Arthur Grey's dark hotel room, silently apologizing for bursting in right in the middle of the older man's only decent stretch of sleep in days. They'd hired spy after spy and turned up nothing until now. Finally, after all the anxiety and the tension and the worry, he had something tangible to tell Jessica's father. At least he would be able to tell Arthur that Jessica was still alive. At least Jessica had been kidnapped for some real purpose and was being kept alive. For a while he and Arthur had faced a horrible possibility—that Jessica had been kidnapped by some madman who would brutalize her, then kill her. Charles's whole body quaked with the tidbit of hope delivered to him that morning by one of the natives he'd hired.

"Arthur, I have news from one of the spies," Charles said breathlessly, squinting in the darkness. "It's not much, but it's a start." He ran past the bed and drew back the heavy draperies, which until now kept the blazing morning light out of the room. "She's not in Damascus anymore. In fact, she's been taken out of Syria entirely."

When the cocoon of sheets on the bed failed to rouse Arthur, Charles realized that he was still soundly asleep and crossed to the bed, shaking the older man's shoulder. "Arthur— wake up. Arthur?"

Charles shook him again. This time the force made Arthur roll over. His eyes were open, glazed, like stones in sand.

"Arthur?"

Stones in the desert.

A scream cleaved the morning air. Jessica sat up, gasping. Instantly her mouth was covered with hands emerging from veils—rather a nightmare in itself. A moment of deep breathing told her the hands belonged to a bevy of veiled women. How had she gotten here? The past few days—so confusing. But not a dream, since she still wore the dusty Bedouin robes. Yes, it had happened . . . was still happening. She didn't remember how she got here. The last few hours of traveling were nothing but a blur now. She vaguely recalled the first glimpse of the city on the horizon and recalled her captor's hands gently lifting her onto the camel's back when she finally collapsed from exhaustion. After that, she remembered nothing. She awakened here, now, without the slightest idea of where she was or why she was here.

The women around her chattered at each other in Turkish and signaled to Jessica that she was supposed to get into a large wooden bathtub, then put on the clothes they were holding. She got to her feet, nodding to them and trying to appear cooperative. When they let go of her, she followed one of the women toward the tub, waiting until the last possible moment. The primitive tub looked too small for a human body. She needed something to test it on. Well, the woman in front of her was human, wasn't she?

Jessica plunged forward and heaved the unsuspecting woman into the tub headfirst, then bolted toward the door at the opposite side of the room. She easily downed several of the other women, who flinched at the determination in her face, a characteristic foreign to them except when displayed by a man. She reached the door and yanked it open, only to run flush up against a wall of muscular Turkish guards.

The veiled women were waiting for her when she went back to the tub. They calmly began undressing her.

"Tell me his name," Jessica asked firmly. "The one who brought me here. Tell me his name."

The women looked at each other, but the glances were not questioning. They were more like glances of guilt, Jessica noted, and she suddenly realized that they did indeed understand her words, even if they weren't speaking English to her. They had probably been told not to talk to her. She narrowed her eyes. "I know you understand me," she said firmly. "I deserve to know the name of the man who controls my life. Let me have honor if you cannot give me freedom."

Evidently she had spoken on terms they understood: an age-old Eastern dedication to the purity of the soul. If the women allowed her to leave this place without her honor, she would be taking some of theirs with her.

Several of the women looked away or down. Then one of the older ones—she was at least in her twenties—swallowed to clear the way for a muted whisper. "I tell you," she said, fearing the power of being radiating from this light-haired woman who acted like a man. "He name Tarik Pasha. Tarik Pasha," she repeated.

"Where is he going to take me?" Jessica pressed on.

Now the girl met her eyes fully. "Don't know,

miss. Nobody know." And the eyes went down again.

"It's done." Radik met his leader in the darkness of an interior room downstairs from where their captive prize awaited her fate. "You meet with the Kislar this very afternoon."

Tarik nodded in satisfaction but continued staring out the same window out of which he had been staring half the morning.

"What is it?" the old man asked him.

Tarik shook his head, hypnotized by some unseeable thing. "This is wrong. I can't—"

"Can't what?" The tone was sarcastic. "Maybe you do her a favor with all this, eh?"

Tarik turned sharply. "What right do we have to do this?"

"Do you want your men released?"

The answer was obvious in Tarik's eyes.

The old guide nodded. "Then we worry about rights after the revolution. Come now. I have the clothes of a gypsy for you to wear."

Jessica still didn't know her destiny even as her kidnapper led her through the tight streets of Constantinople. Tarik Pasha, as the girl had called him, was disguised as a gypsy with baggy trousers and a madly colored waistband in which he had stored a stock of pistols and razor-sharp *yatakans*. Now dressed like the other Turkish women, Jessica felt no grandeur in her flowing *feridje* cape or the *yashmac* headpiece. Her face was veiled till she could barely maneuver, but she guessed that this was part of his plan. Beneath her robes her wrists were once again bound. When they reached a turn that took them off the crowded main street, her captor twisted her arm and forced her into a dim corner between two buildings.

She backed into him when a tall, elegant black man appeared in the dimness and approached her. He was richly attired in silks and brocades, and on his fez rested an expensive jeweled pin. He had a broad face and large eyes whose white rings shone as he stared at her.

The voice behind her was soothing even though it came from her kidnapper. "Whatever happens, don't say a word. Your life depends on it."

She believed him.

The tall black man gestured to the alley between the two houses, and that was where they met. Jessica stood patiently, nervously, enduring an argument between the two men, all in Turkish. Rather than waning and landing on an equitable price, the argument heated up steadily. Soon it became clear that the two men could not agree on a price. Tarik Pasha, a man whose integrity had come to disturb Jessica very much over the past few days, finally fell silent. The black man had made his final offer and it was not enough.

As if this humiliation were not enough, her captor redoubled it by slowly raising the veil over her face. Jessica actually *felt* the impact of her Western features, her blue eyes, and her bright blond hair on the big man with the fez. And more—not just her coloring. She raised one eyebrow, knowing her own worth. Much more than anyone could actually pay. And she knew how impressed he would be by her self-confidence, by her complete absence of shame at having her face unveiled. Though she knew she was being passed from hand to hand, she couldn't help but radiate that confidence. It might seal her fate, but it might save her too.

The beauty of it dropped abruptly when the big black man stroked her face with his hands, holding it in the light, and did all but check the condition of her teeth. Seething, Jessica yanked her face from his grip. Damn him for liking it.

The big man stepped back. "Your way, then," he said in Turkish. "All the prisoners for the girl."

Tarik Pasha bowed in agreement.

The black man stepped out of the alley and clapped his hands in summons.

Jessica spun around, bearing down on her kidnapper. "What have you done? Who is that man?"

Five white men crowded into the alley, but not before Jessica had gotten a good look at the obvious regret tearing at the dark eyes of her captor. Remorse and apology tightened his face as the five men led her away. She looked back at him as long as possible, hoping against hope that he might give in to that remorse.

"Tarik . . ." she murmured, just loud enough for him to hear.

As the sunlight struck her once again her only hope sank back into the alley and was gone.

Salim had prepared himself for death long ago, back when he and Tarik first made that crucial decision to leave the comfort of England, the civilized atmosphere of learning and culture at Cambridge, and return to the turmoil of their homeland. They'd hoped to ease the turmoil, adjust it to better ends, and knew chances were better than good that they would not live to see the full realization of their cause. But when the Turkish guards came to unshackle him and drag him from Sultan Hasam's torture chamber, he assumed his time had come. Could death be any worse than the lashings he and the other prisoners had been receiving? And why were they taking him in particular? His death had probably been designed to be an example to the other prisoners. His heart choked him as he forced his exhausted mind to come to that deduction, for it meant he faced a supremely agonizing death. For days now he had heard the screaming of the parrots in the aviary, a sound designed to cover the screams of more precious cargo within the palace walls. The Sultan's men already knew Tarik's name; one of the prisoners had weakened. Salim no longer held in contempt the man who had broken down. He was only sorry that he could not live to get word to Tarik that the secret was out.

He emptied his mind. Guessing about how they planned to kill him would only prolong the torture. He pitied the other Young Turks, who would have to listen to the details of his death, perhaps even view his mangled corpse. He fortified himself, yet his hands and feet were chilled with uncontrollable fear when the two guards dragged him into the central audience chamber of the palace. Salim forced his head up. He forced himself to walk on bruised legs and swollen ankles and found himself walking toward Sultan Hasam himself.

This shocked him, and his knees buckled, forcing the guards to drag him once more. They threw him down at the feet of the Sultan's divan.

Salim struggled to his knees.

The Sultan waited until they could look at each other squarely. "When you are free—"

"Free?" Salim gulped. A cruel jest this was.

"When," Mustapha began again with great deliberation, "you are free, I expect you to continue with your writings." His large, soft hands, pampered hands, tossed the pile of papers on the carpet beside Salim. "You are very talented. It should not be wasted, so I want you to continue. And in those writings you may speak of everything."

Salim waited, unwilling—unable—to speak. There was more to this. Only a fool would believe otherwise.

"Everything," the Sultan continued, "except, of course, revolution, liberty, rights of the people, rights of women, the harem, foreign policy, domestic policy, nationalism, internationalism, constitutions, plots, bombs, the crescent or the Cross, Mohammed, Jesus, or Moses."

Understanding, Salim supported his weakened back by pressing his hands on his thighs and noted, "And may I ask His Imperial Majesty what remains to be written about?"

Sultan Hasam smiled. "Absolutely everything, my son. The rain, good weather, the dogs in the street. You may write of the Sultan"—he lay a hand against his brocade-covered chest—"if it is to sing my praises. In short, you have full and entire liberty to speak of whatever seems good to you."

And nothing that seems bad. The implication was clear enough.

"I don't understand you," Salim breathed, exhausted by the effort. "You're freeing me?"

"And I suggest you remember," Hasam went on, "who it is that is freeing you. Take him."

While Salim was being taken back to the other prisoners and dressed in clothing much too decent-looking, the Kislar Agha's gilded carriage was approaching the acreage on the edge of the Bosporus, coming nearer to the twenty-foot-high stone fence and its guards. The white marble gates, shimmering with gold decorations, slowly parted and swept open. The carriage casually moved down a steep, twisted road toward the Palace of Yildiz. The palace, a marble epic of fountains and columns and open-air courtyards, seemed to have dropped from the clouds to rest on this high escarpment overlooking the strait where two seas meet. Vines draped its walls and latticework partitions, separating the gardens from the courtyards, the women's quarters from the aviary, the aviary from the torture chambers. Only the birds wheeling overhead could see the links between serenity and brutality.

The carriage stopped at the top of the hill, at the inner gates leading to the seraglio. The footman stepped down and hastily opened the carriage door. Hesitantly he put his hand out, and it was taken by the soft hand in the carriage.

Jessica stepped out and blinked into the brightness. The sun reflecting off the marble walls blinded her for a moment, so she looked down until her eyes adjusted. Below, she saw the rapid, blue Bosporus flowing between the shores of Europe and Asia. Her lips fell open in amazement. This was nothing like the dirty scene she had left behind in Constantinople's bazaar. She moved only when she was prodded onward by half a dozen robed men.

They led her, flanking her on both sides, through a maze of gardens and patios, past the lattice-surrounded courtyards, past the aviary. The movement caused the birds to flap around in crazed patches of color and caw furiously at the disturbance. She went along quietly. This was not yet the time.

The birds who flew free above the palace—birds not trapped in the aviary—circled in confusion. They had heard the screams of the tortured men and, being birds, could separate the sound of death from the sound of other birds. They saw the carriage come to a halt, saw the woman emerge, saw the train of people walking through the gardens. They also saw, as no one else did, the irony of another procession, a procession of twenty battered young men in new clothes moving in the opposite direction from the woman and her party but on the other side of a mosaic wall. While the woman was led toward the seraglio the young men on the other side moved toward the gates and freedom. The parrots continued to shriek.

CHAPTER SIX

"They're here," Misha called from the balcony to the dim recesses of the hideaway.

Tarik heard the younger man's voice and its quiver of anticipation, and he also shuddered slightly, wondering what would come through the door. Sultan Hasam's methods of torture were effective and often permanent. Through a series of spies he knew that Salim lived, but in what condition? The other Young Turks also lived, which indicated that their dying had not been part of the Sultan's plans, which therefore proved that there was indeed some plan afoot, probably aimed at Tarik himself. And the past days had been difficult enough just trying to deal with the guilt of what his backward nation's traditions had forced him to do. Could a man easily betray the principles he was risking his life to establish? But could he have allowed twenty men to die when he could save their lives by working within the old system just one more time?

The woman called Jessica haunted him. He saw her face in his dreams, in the sunset, in the sunrise. He saw it in the wine he drank and heard her voice behind his own words when he spoke of freedom and personal rights, when he spoke of moving forward into the twentieth century. He had condemned her to the shackles of the past in spite of his bold words and all his ideals. Sacrificed her, made decisions for her, condemned her. It was nothing less then condemnation, and she had proven herself worthy of better treatment.

Tarik clenched his fists and begged his soul to be calm.

The door latch clicked, and three men came in. The second was Salim.

Tarik stepped toward him, inhaling sharply when he saw the bruises on his friend's face, but by the time he could think about it, Salim was embracing him. His own arms went humbly about the battered shoulders and he felt Salim wince, but they could not help squeezing each other. Tarik had to force himself to let go, to realize that Salim had probably been lashed and was in pain now.

"Salim," Tarik rasped, cementing the fact that his friend had survived. He held Salim by the arms and surveyed him. "Tell me everything."

Salim nodded, still weak and finally ready to relax the defiant posture he had somehow managed to maintain as he and the others were led to freedom. He held on to Tarik for support and human contact and said, "They know your name.

You are a clear target now. Your life is in great danger, perhaps too much to do us any good for a while. I talked with Sultan Hasam myself, Tarik."

"You *what*?" Tarik led Salim to a rickety wooden chair at an even more rickety table, sat him down, and sat beside him. Misha and the other men gathered around to hear this incredible story. "The Sultan himself?"

"In all his glory," Salim mocked. "He read my writings. He told me I could write about anything except revolution, domestic policy, constitutions, Mohammed, Moses . . . He actually encouraged me to keep writing, and I intend to."

Tarik smiled. "And what will you write about?"

"Oh, revolutions, domestic policy, constitutions, Mohammed—"

The room broke into laughter, and the self-conscious tension slid away.

"Did you try to reason with him?" Misha asked.

"He's not a man to be reasoned with," Salim told him.

"I still don't understand why we can't present our list of demands to Sultan Hasam and—"

"We've spent too much time asking the Sultan for rights men should be born to," Tarik said sharply. He turned to Salim again. "And we've spent too much time fighting in Bulgaria and Damascus and distant parts of the Empire." He stood up and wandered to a dark corner, his back to the others. Several moments passed while he tested and retested his own thoughts. Then he returned and pressed his hands on Salim's injured shoulders. "It is time to bring the war home."

But for others—those living in the seraglio on the edge of the Bosporus—the impending war between their Sultan and the revolutionaries had little meaning. Seldom did affairs of state touch those who concerned themselves with the Sultan's Imperial Harem. The Kislar Agha lived with one foot in each world—a little tampering with the state affairs, a little juggling of the palace's internal politics. The blond woman would cause trouble, he suspected as he walked through the seraglio courtyard toward a meeting that might reestablish his influence with the Sultan. Wrangling the freedom of the twenty revolutionaries had been far from easy. It meant pulling strings and drawing upon unpaid favors until he had hardly an advantage left. The American woman had to please Sultan Hasam more than any other woman since the Kadin; Agha's life depended upon it. As did hers.

Even for a eunuch, the sight of the Hazinedar Usta caused a flutter in the core of his loins— more memory than sensation. Even in her forties, she was still a beautiful woman, still a dark gem of Islam. She approached him from across the courtyard, wearing an exquisite European gown and a dog collar of white pearls with an emerald clasp.

"You have seen her?" the Kislar asked as

they drew close and began walking together aimlessly through the garden. It was safer to move than stand still and talk.

Usta nodded.

"Well, what do you think of her?" the elegant black man pursued.

"She's lovely, but she's here against her will. It shows in her face."

Now the artistry began in his tone. "She needs a special teacher."

Usta looked at him with a practiced coquettishness. "And whom do you propose should be her teacher?"

The Kislar gave her an equally practiced look.

Usta waved her long, dark hand, making the rings glint in the sun. "But I was only the Sultan's mistress. Never his wife . . . never the Kadin."

"You were his favorite."

"Are things going so badly for you?"

The Kislar tried not to sigh—so undignified. "Every day the Kadin's influence over Sultan Hasam grows, and mine weakens."

"And you will restore your position by giving the Sultan the right woman?"

Agha shrugged briefly. "With your help." He turned to her and paused. "You owe your position in the harem to me. I made the Sultan take notice. And I protected you."

Usta was not so easily shaken. "And I kept *you* powerful by remaining his favorite."

The Kislar's thick lips turned up at the corners. He took her arm gently, and they began walking again. "As always, Usta, our fates are intertwined. You must help me."

The sun saw itself in the woman's jewels. "I will think about it."

In the concubines' quarters the subject of the Kislar's concern was fumbling with a bar on the window that moved in its mortar. Now wearing a simple Turkish dress, Jessica grated her hands on the iron bar and leaned into it with determination. Behind her, on a grass mat, a girl of eighteen watched her with curious misunderstanding.

"Don't . . ." the girl said. "Those bars are there to protect us."

Jessica turned around. "Protect us?" Unconvinced, she crossed the room and sat down beside the slim girl. "Geisla, if you help me, we could pry the bars open. We could escape together."

Immense brown eyes widened. "I don't want to escape."

"You don't want to go home?"

"But I *am* home. I've lived here since I was ten."

"Then what are we supposed to do?"

Geisla shrugged. "We wait. For Sultan Hasam."

"You mean we just sit here and wait to be taken by the Sultan or raped by the Kislar or—" Jessica stopped. Geisla was laughing. "What's so funny?"

Geisla giggled. "Many things are possible in

the seraglio, but being raped by the chief black eunuch is not one of them."

"The Kislar is a eunuch?"

"All the men in the harem are eunuchs."

This information drove home the fact that Jessica was actually, as ridiculous as it seemed, stuck in a harem. How completely barbaric. She got up and began working with the loose bar again. She wasn't about to stay here until she started calling this gilded cage "home."

Geisla stretched lazily, got up, and came to Jessica's side. "Don't be foolish. You're wasting your time. Listen to me." She waited until Jessica turned to her, then carefully spelled out, "Escaping through that window will do you little good. The seraglio is only one of Sultan Hasam's palaces. The compound is surrounded mostly by treacherous waters. Besides one hundred eunuchs, there are a thousand of the Empire's fiercest soldiers within the palace walls. No one gets in," she enunciated, "and no one . . . gets out."

Jessica shuddered at how casually fates could be doled out in this culture. And she was a pawn—she felt it. She was worth more than just money to someone, or several someones. There must be more at stake than simple coinage to risk kidnapping a woman so easily set apart from the dark heads of the East. Surely the British consulate would have something to say about it, and whoever had arranged this was willing to risk the wrath of England. Charles would not be sitting around in impotent mourning. Her father would hardly tolerate such an outrage toward British nationals, guests of the Sultan's Empire, without a good stiff fight—if, of course, they had any idea at all where she was. Sultan Hasam's palace was like a country unto itself, and they could easily hide her here for years.

Geisla broke Jessica's thoughts. "Come," the girl invited. "Let's go to the bathhouse."

Jessica considered. "Now, that sounds almost appealing," she said, and followed Geisla.

A steaming, soothing, self-indulgent bath *did* sound marvelous. It would fortify her and couldn't possibly hurt.

Which was why the bathhouse was such a disappointment. Oh, it was richly built—marble-lined, with gold spigots dripping water into huge wooden basins with golden stools to step on. And women, lots of them. All barely dressed in thin linen chemises that were soaked with steam and clung indecently to the outlines of the young, feminine bodies. Gauzy fabric clung to melon-round breasts and dipped inward beneath flat, young bellies. A group of young women passed Jessica and Geisla, chattering in French and splashing water on each other from ceramic urns. The ease with which they exposed their bodies made Jessica aware of her own. Without a thought Geisla peeled off her dress, then looked curiously at Jessica. "What's the matter, Jessica? Don't be shy about it. We spend hours here. Sometimes days."

Unenthused by the brainless activity, Jessica asked, "Why?"

Geisla shrugged. "Because we have to have something to do."

Jessica shook her head. "And cleaning yourself endlessly qualifies as something to do?"

Just then an older girl—though still barely more than a teenager—came hurrying toward them from the other room and babbled to Geisla in Arabic. Geisla then turned to Jessica. "The Kislar is waiting in the court for you. He says the Kadin has asked to see you."

"Why? What's a Kadin?"

Some things are better left unknown, but when the Kadin demands to see someone, someone will be seen. Jessica discovered this in short order, and it sank in completely as she was led into the Imperial bathhouse, a marble room with an elaborate glass dome overhead. The Kislar Agha was already there and eyed her critically as she approached a vast divan of green silk and the stunning woman who reposed upon it. The woman appeared Greek, Jessica guessed, judging by her face, which was made of straight lines put together in a classical motif, her rich umber hair piled high and coiffed with diamonds. Behind the divan was a line of older women, elegantly dressed, and on a platform above were a handful of slaves wearing brocaded robes or short silk jackets over their bath chemises. To one side a young girl sang a high-pitched Eastern song, accompanied by a mandolin.

All around wafted the scents of womanhood. The domain was female. Only the ever-silent eunuchs provided any hint that this was a matriarchy within a larger structure.

All eyes turned to Jessica as she fearlessly approached the reclining woman and stood before her, wearing a fine edge of defiance.

The Kadin gave her an empty glance, then selected a sweetmeat from a brass tray brimming with pilaf, minced meat rolled in grape leaves, and candied fruit. She popped it into her heavily defined lips and chewed leisurely. Only when she had swallowed and decided not to try another delicacy did she address Jessica. She said something in Turkish to which no one reacted.

Finally, assuming she had been spoken to, Jessica informed, "I don't speak Turkish."

The Kadin sat up abruptly. "Come closer," she said. "Hmmm . . . I don't know if you please me. Take off your clothes. Let me see you."

"What?" Jessica squared her shoulders.

"As Sultan Hasam's wife," the Kadin said, "his *only* wife, I decide who will please him. Take off your clothes."

At this the Kislar Agha stepped forward, his deep voice booming. "It is my job to provide the Imperial Harem with new girls."

"Not anymore," the Kadin said, practically yawning. Then she repeated, "Take off your clothes."

When Jessica stood her ground, the Kadin

waved to her slaves, two of whom immediately took Jessica by the arms and began to disrobe her.

Jessica glared at the Kadin. Every muscle in her body tensed but not only in humiliation. Her shoulder was bared as the slave tugged at her dress, and she was engulfed by a wave of self-determination. Viciously she pushed the slaves away, in two different directions. The court fell stone-silent.

The Kislar Agha looked worried, Jessica saw in the periphery of her vision, though she refused to take her eyes off the Kadin. She brought her fingers to the buttons at her breast and worked them open. First the dress came off, then, one by one, the undergarments.

A second hush fell over the court. Jessica raised her chin, ever so slightly, at the Kadin.

Never in the Sultan's court had shined a nakedness so special, so alabaster, like a sculpture in marble beneath the tanned face, with its own kind of uniqueness. Her skin was pale and had a fine sheen that glowed in the light from the dome above. Fine blue veins showed faintly along her inner arms, her thighs and breasts. Protected for years by stiff undergarments, her breasts were impossibly firm and soft, paler than the palest eggs from the most delicate songbird. Under the streaming sunlight from the overhead dome, the fine platinum hairs glazing Jessica's body created an aurora and outlined her like a halo. To people used to dark complexions and coarse black hair, Jessica was breathtaking. All around her, the people stared. Even the older women, who had seen women's bodies all their lives, were awed by the ivory prize standing so bravely before the powerful Kadin. Jessica squared her shoulders and bent one knee over so slightly, then, with eye-catching deliberation, she raised her chin ever so slightly. She glared straight into the Kadin's dark eyes.

"How very ordinary," the Kadin uttered. "Get rid of her."

Caught between hope and insult, Jessica gawked at this unbelievable woman.

Then one of the older women stepped forward with careful patience. "She suits me. I need a girl to help me look after the dresses." She leaned toward the Kadin. Jessica wondered what interest this woman could have in her when she said, "Surely you won't deny me this girl . . . whom you obviously have so little interest in."

The Kadin was forced into a public decision. To deny Usta the girl would be to admit that she felt threatened.

Once again the bejeweled hand waved. "Whatever pleases you."

In Usta's quarters Jessica found herself the hub of a flurry of harem girls eagerly opening boxes from a huge crate that had just arrived from Europe. The apartment around her was furnished in European style; evidently Usta had been clever in her new ways of entertaining the Sultan—European ways, judging by the surroundings and the clothes Usta wore. The girls around Jessica were fascinated by the treasures drawn from those boxes—hobble-skirted evening gowns in gold and silver, flouncy petticoats, bolero jackets, taffeta vests, and turbans trimmed in osprey feathers. The squeals of delight were difficult to take. Jessica frowned and tried to retreat.

Geisla came running up to her and grasped her arm, waving a whalebone corset in front of her. "Do you have any idea what this is?"

Sympathetically Jessica said, "Believe me, you'd rather not know. It's the only thing about England that I don't miss."

As Geisla tried to figure that out, another girl, a tall redhead named Rosemary, rushed to Jessica with an open book in her hand. "Jessica, can you read? Tell us what this says."

Jessica looked over Rosemary's shoulder. "You mean the inscription? It says, 'Glory to the Lord, who adorned the virginal bosom with breasts and who made the thighs of women anvils for the spear handles of men—oh, dear . . .'"

Rosemary cooed, "Hoooo! I think I'll learn to read!"

One of the other girls said, "I'd rather look at the pictures."

Only then did Jessica get up the nerve to look at the picture, and it sent her fleeing red-faced from the salon.

Usta followed her.

"It will take time," the old woman said quietly, closing the doors between this chamber and the other. "I can train you. I will teach you what I know about pleasing men, and you will learn how to gain power within the seraglio."

Jessica whirled around in attack. "Train me? Teach me?" she shrieked. "I won't be one of his whores!"

"Of course not," Usta said calmly. "Neither the Kislar nor I intend to let that happen. You will be a very special girl. The same way I was once special."

"I can't be like you."

"You will learn to be *exactly* like me."

"Have you forgotten your past?" Jessica accused. "Don't you remember what it's like to be free?"

Usta had talked to her, told her that she, too, once knew the freedoms of the outside world, that she remembered the beauty of Europe and the entrancing vitality of Western ways. Usta had once been free, had been educated in France, and had planned for herself a life of her own reckoning—until the time of change. They had much in common, she had told Jessica, for Usta also had been kidnapped and placed in the harem. She, too, had resisted and had spent untold hours mourning the loss of independence. But that had been years upon years ago, and she was not that person any longer.

Sensing that this would take a deeper kind of convincing, Usta moved to her and took her hand, making her sit down, then sat beside her. "Completely. I know you must feel like those caged birds. But . . . you must learn to fly within the cage."

Jessica turned her head away and found herself staring out a low-silled window at the surging Bosporus. "It's demeaning."

"What is?"

"The things those girls talk about."

"Ah . . . you're afraid of sex."

"I'm not afraid," Jessica defended, "but I know this is wrong."

"How can there be anything wrong with knowledge?"

"These kinds of things take care of themselves," Jessica said in a rehearsed way, the way she had been told. "With the right man at the right time . . ."

Usta tipped her head, searching for the best words. "This is a matter of manners, not morals. The problem is in the way you've been raised. It's said that the English have the finest women in Europe and least know how to use them. Perhaps that is why they choose to keep them so ignorant."

"I'm not completely English," Jessica said belligerently. "I'm half American. And I'm not afraid. I won't compromise my morals."

Usta shook her head. "You were not brought here to dance a little dance or sing a little song. You will learn how to make love to a man," she said, then leaned closer, intimately. "You talk so very much about wanting your freedom, but you will never be free until you free the soul inside you . . . until you stop fighting the differences. You will learn how to please a man beyond all pleasure. You will learn the mindless tug of the flesh and how to make it do your own bidding, Jessica. Making love to a man is a special art. Only women possess the gift of touch and stroke that makes a man lose himself. You have the power already. You must only learn to use it so that you can draw a man out of himself and show him a surging more intense than the ocean. I can teach you these things. I can help you realize the gift resting within your body, waiting for a man's response. You will learn these things, Jessica. It is my promise to you." Usta moved to a cabinet and took out a large brass vial. She turned to Jessica. "Let the lesson begin."

She tipped the vial. A silty dust of gold powder spilled into her hand. Usta then put down the vial and carefully began spreading the gold dust on her arms, from wrist to shoulder, covering every inch of skin. Soon her arms glowed unnaturally with the shimmering powder. At last she applied it to her hands, the palms, each finger, between the fingers, the knuckles. "See how it emphasizes the lines of the body," she said, gracefully moving her golden arms and hands. "When you move, it is as if you see every muscle. We have secrets, we women of the harem. Age-old secrets to make a man weep with desire. Look, see my hands, my arms . . . see what a man would see by the candlelight. But not just any man will take you, Jessica Grey. You will be the prize of Sultan Hasam, man of men, ruler of the Empire, a man who has known the finest women, the most subtle bodies, the most tempting seductions. That is the gift he will give you when you give of yourself. He is the embodiment of all Eastern lovers, and he will make you his work of art. Before you bed the Sultan, you will learn how to move with practiced grace, like a dancer in a garden. Come." Usta lifted the brass vial and moved toward Jessica. "Give me your arm and let me show you how a woman's skin can sing."

Disturbed by an international kind of truth, Jessica stood up and moved to the edge of the balcony. Far below, the Bosporus roared.

"I have chosen all of you to give to my husband."

The Kadin strolled casually amid the marble slabs that held thirty young girls being perfumed and massaged by the eunuchs. She walked in long, slow steps, keeping about her an aura of divine separation. "Tonight," she went on with inflection, "you will become my hands, my breasts, my very soul. And you will give him pleasure beyond anything he has ever known. Rise now, and follow me toward your destiny."

To the jangle and twang of Oriental music the Kadin led her string of chosen women—for truly they were women and no longer girls— to Sultan Hasam's viewing chamber where the ruler of their Empire reclined upon his divan and smoked his water pipe, knowing that soon he would be the center of the universe. Some of the young female bodies that passed him were dressed in traditional Turkish attire, others in European dresses, each passing before him with her best, most seductive walk. His brows rose once or twice, but other than that, there was no sign of interest. Finally the last woman passed him and came to stand in a queue behind the Kadin.

The Kadin stood as straight as a Nile reed. "You are descended from Suleiman the Great, and you will make the Empire greater still," she chanted.

Sultan Hasam drew the stem of his water pipe from his lips. "And whom do I make the Empire great for? Myself or your son?"

The Kadin raised her head even higher. "*Our* son."

The Sultan shrugged. The Kadin gestured to several girls. The girls then went to the Sultan and began to caress him—his forehead, his hands, his arm, and one of them worked on his feet. While they worked their magic the Kadin tried to work her own, whispering obscenities into Sultan Hasam's ear.

The Sultan pulled away and looked at her. "Would you deny that the boy could make you great? You who would be the Sultan Vadide?"

The Kadin looked amazed. "You were my passion before he was conceived. That begins and ends it."

For a moment something passed between them—something of the past, never to be retrieved. Hasam said, "Perhaps you do still love me. Perhaps it is not so impossible."

The Kadin leaned closer. "A woman is not made like a man. Power is not enough." Her whisper was sultry.

Sultan Hasam raised his brows again. "Sometimes I wonder." He turned back to the girls who caressed him and noticed something peculiar: the girl who rubbed his feet. Over her harem trousers she was wearing a whalebone corset. Very . . . appealing.

"What is your name?" he asked her.

"Geisla."

He nearly felt the girl's heart pound as he stood up and took her hand. To the Kadin he said, "Write Geisla's name in the great book."

Geisla followed the Sultan from the room, hesitating only long enough to see that the Kadin was writing her name in the great book.

Hours later—long hours—Geisla walked proudly through the gardens with Jessica, dreaming of future greatness.

"Don't you understand?" she tried to tell the American woman. "Being written in the great book makes it official."

"Makes what official?" Jessica asked, though she had already guessed.

"That Sultan Hasam is the father of my son."

"What son?" Jessica's voice belied a scolding undertone that Geisla was counting her chickens before they were hatched, rather literally.

"The son I'm going to have in nine months."

"You can't be sure, can you? Certainly not this soon. Not in just a few hours."

"Of course I'm sure. It has to be a boy," Geisla said dreamily. "Boys become heirs, and their mothers become Kadins. But girls are worthless. They are killed or, even worse, sold as slaves."

Jessica sighed, her face damaged by a knowing sorrow. "Oh, Geisla . . . why can't you understand? That's all we are, you and I. Slaves."

And the word echoed in her own mind.

CHAPTER SEVEN

"Two years ago only twenty people would have listened. Now look." Salim followed his own suggestions and gazed out over the marketplace, crowded with a staggeringly large number of people. It was as though the heavens had split and humanity had fallen out onto the Earth. All had gathered today to listen to a promise Salim could only hope lay within their power to fulfill. Beside him, Misha also stared at the amazing sight and realized the drawing power of the man he had decided to follow in a life-or-death quest. The crowd was completely silent, spellbound by the charisma of a man they sensed could lead them as he was promising to.

Tarik stood on the balcony of a decrepit building in Constantinople's central marketplace, framed by erosion indicative of the claims he made and the government he condemned. He spoke slowly and clearly, his dark head bared so that people could see his European haircut and realize that he had seen other worlds, other ways, and might know something they did not. He tried not to think of the weeks gone by since he had compromised himself and the very principles he claimed to espouse by handing Jessica Grey over to the people who would abuse and degrade her for the rest of her life. Still, his one huge betrayal of himself pushed its way to the front of his mind as he knitted these grand words and promised these bold promises.

"We have lived too long without hope," he told them. "We have accepted oppression as a way of life. I have seen other places in the world. Places where people live freely, with hope instead of resignation. Promise instead of despair. Freedom instead of slavery." He paused for the words to sink in, for the people to form in their minds a vision of such a place here on Earth. "There are places where men have a choice, a voice in determining the direction of their country. There are countries where women live without fear. There are governments who give their people schools for their children. Our children are starving! Our men are dying! Our women are mourning. It is time to break the chain of oppression! Time to be heard! Time to fight!"

The marketplace pealed with a rush of applause and cheers. Tarik made eye contact with as many individuals as he could, then waited for the wave of cheering to die down.

"I believe in the Ottoman Empire," he announced. His voice echoed, carried to the edges of the throng by the stone buildings on either side of the marketplace. "I believe in its people—*all* of its people. I believe we can live together as Jews, Christians, Muslims—that we can be one under just laws and still be separate within our own families and our faiths." He paused to let his words soak in, indulging in effective eye contact with the throng. "I believe that in order to live in freedom, men should be born to freedom. We will do . . . what we must do."

Again he stopped, signaling a round of dubious applause that rustled across the marketplace as people exchanged glances to see if anyone else approved. He must capture them now, or never.

"We will resist Sultan Hasam in every way. Resistance on every front. Passive resistance . . . active resistance . . . whatever it takes, because we will do what we must do. We will say no to the tax collector who asks for more than we should pay! We will move within the army itself, convincing soldiers to refuse to march against the people. We will *do* what we must do! We have accepted oppression as a way of life. We will accept it no more! And when the time comes and if there is no other way, we will raise up arms against acts of oppression because . . . we will *do*"—a long, effective, ardent pause—"what we *must* . . . *do*!"

The crowd dissolved into wild cheering and applause, an angry cheering of blatant, furious, ready enthusiasm. Yes, he would do whatever he had to do, as he had said, and if he would, then they would also. They sensed his integrity above and beyond his ability to capture them with his words, felt his willingness to die for them, and they would not allow him to die alone.

Tarik's face grew rosy with emotion. He glanced at Salim, and moisture gathered in his eyes but he refused to smile—a smile would make happy a moment that should be intense and defiant. There would be time for smiling later. But Salim, knowing Tarik too well, winked at him, anyway.

They did not hear the underlying clatter of hoofbeats on the cobblestones until it was too late. The sound blended too well with the roaring of the crowd. Nor did they hear the gunshots right away. A few bullets ricocheted off the stone walls around them before the people began to understand what was happening.

Tarik's expression of ardor for his people faded into a grimace of confusion as several people in the crowd crumpled to the ground. He leaned forward over the balcony rail, trying to understand what was happening.

The sound came, it seemed, from the bowels of the Earth itself. From all directions—every avenue or alley leading into the marketplace—an ominous hum. The multitude sensed it first, then, as they became quieter and more suspicious of the hum, heard it.

Tarik tensed. He felt something. The sound was like an approaching windstorm on the desert. He gripped the balcony's rail.

Below him, the people saw something he did not, and began to scramble without direction. Their very numbers prevented them from moving. Thus they were trapped by each other when the alleys and streets in every direction roared like lions' mouths and vomited a flood of mounted Imperial troops. Hundreds of them—bayonets mounted, rifles ready, pistols and swords drawn. It was an ocean of red fezzes and Imperial uniforms—a thunder of hooves and hungry steel.

The multitude's swelling enthusiasm disintegrated. The intrusion became a pattern of death as the legion trampled everything and everyone in its path, firing freely from the vantage points of their saddles and mowing down scores of helpless people.

Tarik froze, astonished, horrified. At first his mind could not absorb the carnage below. Surely he was dreaming. He must have fallen asleep after drinking too much or eating the wrong piece of meat. Paralyzed, he watched as the Turks whittled the crowd from a swarm into a heap—and realized it was real only when he saw a human leg fly across the marketplace like a distorted bird.

Endlessly they came, the soldiers, pouring out of every street that might have provided escape for the people, a flood of humanity and horseflesh primed for mutilation. The crowd shriveled into mindless panic. The soldiers pushed their screaming horses through the crowd, haphazardly hacking and shooting, head-

ing for Tarik. He watched, powerless, as people
in the streets fell by scores before the barrage of
trained fighting men. Bile rose in his throat,
and his stomach collapsed upon itself as women
and children fell as easily as the men and with
no more regret or restraint from the Turks. Hundreds of them. Thousands. Dying because they
dared listen. And when his eyes fell upon the
writhing body of a child barely more than six
years old, Tarik's heart snapped.

He reached into his robes and numbly drew
his pistol.

"Tarik!" Salim's voice barely penetrated the
pandemonium below. "Tarik! No!"

Salim knew Tarik would stand and fight, die
as he had promised to. But before he had time
to react, the most horrible possibility happened—
Tarik staggered backward, driven by the impact
of a bullet in his shoulder. He wavered, then
fell. Salim gritted his teeth and climbed from
the ground to the balcony by going from window to window, then dropped beside Tarik. He
lifted his leader and friend, wrenched the gun
from his locked fist, and forced him to his feet.
"Misha!" Salim called, but others were already
on their way to the balcony. Immediately other
revolutionaries appeared to help him whisk their
leader away. They were unwilling to lose him,
even if he was willing to sacrifice himself to the
carnage his presence had caused. They hustled
him down from the balcony without going into
the building itself, for that would be a trap.
Soldiers were on their way, a select troop of

Imperial Turks trying to slice their way through the crowd to the balcony. They wanted Tarik Pasha. Dead or alive, he would be their prisoner before the day ended.

"This way!" Salim pulled on Tarik's bloodied arm as the other revolutionaries pushed and dragged him through the alleys. People in the crowd cleared a path for the man they believed would lead them from oppression, and it was as much as committing suicide so that Tarik Pasha could live.

"I can't leave them—" Tarik gasped, straining back toward the massacre, his senses lost to empathy and intense loyalty. He crushed one hand over the wound in his shoulder and tried to turn back.

"We can do nothing for them," Salim insisted. "Your time will come, Tarik. We have to get you away. Stop fighting me!"

Salim and the small group of revolutionaries succeeded in forcing Tarik to leave the marketplace as the streets began to run red with blood. They shuffled through the booths and panicked people, the horrible sound of screams drumming upon their ears. Behind them, surging through the chaos, soldiers of the Empire spied their targets and spurred through the people toward the one man who was their ultimate prey.

Tarik accepted Salim's words with redoubled agony. Not only must he find some way to live beyond this brutality, but also he must rise above it to become the leader again. They skirted the undersides of old buildings, pulling themselves through dusty cellars and stinking animal droppings in the ditches, ever driven by the rising shrieks from the marketplace. The soldiers pursued them, but once clear of the crowd, even the finest tracker would have been confused by the winding route through the city on which the revolutionaries led them. Tarik and his men were driven more by pain and fury than by desperation. They would live, even in this wake of death. They would live to return, to continue the fight, and to let Sultan Hasam know that ideals are not cut away as easily as arms and legs may be hacked off.

In the marketplace far behind them the random attack continued. When the soldiers realized Pasha was lost to them, they released their frustration on the people in the street. The piles of bodies grew. Some were as tall as the men on horseback, as fleeing citizens were hacked down or shot down as they tried to scurry over their dead neighbors. They were defenseless, but their deaths would prove a point that Sultan Hasam desired to prove.

The massacre went on for two solid hours. The old Empire had chosen this opportunity to reestablish its supremacy. Long before the Turks had finished the slaughter, the stink of death had begun to rise over Constantinople.

Some were dead. Some were mangled, waiting to die. Blood ran freely between the cobblestones. The sound of moaning grew louder than even the roar of approval they had just hours ago given to a man who spoke their hearts. All who could escape had done so, and all who could be massacred had been massacred. The unprovoked attack would dominate the whisperings in the streets for years to come. Thus had it been designed.

The Chief Commander of the Turkish Imperial Troops surveyed the carnage with an impassive eye. Then he beckoned to the waiting crowd of beggars and scavengers who peeked out of the alleys at him. "Take what you want," he told them. "And spread the word of where you acquired your prizes."

He waved to his mounted soldiers, and they wheeled away at a casual canter. The beggars moved in and began picking the pockets of the dead and dying.

The Commander felt little victory, even though his attack had clearly made its own point. He now realized his mistake. The wild offensive had indeed shown the people who was in control, but it had also lost him his quarry: Tarik Pasha. Unless Tarik Pasha was captured soon, this massacre would become a tool of martyrdom. This victory could quickly backfire into a rousing defeat for him if the people still had a leader. The populace would rise again behind Tarik Pasha, using this slaughter as a springboard for their emotions. A man such as Pasha would know how to use such a weapon.

The Commander sighed and reflected upon how effectively the dead could summon the future for the living. Next time he would have to be more subtle. And there *would* be a next time with a man like Pasha. Such men are fueled by this kind of defeat.

But for now . . . there was the Sultan.

A less than appealing duty, having to tell His Majesty.

"What . . . about . . . Tarik Pasha?" Sultan Hasam's neck bulged into angry cords as he sensed what he was about to be told.

The Chief Commander tensed within his uniform. "He escaped."

The Sultan leaned forward, one eyebrow raised like a poised lance. "Again?" The insult burrowed home. "I see. Is this man some kind of super being? Is he made of something other than flesh and blood?"

The Commander breathed deeply to steady himself, unwilling to explain his blunder. It was enough that Pasha had escaped. The details would only compound his problem. He was tensely aware of the other presences in the room— the court astrologer and the Kislar Agha, two men constantly vying for the Sultan's favor.

"How difficult can it be to find one man?" the Kislar wondered.

This was part of an age-old game—make oneself look good by making another look bad. The Commander shot him a sharp glare.

But it was the astrologer who took the opportunity to put down Agha by noting, "Obviously as difficult as it is to train one woman." On his skinny hands he displayed seven upright fingers, indicating the number of weeks the American prize had sat ripe but unpicked in the harem.

The Sultan glowered. "Where would the revolutionaries hide this Pasha?" he demanded.

"On the outskirts of the Empire," the Commander guessed, trying not to shrug. "Syria . . . Bulgaria . . . Cyprus . . . or Macedonia."

"Search them all."

"But that's—yes, Majesty. At once."

After all, quick retreats were worth something.

In Macedonia, deep in the shadows of the Mediterranean evening, Murat walked across the military encampment, looking forward to taking off his dress uniform and trying to get some sleep. This outpost was ordinary and boring and gave him much time to think, too much time, perhaps. He thought of the Empire and of the strangely uneven method of rule—a method that forgot the people and thought only of the Sultan and his military. A soldier's mind should not be so filled with politics, Murat would tell himself on dark endless nights like these. Perhaps the life of a soldier had been the wrong choice for him, after all.

When he heard the whispering voice from the folds of a nearby tent, he thought it was his conscience calling to him. But he stopped and looked and drew his pistol.

"You are Murat . . ." the voice whispered again.

He squinted into the blackness. "Come out. Show yourself."

The tent rustled. A young man, a stranger, appeared in a shaft of moonlight shining through the clouds. Murat put his pistol to the other's throat. "Why do you speak to me?"

"You don't need the gun. I am unarmed."

Murat pressed the gun tighter to the younger man's throbbing neck. "Perhaps I should call the guards."

Keeping his voice low, Misha stiffened and convinced himself that Tarik would not send him here unless there was an excellent reason. He swallowed hard and went on talking. "There are many others like you. Many who believe that Sultan Hasam should lead the army and not retreat into his harem."

Murat drew the pistol back. "How do you know what I believe?"

"Your soldiers respect you," Misha said, "but they also know how you feel. Your attitude is transparent."

Murat frowned, thinking. An odd way to say it. Slowly he put together what the stranger was saying—and not saying. "And where do I find these men who think like I think?" he asked slowly.

Misha turned to him. "I can take you there."

The meeting took place in the hollow of a hill nestled in the breast of the Earth. Two riders approached a third rider, who awaited them. They surveyed each other from a suspicious distance, then Misha turned his horse away, his duty dispatched.

The two leaders were left alone beneath the Macedonian moon. The sling on Tarik's arm was the only evidence of the wound he had received in the marketplace. He still felt weak but refused to show it. The two rode toward the lee of the hill. As if by agreement, they simultaneously dismounted and began walking their horses as they talked.

"The first time we met was in Syria," Tarik said slowly, "when you captured Salim and the others. But what I remember most is how your men followed you. Such loyalty is rare."

"Why have you come to Macedonia?" Murat asked abruptly.

"To find out if they still follow you."

So the two men began talking. The talked half the night while the camp fire flickered under darker and darker skies. Tarik stole Murat's sensibilities when he told, firsthand, of the massacre in Constantinople. He spared no detail, for they would have to be strong, and the horror could give them strength.

"Hundreds of people were slaughtered. It was unforgivable, and I do not intend to forgive," he said through a tight throat. It was the end of his story, a long and painful story indeed, one he hated reliving. But Murat must know.

"Were there many Turks among the victims?" Murat asked after a long pause.

Tarik shrugged, not understanding the question. "Most were Bulgars, Kurds, and Albanians."

Murat leaned back. "Then it was a more acceptable loss."

Astonished by the bald bigotry, Tarik spat back, "There are no acceptable losses when women and children lay dying in the streets!"

Murat gazed at him emptily. "How are you going to protect women and children if you advocate general insurrection? If you are going to overthrow Sultan Hasam, you must learn to think like a soldier."

Settling down perforce, Tarik licked his lips before answering. "The people are with us, but the people can't fight against the Sultan's army. We have men all over the Empire, men willing to fight, men ready to fight. But without the support of the army we cannot take a stand. That is why I am here. We need real soldiers. So tell me honestly . . . would the Third Corps follow you against the Sultan?"

Flattered by the idea, Murat admitted, "I cannot be sure. Some would."

"And would you ask them?"

"If we find ourselves in agreement, and if I believe the time to be right . . ." He paused and began again. "Lives lost in victory are acceptable losses, but I will not risk my men for a political exercise."

Tarik nodded. "I understand you. I will do everything in my power to make this more than just a political exercise. The days of the old Empire are limited. As I am alive, I swear it."

When Murat had gone and the first pink-yellow rays of dawn began to glimmer upon the

Macedonian horizon, Salim found Tarik still beside the glowing embers, his head buried in his arms, which were coiled upon his knees. Salim sat down beside him and shook him gently, only to find that Tarik was not asleep, after all.

"So," Salim began immediately, "what do you think?"

Tarik sighed. "His attitude is annoying. He's a bigot."

"The two of you are very much alike," Salim observed.

"How can you say that? He's a pro-Turkish nationalist. He may have rejected the supremacy of the Sultan, but he still holds on to the supremacy of the Turk."

"So?" Salim bumped him shoulder to shouler. "You believe in the rights of all Ottomans. In the rhetoric of revolution it's a minor distinction."

Disgruntled, Tarik stared into the dawn. "I had a feeling that he would sell his own mother."

"And you would sell me if you had to," Salim pointed out.

Tarik looked at him.

Salim did not smile. He wasn't joking. "Tarik, I love you like a brother, but I know you have always been able to sacrifice the individual to the cause."

The truth of it weakened Tarik as he turned back to the dawn, and in it he saw the yellow hair, blue eyes, and undaunted courage of one he had sacrificed to the cause.

Her blond hair barely shone through the shimmering veil. Her eyes were now lined with kohl in the usual Eastern style, making the blue color especially striking. Jessica sat with unexpected complacency beside Usta in their cart, and behind them, nineteen other carts drawn by garishly decorated young bulls followed them through the bazaar. Above the procession, the city's ancient spires spoke of past greatness and fading glories, the freizes and mosaics and tiles depicting magnificent conquests of the past.

At the head of the procession rose the Kislar Agha, astride a thickset black stallion with heavy legs and a short gait. Upon each cart were two drivers, and beside each rode four eunuchs. Within each cart rode several women of the Imperial Harem, bedecked with bead-fringed *yashmacs* made of gold fabric confined to their heads by crowns of blazing jewels. Upon their shoulders they wore brightly colored, heavily brocaded *feridje* cloaks, and at the sight of them the tradesmen in the bazaar began to hawk their wares and confections and treasures with superfluous flourish. As the procession rode slowly past the booths and wagons, the harem women were shown an endless array of bolts of fabric, brass trinkets from India, Italian glass beads, Persian rugs, ceramic and earthenware pottery—everything that could be sold was for sale here.

And Jessica adored everything she saw. Not because she wanted those things but because every item, every huckster, every inch that passed beneath the carts put that much more distance between her and the Palace of Yildiz. She knew her plan, knew her place. She would shop happily, as she was expected to do. She would make Usta proud. Proud and incautious.

From early morning until late in the afternoon the women of Sultan Hasam's harem combed the bazaar for whimsy's sake, and though Usta stayed close to Jessica, she finally began to wander a little farther away each time something new caught her eye. Jessica seemed to thrive on the shopping spree, nourished by the outing. The two of them walked casually through the bazaar, followed by two eunuchs who carried their bundles of purchases.

"If you were in England," Usta told Jessica as they examined a display of rings and bracelets, "you would have to look at the prices. But here, no extravagance will be denied you. Eastern women control their own fortunes. Anything you want is yours."

Jessica inhaled deeply, as though actually trying to absorb the idea, to get used to it and learn to enjoy it. Usta seemed pleased.

Jessica looked back over her shoulder. "There was some fabric we passed . . . exquisite green, like the sea when the sun is just right. I thought it would make a luxurious nightgown."

"Show it to me."

Jessica led Usta and the eunuchs through the lines of stalls, away from the rest of the women and their servants. She glanced around and measured the distance between herself and the other harem women. "I think it was over that way," she said, and started off again.

Ready to indulge her, Usta followed, beckoning the eunuchs to come after her. They trailed after Jessica through the bazaar, around a corner, and toward one of the dozen or so textile merchants selling their fabrics. Jessica picked out the first green bolt of fabric she could find. "This one, Usta. That's the one I saw."

Usta bubbled off a phrase in Turkish to the tradesman behind the stall. The turbaned man freed the bolt from the display and presented it to the two women, sensing a juicy sale.

Jessica wrestled the heavy bolt into her arms. "Feel this, Usta. It's absolutely . . . divine!"

The bolt rammed hard into Usta, driving the older woman back into the eunuchs, who were thrown off-balance by the heavy bundles they already carried. Usta and the two servants piled backward into a clattering display of painted tin bowls and vases. The display collapsed and rang like an alarm.

Jessica climbed over the table of fabric bolts and flew down on the other side, in the next aisle. She scrambled to her feet and ran for her life, for her freedom. Behind her, Usta screamed for the Kislar. The sound drove Jessica onward as she crashed through the bazaar, toppling urns and tearing down displays as fast as she could grasp whatever appeared within reach. The trail of havoc grew behind her, slowing down the eunuchs who pursued her at the Kislar's panicked order.

"Find her!" The Kislar's booming voice echoed through the ancient streets. The bazaar swarmed with eunuchs, but Jessica was gone.

A hanging row of copper pots and trinkets hid her quite well as she peered between the cookware and watched the eunuchs combing the bazaar for her. They were asking questions of the tradesmen. Good—that meant they had lost her trail completely.

She watched, barely breathing, as the eunuchs moved on. Knowing she was still too much out in the open, Jessica opted to find a better hiding place. Soon it would be sunset, then night, and in the darkness she could escape. She would find a horse. She would get away to freedom.

When the eunuchs disappeared behind the next building, she carefully emerged from her hiding place and hurried down the street the opposite way, scurrying through rows of bazaar stalls and ignoring the appalled stares of men who dared not look at an unveiled woman. She rounded a corner and ran flush into the corner of a booth. Recovering, she tried to pull away, only to have her neck wrenched back. "Oh, damn!" she gasped. Her *yashmac* had caught on a piece of splintered wood. She tugged at it, but that only compounded the problem as the veil twisted around a loose nail and embedded itself into the splinters. Her chest tightened. She began breathing too fast and yanked desperately at the veil, each yank drawing a gasp from her. Her hands shook as she sought the clasp that held the *yashmac* on her head by the strip of silk looping under her throat. The pressure began to choke her, but she kept yanking. The stall's wares—brass tea sets—shook and jangled as her desperation drove her to violence.

A strangled yell bolted from her throat as she tumbled backward, and several numb seconds passed before she realized she was free. Her veil hung too short over her shoulder—cut.

And the knife that had done the deed still gleamed in the sun before her. A man in Muslim garb, with a scar on his face and a narrowed left eye, stood over her. With a grin he reached down and grasped her hand. "You come with me," he said.

Jessica lashed out at him with her foot and scrambled up, but he still had hold of her wrist. "Let me go," she said, choking.

He held her tighter. "I will take you to the English embassy. To Charles."

Jessica stopped. Stared. Charles? How did this ball of rags know Charles?

The eunuchs were drawing closer. She sensed them, she saw them, and she made her decision.

The Muslim spy led her through the maze of bazaar stalls, only seconds ahead of the eunuchs as they searched for her. They headed for the open, teeming streets where they could disappear into the crowd. Just as they would have reached the streets, the Muslim spy suddenly stopped and pushed her back.

"What's wrong?" Jessica demanded. "What are you doing? Take me to Charles, do you hear?"

"Can't," the man said."Look."

Their way was blocked by the carts of the Imperial Harem, which had moved in to surround the bazaar.

Jessica began to shake. The Muslim spy gestured her to fall back into the shadows of a partially collapsed tent. There they waited.

Inside the folds of the tent Jessica curled into a ball and tried to keep from panting. Charles . . . Charles was looking for her. She had known he would. He hadn't lost faith. He didn't care what had happened to her in all these weeks. He didn't care what reputation she would have once word of her captivity in an Eastern harem trickled back to England. Freedom. Freedom. She would possess herself once again. She had possessed wealth and riches and a chance to bear a child who would rule a nation, but nothing could stand against possession of herself. *Freedom.*

"Attention! Attention!"

Jessica jolted. It was the Kislar's thunderous voice calling in English.

"There is a reward for this woman who hides among you. A reward that will make you rich. Never again will you have to sell wares in the bazaar. Look at me and say I cannot pay such a reward as I speak of."

Tempted, the Muslim spy peeked out and indeed saw the brocaded magnificence of the Kislar moving on his priceless, overfed black horse through the stalls.

"This woman," the Kislar announced, "is the

property of your ruler, Sultan Hasam. And no one can pay a higher price."

Jessica leaned forward, hissing to the Muslim spy, "Charles will pay you more!"

But she had already lost. The Muslim's face gleamed with realization. No one in the Empire could outbuy the Sultan. Especially not an embassy clerk.

"No!" Jessica rasped. "Where's your sense of honor?"

The man took her wrist. "In my purse." He dragged her out of the tent. To the Kislar he called, "Is this the one you search for?"

The Kislar reined his black steed around. And he smiled.

CHAPTER EIGHT

"Why do I have to watch this? What difference does it make?"

Jessica pulled against the Kislar's iron hand as he bullied her down a marble corridor toward the chambers of the Kadin. Wasn't it enough that she was back in this world of cages? Must she also be subjected to another audience with the Kadin? But, halfway down the corridor, the Kislar stopped and signaled to the three eunuchs who followed. He wrenched Jessica to a halt. The three servants immediately put their shoulders to a section of the wall. Jessica thought they'd gone mad, until the wall moved. A passageway, black and forbidding—leading where?

"What are you doing with me? I demand to know." The quiver in her voice depleted Jessica's attempt at forcefulness.

"You may demand nothing," the Kislar told her. "If you had dark hair, you might not even be alive."

The passageway was unlit and cold as Jessica

struck the moldy wall and recovered her balance, sending back to the Kislar a glare of both contempt and contrition. He followed her in. The marble column rolled closed behind them. Darkness became blackness.

"Walk."

She straightened. "How? I can't even see."

"Walk and you will soon see."

She felt her way along the wall, her skin crawling at the sensation of lichen and slime and the Kislar's nearness behind her. Soon her eyes began to adjust—no, there was light ahead, around a corner. She hurried toward it.

A face appeared, glowing yellow and etched in shadow. Jessica caught a scream with both hands and bumped backward into the Kislar.

"No matter what happens," a deep female voice told her, "no matter what you see, you will not make a sound. And you will not break."

"Usta," Jessica whispered, finally seeing form behind the distortion caused by the glow of a single candle in Usta's hand.

They led her down the corridor toward nightmare.

At the end of the corridor there was light and latticework screen above the domed chambers of the Kadin. Jessica hadn't realized the passageway sloped upward, but they were now high above the Kadin's audience room, gazing down upon judgment.

Below, the Kadin was reviewing Geisla, who stood before the elegant Grecian woman and between two eunuchs twice the girl's size.

"There are rumors," the Kadin was saying, "that you are pregnant." She rose, smoothed her voluminous robes, and walked toward Geisla. She surveyed the girl to put her in her place, then pulled the robe from Geisla's shoulders and pressed her hand across the girl's abdomen. "Perhaps they are more than rumors."

Geisla dropped to her knees in a salute of subservience. "It has been more than two months. I am certain I am with child."

In her high cubicle, Jessica inhaled slowly. Two months? It seemed more like two years, but two months was a long time for no one to have come looking for her and nothing to have happened to advance her chances for freedom. Only the untrustworthy spy in the bazaar showed any indication that Charles was interested in finding her, and it proved conclusively that he had no real idea of how to go about it. She was on her own.

The Kadin tipped her head and moved fluidly back to her divan, reclining upon it and observing, "You must be very happy."

Geisla nodded emphatically. "I am. Very happy."

The Kadin smiled. Jessica shuddered at the quality of that smile.

"And who is the father?" the Kadin asked.

Geisla's face became a matt of shock. "What do you mean?"

The Kadin turned lazily to the other women lining the room and said, "There have been so many, the girl is uncertain who the father is."

The ladies laughed, but their eyes were cold, frightened.

Jessica linked her fingers into the latticework and strained to see better. Her hands were suddenly cold.

Geisla stood up and took two measured steps toward the Kadin. She looked more adult than when she had gone to her knees. "There is only one father. There can only be one husband—"

The Kadin interrupted, "Husband? There can be no husband until you've produced a son."

"And when I do," Geisla's crisp, young voice announced, "everyone will know the father is the Sultan. Our union is recorded in the great book. Therefore I am protected—even from you."

The Kadin's thick, painted lips pursed in an ugly way. She lowered her eyelids. "Bring me the great book."

Jessica felt a thin veil of sweat break out beneath her robes. The rules . . . did they work? They must work.

The great book was presented to the Kadin. The woman rested it on the divan beside her and casually turned each page, scanning the script. "I find nothing . . . no record of you, my dear."

Geisla's eyes grew painfully wide. "But there must be! I watched you write the entry myself!"

The Kadin shrugged with one shoulder. "Perhaps I missed it. Let me look again. Ladies, come here. Do you find any record of Geisla in these lines?"

The women crowded around the book, studying the pages. One by one they backed away, shaking their heads.

"But they can't even read!" Geisla shrieked.

The eunuchs pulled her back.

The Kadin slammed the book shut. "Perhaps one of you ladies remembers the night when Geisla caught the Sultan's eye? Does anyone remember such a night?"

More shaking of heads.

Jessica gripped the latticework and opened her mouth to shout the truth, but a dry hand closed over her lips. "You have no power here," the Kislar whispered in her ear. "Death is easy recourse in Sultan Hasam's palace. Keep quiet and you may not die."

The chilling reality stiffened her.

Geisla's voice became thready. "Why are you doing this to me?"

The Kadin said, "I am only following the law."

"But you are the first Kadin! No one can take that away from you!"

"There is no record of your union with Sultan Hasam. That makes you either unfaithful or a liar. Or possibly both."

"My child is no threat to you!"

The eunuchs dragged her across the chamber toward the Kadin's immense marble tub as the court ladies formed a ceremonial line. Geisla, whimpering, was stripped of her chemise and lifted over the side of the tub with utmost gentility. Even from the second floor Jessica heard the soft sobbing as though Geisla stood only inches away.

Only the Kislar's echoing warning kept Jessica silent. She pressed her knuckles into her mouth until she tasted blood.

Geisla screamed.

The eunuchs forced her head under the scented water. Next came the awful, panicked splashing. Another scream—this one followed by sickening gurgles.

Jessica spun away, coiling her arms around her head, shaking like beads on a dancer's wrist. Inside her head she still heard the screaming, the splashing.

Then there was a terrible silence. A peace of no real peace.

Hands collected her and pulled her back into the passageway. She barely sensed herself walking and knew only her own racking sobs.

Usta's voice came out of the darkness and shook her. "Stand up straight. Get control of yourself. It is all over. You must learn. Do you understand now that you *must* learn?"

Jessica held herself up against the slimy wall and demanded of herself that the sobbing stop. Her eyes, now red, stared into the dim light from the one candle.

The Kislar moved beside her. "Now you know what happens to unprotected girls."

It seemed that, for today at least, Kislar Agha had reality in his pocket. Anger swelled within Jessica's chest, an unbridled rage toward the

Kadin and toward the strange customs that gave power to those clever enough to use it. For herself she felt contempt. She would never gain her freedom working outside of this system. And she could not protect her friends as Geisla needed to be protected. Or protect herself. The system had to be penetrated. Power dangled all around, like golden apples ready to be plucked by the wisest, the most cunning. . . .

She shuddered down her fear, her revulsion. She made herself cold and vowed to remain so.

To Usta and the Kislar she turned a face of convincing submission.

"Teach me what I need to know."

Foolish is the man who tries to spend only one side of a coin. The Muslim spy reveled in his newfound wealth and quickly formulated a way to compound it. Without a moment's hesitation he left the Kislar's side and headed straight back to the English embassy where he found Charles Wyndon not at his desk but staring out a window.

Charles turned when the door shuffled open and took anxious note that his spy entered alone. "Anything?"

"I know where she is," the man told him.

"Sit down," Charles said, "and tell me what you know."

The spy remained standing. "First," he demurred, "the money."

The transaction was completed immediately, without question or hesitation. This was satisfying for the Muslim, who knew better than to try to squeeze payment out of his own kind without first providing the goods, but these English knew no better and were easy to subjugate. So he told what he knew, leaving out only those details that would save his skin.

Without pause Charles took the costly information before his superior, sure he had advantage now.

Ambassador Grant sat in his immaculate velvet chair behind his immaculate desk—easily kept immaculate since Randolph, his attaché, did most of his work, anyway—looking patriarchal. Randolph sat near the desk, taking notes, then looked up when Charles interrupted them.

"Sir," Wyndon said quickly, "excuse me. I'm sorry for the interruption, but I have very important news."

"Go ahead with it, then," Grant said, raising his bushy white eyebrows. His tone had a polished sympathy about it, a perpetually ready tool.

"I've just received word of my fiancée's whereabouts."

"Indeed?"

"She's being held against her will in the palace of the Sultan."

Silence dropped like a sledge.

Grant cleared his throat and glanced at Randolph. "Sit down," he said to Charles, and waited until the invitation—order—was accepted. "Now, tell me where you got this information."

"I hired a man. A native."

"A native. I see. . . ."

"I deduced that someone indigenous to the area would be more likely to provide accurate information than—"

"And how much did you pay for this so-called proof?"

Charles sat back, catching Randolph's warning glance in his periphery. "Rather a lot, sir."

Grant rolled his weight onto his elbow as it rested on the leather top of his desk and said, "This is very disturbing. Very disturbing indeed."

"What are you prepared to do?"

"Do?"

"Sir," Charles began again, sensing evasion, "I now have proof that Miss Grey is a prisoner. Certainly we must prepare to demand her release."

Ambassador Grant spoke slowly. "We cannot move on such a grave accusation unless we are absolutely sure. And your 'proof,' as you call it, is at best highly questionable. I mean, really, Charles—are we to take the word of a man who makes a living selling secrets, who demands money for information?" With a bad-taste sort of grimace he added, "A Muslim? No, we must proceed cautiously. I suggest you continue with your search and try to find more substantial proof that Miss Grey is in fact even *in* the palace. Now, if you will excuse me, I have a luncheon engagement, do I not, Randolph?"

Randolph stood up. "Yes, sir. With Mrs. Bridesley and her nephew."

Grant got up laboriously and checked the position of his tie in a gilded mirror behind his desk. "Isn't your fiancée American, Wyndon?" he asked the question as though it were half the reason for Jessica Grey's disappearance.

Charles bristled at the implication. "Her father is . . . was English."

"Ah, yes." Ambassador Grant moved toward the door. "Of course."

He moved slowly, with careful aplomb, but took care to close the door behind him, leaving a definite impression on the two young men left in the office.

Charles closed his eyes and his fists. "You can tell that pompous, supercilious ass that I'll get him his proof."

Randolph put his pen in his pocket and gave Charles a grin of genuine sympathy. "Do you want that on or off the record?"

Charles turned to him with a response, but from the doorway, Ambassador Grant's voice stopped him cold. "It seems I've forgotten my cigars."

"They're in the top drawer, sir," Randolph covered quickly, "on the left, I believe." He shared a guilty glance with Charles as the ambassador rummaged through his desk.

"Ah, here." Grant straightened up with a box of specially blended Turkish cigars. "I assure you, Charles, when you are able to offer substantial proof, this 'pompous ass' will immediately begin negotiations for Jessica's release."

Charles turned the shade of the velvet chair and nodded. But before the ambassador had left the room a second time, Charles had formulated a new plan.

The turf slope, having been tended and fed and groomed, glowed a perfect jade-green beneath the noonday sun and provided the foundation for a natural amphitheater. Above, between the grass and the sun, workmen's brown shoulders gleamed with sweat as a monstrous bird cage took form, a cage that would be completed in record time, whitewashed, bedecked with vines, and ready to house Sultan Hasam's entire harem. Here the royal concubines would sit to watch the ballet being rehearsed in the theater below. The workmen slaved without pause, insensible to the shining bodies of prepubescent boys rehearsing a sensuous dance they did not yet understand. In eight days it would be the Sultan's birthday, and the celebration would ring across the Empire, whether it brought joy or condemnation.

Within the palace other preparations were being made. Other rehearsals.

In a darkened room, lit only with the rosy glow of a single lantern, Jessica sat upon the edge of Usta's quilted bed and watched her mentor demonstrate a sexual ballet. Usta's body was draped in sheer gauze, shimmering golden in the rosy light, and the undulations she showed Jessica were plain to see. As a classroom, these chambers held a particular aura of submission tonight: Jessica's submission to her training, a woman's submission to a man. Usta spoke not a single word but described the shapes of a man with her beautiful hands. Beneath the thin gauze, a body that once had been firm with youth now molded itself to an imaginary man with the elegance of experience. Age became a thing of desire, for no teenager could move with this special allure. Even to another woman the movements were arousing, tempting.

Usta arched and bent and rotated with practiced grace, and Jessica demanded of herself a personal steadiness—she refused to blush or look away. She would indeed learn what she needed to know to gain power within the structure of palace politics. If her freedom could not be gained by stealth, then it would be gained through power. For that she would have to win over Sultan Hasam, and Usta knew the formula. For the next few days—perhaps weeks— Jessica Grey would forget her civilized upbringing and retreat into a world of the past where power belonged to the most charismatic of men and women.

She watched the sexual poetry and committed every act to memory, forcing herself to envision herself in that role, with the Sultan beneath her body. She imagined the shapes of Sultan Hasam's body as Usta's hands and legs described what the Sultan enjoyed most. Jessica captured all those movements and pressed them deep into her memory, committing herself to what must come.

"It is a pleasant thing," Usta finally said, very quietly. "You can easily learn to love the loving, even if you do not entirely love the man. It is a woman's way, Jessica. Lie down upon the bed and close your eyes and I will tell you."

Uneasy, Jessica rolled onto the brocade cushions and tried to relax.

"Close your eyes," Usta repeated gently, "and listen to the value of womanhood. That's right . . . that's right. I am nothing and you are all the future, my dear. As a woman, you will learn about yourself—how to please yourself as you please the man. You will learn the special control we have over men. They think they make love to us but—ah, no. It is quite the reverse. As a sensual being, a woman carries with her the wholeness of life and all its fruits. Without a woman there can never be love. All that is yours to take as you will, to cherish to your heart . . . ah, so glorious! The knowledge is frightening, I know. But without it there is nothing. An intelligent woman knows how and when to use all her assets—her mind, her legs, her thighs, her breasts, her hands from finger to finger. It is a symphony, Jessica, a symphony."

Jessica's arms tingled as she listened to Usta's emotions pour all around her, her eyes closed. The elder woman had an incredible past to share, and still she was not jaded by it all. Usta's voice still quivered with excitement at the prospects of womanhood, of making love to a man as that one special art.

With those images in her mind Jessica remembered the man who had brought her here. Tarik. Tarik Pasha, they called him—a disturbingly foreign name for a man so disturbingly civilized. He spoke of moving into the twentieth century, yet he retreated into the past in order to enslave her for some profit. But he hadn't liked it—Jessica had spent enough time with him to know that for certain. He had treated her gently, with regret. He had spoken darkly, and with bitterness, of his cause, and she had stopped believing that the profit he gained by selling her to Sultan Hasam had anything to do with coinage. Something else had changed hands in that bargain, something she was *worth* to him. If she could discover what sat on the other side of the scale, perhaps she could buy back her freedom. But for that—power. She must gain power within the palace edifice.

Usta clapped her hands, awakening Jessica from her thoughts. As she looked up, several slave girls filed into the room and waited for Usta's orders. "They will massage you," Usta said to Jessica. "They will perfume you. Pamper you in every way. You will stay here for a week, my dear. The first thing you must learn is to be comfortable with your own body, to relax with your nakedness. You will never be comfortable with a man until you learn to be comfortable with yourself. Now it begins."

Two slave girls moved toward Jessica. Usta moved aside, folding her long hands together approvingly. The girls slid Jessica's robe from her shoulders. She closed her eyes, feeling her breasts fall free before strangers.

That night the cool marble slabs of the Imperial Turkish baths knew a special glow—a few extra candles, new spices in the trickling waters, a rustle of linen chemises—as the ritual began of turning a girl into a woman. Jessica lay half in despondency and half in hopelessness upon one of the marble slabs. Slave girls massaged her shoulders, kneaded the big muscles of her back, caressed her thighs, rolled their knuckles over her calves, and gradually her tension began to subside.

On the second day the slaves made ancient mixtures of rice flour and oil. They made it slowly, with great care, then hurried it to the baths before it cooled, as this recipe had been hurried into harem baths for centuries uncounted. They plied Jessica's ivory body with the mixture, spreading the creamy substance over her stomach and her breasts, her shoulders, her face, even the bottoms of her feet. She leaned back and closed her eyes, unable to resist the tingling warmth. The slaves heated water until it steamed in great pots beside her to keep the mud pack warm and supple.

On the third day they began massaging her feet and hands. They rubbed her neck and ran their young fingers beneath her chin. She drifted to their touch now. Strange how quickly she had become accustomed to it. She could let them touch her now without flinching. Her eyes would drift shut to the sensuality running in her body like blood through veins.

On the fourth day she lounged in the rosepetaled water while slaves' hands ran along her body beneath the surface. She no longer saw their faces as they bobbed beside her. The fragrance here was intoxicating, dream-inducing. She lay her head back and dreamed.

On the fifth day she floated to the baths without summon. She lay upon her silk divan as though it had always been hers. She thought of Tarik Pasha with less contempt, with more pity, with unbeckoned thoughts of touching and tempting him in her own brand of capture, just as he had swept her away into his world without giving her a choice. She dreamed in the baths, inhaling the herbal aphrodisiacs until the eyes of Tarik glowed like black pearls in her mind. An Eastern lover . . . Love could be a kind of revenge.

By the weekend she stood like a queen over her slaves, her robe draped off her shoulders to reveal her back. The slaves dusted her shoulders, her back, and her arms with the gold powder, brushing it evenly over the ivory skin that glowed beneath. The gold dust looked different on her skin than it looked on the bronze skin of Eastern women. On Jessica the golden glow shined like topaz and had a different depth. She raised her arm and surveyed how it shimmered in the noon sun. Yes. Very good. She was pleased. She nodded to the slaves and looked up at the sunbeams with open challenge.

It was the royal birthday. The week of furious building and rehearsing and cooking and preparing finally came to a head.

When the ballet was fully rehearsed and the sun began to set, great rows of torches were lit, as well as gas lanterns, to brighten the stage and the area where Sultan Hasam would sit and where his Imperial Harem would repose within their protected lattice cage.

Usta, now properly veiled and robed, walked beside the Kislar Agha, making sure they were discreetly out of earshot from the workers who were still rushing to complete the last details on the stage and the viewing platforms.

"Is she ready?" the Kislar asked.

"For the Sultan to see her? Yes," Usta answered. "For the Sultan to bed her?" At this she shrugged. Jessica had seemed willing to learn how to make love to a man—too anxious, perhaps, to be sincere about it or to learn it for its own sake, but she had paid attention and not turned away. "She is not the kind of girl who can be read in a glance. I cannot tell how she will behave in the Sultan's chamber. I make you no guarantees."

"She must behave well," the Kislar said thoughtfully. "The price I paid for her is worth my life if she displeases him. If I had paid for her in jewels or coins, things would not be so critical. He will crave her when he sees her. If she does not deliver the passion he wants, blood will flow—hers, yours, and mine."

"We shall see, then." Usta lengthened her stride to keep up with the long gait of the Kislar. He always walked faster when he was nervous, and Usta tried to slow him down with her own stride so that no one would see his tension. "She is being prepared now. The slaves are perfuming and powdering her, and she has submitted to the thin veils that will show her body as she walks. Outwardly, at least, she has become an Eastern woman. We shall have to wait to see about the inside."

"What will she wear tonight?"

"Her best color: a deep peacock green . . . all silk. And no jewels," Usta pointed out. "Just a few rubies for her headpiece." She gazed ahead at the twisting garden vines as they turned magenta in the setting sun. "When I was the Sultan's lover, I never wore my jewelry. I let my slaves carry it. They followed me, stark naked, carrying trays of diamonds and rubies." A smile curved her painted lips and she raised one eyebrow. "It was quite effective."

The Kislar inclined his ebony head ever so slightly. "You are still effective," he told her.

Sultan Hasam's guests began arriving shortly after sunset. They were ushered to their seats for the ballet on either side of the great platform that would hold the Sultan and his advisers, and to the left of the impressive golden lattice cage with its thick vines designed to conceal the women of the harem. Those mysterious women, the stuff of legend and gossip, would appear only as flashes of shimmering multicolored veils between the rows of vines and latticework. The guests were mostly Europeans residing in Constantinople, as well as a large contingent from the British embassy in their preferred seats. As Charles followed Ambassador Grant to their seats, he stared narrow-eyed at the harem cage. Behind him, Randolph gently urged him to move forward. He glared obsessively at the cage.

"Perhaps you shouldn't have come," the ambassador suggested when Charles bumped into him without noticing that they had reached their seats.

Charles pressed his lips together. "She's in there. I can feel it. And maybe somehow she'll sense that I'm here . . . that I haven't given up."

The orchestra, clustered in a wide cubicle at the base of the stage, struck up a stirring Oriental march, and the spectacle began. All but Charles were caught up in the elegance as a procession of people in various native costumes strode gracefully across the stage, met at center, and descended into the audience to pass down the center aisle. The spectacle had been carefully designed to showcase the heterogeneity of Sultan Hasam's empire, and every group, from the elemental Greeks to the nomads of the desert, were represented. Serbia, Syria, Bulgaria, Arabia, Armenia, Turkey—all were here in effigy tonight, framed in pageantry, each costume modeled by the most beautiful or most handsome of its native race. The audience was awed, all except a single young man in a pinstriped suit.

He was watching Sultan Hasam with a deadly contempt.

The Sultan observed the pageant with a practiced regal boredom. His black robe glittered with meaningless medals and decorations, sharply contrasted by the giant white egret feather in his red fez, anchored by a random cluster of diamonds and saphhires.

Charles glared.

Randolph began to sweat, and nudged Charles when the music markedly changed, gesturing to the stage where a portion of *Madame Butterfly* was being performed by lithe young bodies all powdered white-pink. Elaborate Oriental costumes flickered beneath the harsh stage lights, and all Charles could manage was a noncommittal, "Yes, they're quite lovely. . . ."

Ambassador Grant smiled beneath his mustache. "What they are," he said scandalously, "are boys."

Charles turned his gaze back toward Sultan Hasam and wrenched to his feet. The Sultan had disappeared. Desperate, Charles scanned the crowded amphitheater until he spied the white egret feather moving within a ring of fezzes toward the gilded harem cage as the guards moved with their ruler. Charles's fists knotted.

"I hope you're not thinking of doing anything foolish," Ambassador Grant advised. The heaviness of his tone succeeded.

Charles lowered himself, stiff as an ironing board, back into his seat.

Sultan Hasam disappeared into the gilded cage.

Through the bevy of women, the most stunning women in all the Empire—and beyond—there ran a flurry of thrills. They rippled like a veiled ocean, their indescribably varied jewelry glittering as they immediately dropped their veils and turned on their most seductive expressions.

By reflex, Jessica started to loosen her own veil. With a subtle gesture Usta stopped her. Jessica's silent question soon turned to the beginnings of understanding.

Even the line of black eunuchs noticed her—the only veiled woman among a sea of beauties. Even the Kadin, surrounded by nearly naked preadolescent girls as bait, was no match for this subtle tactic. The Sultan looked across the shimmering panorama at Jessica.

And so did the Kadin. And so did the eunuch. Jessica continued to look down at the ballet. She felt the Sultan's eyes upon her and forced her heart to steady its apprehensive thudding, but she never took her eyes off the stage.

The Sultan, who had paused near the Kadin, now changed his path through the herd of women. He moved, hypnotized, toward Jessica.

Only when he stood over her did she turn her gaze upward.

"Why," he began, "do you continue to cover yourself?"

She wondered if her apprehension would come out in her voice. "It does not please you?"

"It would please me to see your face."

Her eyes changed over the veil as she smiled, and in a single elegant gesture she freed the shimmering fabric. It billowed to her shoulder. Where once there had been the disguise of the gleaming gold-threaded veil now shined a face stunning in its simplicity and its ivory pureness, a tinge of sunny rose upon her cheeks.

To the side, the Kislar nodded at Usta. The other women of the harem gasped as Sultan Hasam took a seat beside Jessica.

The Kadin silently raged.

Below, the dance went on. A single Roman candle lanced across the sky over the harem cage and burst into a million stars.

Jessica forced herself to relax. Sultan Hasam's presence beside her was electrifying. She felt the ruler's curiosity and arousal, felt the Kadin's bitter hatred, felt the jealousy and awe of the other harem women, and felt as though she were sitting in the middle of a maelstrom of potential energy. It could drown her, or it could carry her high up over the threats circling below. But, as Usta had said, it all depended upon Jessica's own abilities as a woman, both sensual and intellectual. Her entire self must play this game or she would lose.

She hardly saw the ballet, though her eyes remained fixed upon it most of the evening. Only twice did she give in to the tension and look toward Sultan Hasam. Each time he immediately turned his eyes to her. Yes, he was just as aware of her as she was of him but in different ways.

Finally the long evening ended. Without a word Sultan Hasam rose, turned away, and strode out of the harem cage to preside once again over the celebrations. Jessica watched him go. She felt weak all of a sudden. She felt drained, and amazed that he could spend the evening beside someone and say nothing at all when he left. Now what? Was it all over? Had she fortified herself for nothing?

She shook her head slightly. This didn't make sense.

The harem women were immediately escorted back to the seraglio, not allowed to participate in the gala affairs following the ballet. Jessica felt the curious eyes of the people in the stands. How strange all this must seem to them, perhaps even stranger than it was to her now. Emotionally tired, she went back to the seraglio without protest, for protest would evidently not be her way out of here.

She went to her rooms with the other girls and fell asleep with all her veils still on and hardly stirred at all when Lanie came to help her change her clothes.

She awakened abruptly and sat up.

Four white eunuchs glared down at her with impassive expressions. Not even that—more like the faces of the dead. She pulled away in fear. "What are you doing here? Where is Usta?"

They dragged her out of her bed and out of Usta's apartments entirely. Her white lace nightgown swarmed behind her on the marble floor.

"Who sent you?" Jessica demanded, hoping the new tactic would get her some answer. It didn't. "Please let me talk to Usta . . . where are you taking me?"

Geisla's image flashed into her mind. Again she heard the screams, as sharp as horsewhips, as the water closed in. One of the eunuchs gave her a wicked smile—the last thing she would ever see?—and shoved her through a heavily tiled doorway.

She expected a torture chamber, pots of boiling oil, executioners carrying lashes and knives.

What she saw instead was a flurry of slaves carrying flowers, ornamentations, trays of crystal jars full of perfume and rosewater, and furniture as lush as any King Edward himself might hope to recline upon. In the midst of it all the Kislar Agha relaxed upon a silk divan against a background of great tapestries and sprawling draperies with dark and intricate Persian designs. The Kislar slurped grapes and directed the workers with almost feminine affinity.

"The jars go to the bath . . . the flowers go over there. Brass urns and the samovar go beside the tea set. . . ." He looked up when Jessica moved uncertainly into the chambers. "Ah, I hope it suits you. I had to make a lot of decisions rather quickly."

Jessica stared at him. "Why didn't they tell me it was you who wanted me? I was scared half to death. What do you mean you hope it suits me?"

The Kislar rolled to his feet. "This is where you live now. Your new apartments."

"Mine? I don't understand." And she didn't trust appearances, either.

He strode toward her. "You have caught Sultan Hasam's eye. He sat with you during the ballet."

"Yes, for about twenty minutes. How does that—"

"You are *guzdeh*: special under the eye of the Sultan." He led her into the bedroom and pulled aside two buckling doors over twelve feet long. Dresses—an endless closetful of dresses richer than any royalty dared desire. Organza, silk, taffeta, brocade, satin, organdy. They drew Jessica's hands. She caressed them, decided they were real, and tried to find words for this strange turn. Power . . .

"Being *guzdeh*," the Kislar explained, "means you won't be called in like the others to be part of a nameless orgy. It means you will be treated special."

"All of this is mine?" Jessica turned accusatively, as though to catch him off-guard and discover the truth.

"All and more." For the first time Kislar Agha moved toward her in a genuine display of tenderness and put his huge hand on her shoulder. "There is coffee and a tray of sweetmeats awaiting you in your bath chamber. There you will also find a tub of pink marble even more luxurious than Usta's, with cascading fountains of the most delicately scented water. You have only to make a summons, and whatever you desire will be brought to you. There has not been a woman who was *guzdeh* in . . . a very long time."

Jessica repaid his kindness with her first sincere gaze into his black eyes, the first gaze she had given him that lacked suspicion and disgust. "When will the Sultan want to see me?"

He shrugged. "Maybe tomorrow, maybe in a month. Whenever it pleases him. In the meantime *your* pleasure is the concern of everyone around you."

Jessica slowly and thoroughly absorbed the entire truth, the process of power within the seraglio. With that power, she had learned, also came obligation and the terrible, draining process of waiting, a process that could make a woman old.

Entranced by her surroundings and their implications, she moved ghostlike toward the scented waters of her bath chamber. "Yes," she murmured in a tone that confused the Kislar, "in the harem we understand the vocabulary of pleasure. . . ."

CHAPTER NINE

The canaries twittered in the exquisite bird cage dangling from Lady Ashley's hand as she entered one of the rooms in the endless maze within Sultan Hasam's seraglio and strode across the rich reds, browns, golds, and blues of the Persian tiles, passing opulently covered, low-slung divans with their expensive, embroidered scenes of Eastern life, ignoring the inlaid tables in favor of greeting the Kadin. The Sultan's elegant Grecian wife reclined on a silk cushion whose silver threads caught the lights in her eyes as she rose to meet her guest. She got up with a poised purposefulness, a slow and gradual business meant to proclaim her life-style and advertise her position.

"Lady Ashley," the Kadin said in a professionally social groan. "It's been too long."

"Too, too long indeed," Lady Ashley responded, and held out the bird cage.

"How lovely," the Kadin said.

"It was made by an artisan I knew rather well once. He lives in Vienna now."

"How you must miss him."

Lady Ashley smiled the kind of smile women give to each other when they know more than they will say. "Occasionally I rather do."

"Come sit with me and give me news of Syria."

The two women kissed each other on the cheeks and sat on the nearest divan together. The position was perfectly choreographed to set off the Kadin's bejeweled hairstyle and the deep russet tones in the hair itself, showing them against a polished gold-lattice partition behind her.

"Would you like a cigarette?" the Kadin offered.

"Please," Lady Ashley accepted. "Yours are so unique. There's nothing like them in Damascus."

"I shall have you sent two dozen of them immediately." The Kadin beckoned to a slave girl who stood in a corner, absolutely devoid of identity. The girl hurried around the divan and bent before Lady Ashley to light the long Turkish cigarette.

Lady Ashley waited patiently as the girl struggled with a new kind of lighter, and resisted the urge to glance past her to the doorway when she thought she heard footsteps. To find Jessica in this cave of rooms upon rooms would be a feat indeed. Lady Ashley knew very well the chance she was taking—knew that finding Charles's financée here could be more dangerous than not finding her, depending upon the way Jessica reacted. A delicate situation . . . and tricky.

"Perhaps," the Kadin was saying, "you would like to take the baths. The journey from Damascus is especially dusty this time of year."

"Oh, it is, my dear," Lady Ashley agreed readily, "it certainly is. And we were following an elephant caravan for miles at the border—smelly beasts, I daresay. My clothing still carries their . . . aroma."

"They shall be laundered immediately. Come." The Kadin rose fluidly, extending an arm to her guest. "In moments you shall have forgotten the elephants."

The Kadin was true to her words. Lady Ashley's fine gown and shawl were taken gently by slaves of the Imperial Wardrobe, and soon the two women, equal in bearing if not in standing, walked arm in arm through the labyrinth of bath areas. Lady Ashley casually glanced at the delicate faces around her, nodding in distant greeting when some young girl caught her eye. None was Jessica. She continued walking with the Kadin, carrying on a conversation as empty as an upturned jug.

"So Sheikh Medjuel has not taken another wife—when he could have four," the Kadin noted, not exactly intending to compliment Lady Ashley. "You have done very well."

Lady Ashley squeezed the Kadin's arm and said, "Me? What about yourself? The only Kadin. Women all over the Empire wonder how you've managed such a coup. Some even say you do magic."

The Kadin laughed, immersing herself both in flattery and in the victory that her baiting had succeeded.

"But still," Lady Ashley went on, "with new girls arriving all the time, it must be very difficult to remain Sultan Hasam's only wife."

The Kadin's huge Grecian eyes became even larger with subtle amazement. "There have been no new girls. You must know that the slave trades have been abolished."

Lady Ashley leaned nearer. "But we both know there are ways. And I think I see a few new faces."

"Only young faces that have grown older. More mature. You have stayed away too long."

With conspiratorial girlishness Lady Ashley leaned even nearer. "But there have been kidnappings outside of Damascus. And rumors say those girls are in the palace."

"And I've heard they're still in Syria," she said, countering Lady Ashley with a little gossip of her own. "Don't let your husband be gone too long in the desert."

Lady Ashley let her own laughter ripple through the marble bath chambers, merging it with subtle looks this way and that, and a not too obvious effort to see through the lattice-work walls to the other chambers where ethereal beings moved and bathed. But the lighting here was deliberately dim, and the lattice work difficult to see through.

And it was early. She would be here all day.

Jessica dried herself off. She was beginning to feel more like a turtle than a woman. How much time could anybody spend up to her neck in rosewater? Beside her, Usta continued with the lesson of the day, a discourse in the benefits of Jessica's position as *guzdeh*. Jessica had been listening only sporadically but had carefully pretended to listen all along. She would have to learn many pretenses if she was to survive here. And she *would* survive, whatever the cost.

"You have been lucky," Usta was saying as she presented Jessica's robe. "And there are worse things to face than making love with Sultan Hasam. Some call him tyrant, but this is not your concern. Whatever he is on the outside, you shall be involved with only the inner man, the man he becomes when the veils draw around his bed. And I can tell you better than anyone—the man within the veils can be many kinds of lover. . . . Eastern men study the art and mystery of satisfying the physical woman, and the Sultan is an intelligent man. His greatest pleasure is to talk to an intelligent woman." Usta's eyes grew misty with nostalgia, recalling a time when she might have become Kadin, had things gone better, had fate turned her down a different fork in the road. "He used to say that such conversation was his favorite aphrodisiac."

Jessica gazed at Usta's expression with a touch of wariness. "But the women say he's changed.

That he's a different kind of man now. That it takes special tricks and potions to please him."

Usta waved the idea away, and the mistiness went with it. "Drugs and potions only create illusions of pleasure. Why use them when you can create your own?"

Jessica thought back to the moment when she and Usta had walked past the Kadin's chambers earlier that day, and the cold feeling of hatred returned. They'd seen the row of slaves provided to escort the Kadin's visitor, and Jessica hadn't been able to resist a peek into the open chambers, but all she had seen was the backside of a slave girl bending over in front of the Kadin and her guest. She had seethed inside that someone was able to come and go at will from this beautiful prison. Now, after a long bath, she felt no better about the Kadin and allowed Usta's words to sink in thoroughly. A time would come when she herself would be in a position to meet the Kadin on her own ground. If that opportunity never presented itself, at least she would be able to protect anyone else from the Kadin's falsification of the great book. Geisla had not died in vain, Jessica vowed, nor had the Sultan's child she'd carried.

"There is a careful delicacy with which a lover should embrace her partner," Usta said slowly, remembering. "Every moment, every position can be changed, transformed into something new by the intensity with which it is performed. Performed softly and with restrain, an embrace becomes tempting. Performed passionately and urgently, it becomes something new entirely . . . a thing of wonder, even pain, but so anxious a pain. . . ." Her voice dropped away. Her eyes caressed the marble walls of the baths as though a tapestry of her past lay etched there.

Jessica watched her, saw the love she had for lovemaking, for the Sultan himself, and was stung with an anxious envy. Could those memories, that expression, ever be hers? Not with Sultan Hasam, certainly. Not with a man she still had not really met. She tried to think of Charles, forced herself to see his face in her mind, but there was no sizzling wonder around it as Usta seemed to see around her own memories.

"At times," Usta murmured on, her lips quivering, "I would press my nails into his back— cautiously—just when he least expected it. It added a sharp piquancy to our embraces. Ah, Jessica . . . you have so much to look forward to, if only you can forget your past. The Eastern man is an intelligent lover. He studies the mystery of satisfying a woman. He learns to practice the restraining art. You see, to make love for long periods is a highly prized art in the East."

Usta paused, then climbed from the tub and extended a hand to Jessica.

Jessica hesitated, studying Usta's face and the experience it held precious in its timeless features. As the steam rose from the scented waters the face before her wavered and became a man's face, eyes black as stones and a rough stubble hazing the rounded jawline, framing lips set with determination. She saw him in Bedouin robes, then in gypsy's rags, then—

"Come," Usta said.

Jessica blinked.

"You are thinking of a man?" Usta words surprised her.

"Yes," she admitted. "A very disturbing man."

"The Englishman?"

Jessica felt the water sheet from her body as she rose out of the tub. "It was nothing."

She accepted the soft robe as Usta draped it over her shoulders and stepped to the high tier of marble around the tub. Behind the lattice screen, other women lolled their lives away in the scented baths, but Jessica no longer cared to look. Her curiosity about their bodies—so many different colors and shapes—had lost its edge. The idea of guarded privacy no longer tampered with her thoughts. They didn't care, and she no longer did, either. Whoever wanted to look could just look. What an odd culture—show your body but not your face.

She shook her head in a surge of recurring Americanism and followed Usta into the corridors.

"What happens if I don't please him?" she asked on an impulse.

"You will," Usta told her. "I have taught you everything I know . . . and I have never taught anyone *everything*."

"But what if . . . what if I can't—"

Usta turned to her, standing squarely before her in the middle of the cavernous hall. "Jessica, listen to me. Everything you value depends upon your pleasing Sultan Hasam."

Jessica pursed her lips. "What *I* value or what *you* value?"

Usta seemed to understand. "You must not question what must be done," she said, speaking carefully and with inflection. "It is your only hope for freedom."

The word jarred deep within Jessica, filling a cold and empty receptacle with a wine she dared not hope to taste. Someone else believed she might actually gain her liberty from this place. Someone who knew what was possible and what was not.

Numb, she murmured, "What are you saying?"

But Usta dared say no more.

And other things began, very suddenly, to happen.

Shock descended upon Jessica as she stared past Usta to the great gilded doorway of the Kadin's apartments.

The flowing Parisian frock could have been spotted halfway across Turkey, moving as it did against the Kadin's glittering Eastern robes and harem trousers. Jessica felt the blood drop from her cheeks. "Lady Ashley . . ."

She bolted forward. Usta clutched her arm and wrenched her back.

"Say nothing!" Usta whispered urgently. "You risk your life and hers."

Jessica pulled away from Usta, consumed with

something beyond sense, only to be frozen in place when Lady Ashley's eyes met hers down the long corridor. Instantly two conflicting awarenesses clogged her mind: recognition, death . . .

She couldn't move. Lady Ashley would take care of everything now. She would insist that Jessica be allowed to accompany her out of the palace. After all, Jessica didn't belong here. Jessica was a foreign national, a guest of the Empire, a representative of . . .

Lady Ashley turned her head, falling back into casual conversation with the Kadin. Jessica watched in shock as Lady Ashley accepted a gift from Sultan Mustapha's wife, pecked her on the cheek in a gesture of pure superficiality, and allowed the eunuchs to escort her down the corridor—in the *opposite* direction.

Jessica inhaled for a good long shout. Usta's hand crushed the shout back down her throat. She had no idea Usta was so strong.

She struggled. The *yatakans* in the eunuchs' belts meant nothing, though their curved blades glinted in the sunlight that streamed in the great wooden doors leading out to the courtyard and the carriage that would take Lady Ashley away— without her.

She was still struggling when the sound of the doors grating shut echoed down the corridor.

"It's over," Usta told her. "She's gone."

They were alone in the corridor. Jessica stared down the marble walls, seeing a tomb. "She just looked past me. . . ."

In hopelessness she drifted to the cold white floor, staring mindlessly at the folds of her robe as they ballooned around her. Only when the ornate fabric settled did realization also settle.

She struck out at Usta with both fists. "Damn you! You ruined everything! I didn't even have the chance to make her recognize me!"

Usta caught Jessica's wrists and knelt beside her, forcing her to look into the face of common sense. "I ruined nothing. Jessica, I am your friend. And I tell you that women can't help you."

Jessica yanked back. "Really? My friend? You're just obeying the Kislar's orders."

"I don't care who she is," Usta insisted, "that woman can't help you. The only one who can release you is Sultan Hasam himself."

"But he won't, will he?"

Usta took the younger woman's shoulders and held fast. "He is your only hope."

Usta felt the shudder of rage and misery flow through her pupil, and when Jessica wrenched herself away and rushed down the corridor toward her own apartments, seeking something Usta could not provide now, Usta made no attempt to stop her.

The older woman rose slowly, conserving her dignity as well as the bruised hip Jessica had struck with one of those sharp fists. She knew she was being watched.

She turned liquidly and faced the Kislar as he moved out of one of the antechambers off the corridor.

"You should never have promised her freedom," the Kislar said. His voice rolled with its own brand of elegance down the empty hall. "Why did you lie to her?"

"Freedom is the only thing she wants. Maybe, after a while, she'll want that less. Or something else more." Usta gazed in the direction in which Jessica had gone. "In the meantime her desire for freedom will keep her alive. It is the only thing that will make her give all she can give when the Sultan calls. It will save her life." Usta's thick eyelashes brushed down, then slowly up again. "And possibly yours."

The big leather chair opposite the desk in Ambassador Grant's office had been stuffed too tightly to be comfortable. Lady Ashley adjusted her bustle and sat on the chair's edge to inject solidity into her story. Beside her, too fidgety to sit, Charles shifted from foot to foot. Randolph, also seated, took notes.

"Ambassador," Lady Ashley insisted for the third time, addressing the man behind the desk, who was as overstuffed as the chair. "She *is* there. I've seen her with my own eyes."

The ambassador studied Charles with an unreadable kind of annoyance and waited for Randolph to finish taking notes of that statement. "And you are certain," he said, "that she's being held against her will?"

Charles said gratingly, "There's no doubt of it. She was kidnapped."

Ambassador Grant drew long puffs from his

Art Malik as Tarik and Nancy Travis as Jessica. Separated by different cultures and opposing forces, their romance and sense of high adventure intertwines their lives.

Omar Sharif as the Sultan.

Cherie Lunghi as Usta, Jessica's true friend inside the palace.

Lady Ashley (Sarah Miles) confirms Jessica's presence in the harem.

Barry Houghton as the Astrologer.

Upon her arrival in Constantinople, Jessica wanders through the local market.

The Sultan rules his palace as firmly as he rules the Ottoman Empire.

Jessica is escorted into the palace by the Kislar (Yaphet Kotto).

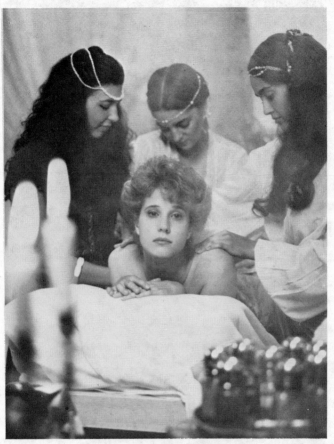

Jessica is pampered in the baths by many servants. Her lessons in seduction and the inner beauty of womanhood are mirrored by her surroundings.

Women who break the codes of harem life meet untimely deaths.

Initially Jessica's kidnapper, the Young Revolutionary Tarik eventually plans for her rescue.

The Sultan falls in love with Jessica's wit and charm as well as her natural beauty, a combination of talents which sets her apart from the rest of the harem.

The Sultan's army cannot hold off the Young Revolutionaries and their growing forces.

cigar and leaned back. "Well, then . . . we shall begin negotiations immediately."

Charles nearly fainted. Somehow he stayed on his feet, and when Lady Ashley looked up at him, he smiled back. Jessica, he certainly believed, was only moments away from him.

Lady Ashley could not bring herself to smile back.

"Thank you, sir," Charles breathed. Weakened, he lowered himself into a chair beside Lady Ashley.

Ambassador Grant finished another draw on the cigar, rolling it between his yellowed fingers. "I suggest," he began slowly, "that we approach the Sultan with gifts." He nodded in agreement with himself. "Let's say we begin with four elephants and two tigers."

Charles gulped. "Pardon me?"

"Four elephants and two tigers."

Lady Ashley sat back in her chair and crossed her legs, holding her chin in one gloved hand. "I don't believe the Sultan cares for elephants."

Grant blinked. "But he does like tigers, doesn't he?"

"Only if they come from Africa."

"Very well, then. Let's begin with six tigers from Kenya."

Charles gaped.

Lady Ashley pursed her lips.

It was Randolph who spoke. "It would be much easier to procure tigers from India, sir."

"What's easy is not at issue," the ambassador advised. "I realize these things take time."

Charles's voice rose. "Sir, with all due respect, I must say I find this whole conversation preposterous. Surely our diplomatic position here must carry some weight, and I don't see why we shouldn't use it. Demand that Sultan Hasam either release Jessica or run the risk of losing British support."

Irritated, Lady Ashley turned her best irony to Charles, saying, "Your approach is far too direct and sensible to be appropriate."

The ambassador chased her words with a stiff broom. "If we had a diplomatic position, then perhaps we could use it. Without access through the Ottoman Empire, we lose our passage to India. Therefore, we need Sultan Hasam—"

"But Sultan Hasam doesn't need England," Lady Ashley finished for him. "In fact, I think we rather bore him."

"But the impending trouble—" Charles nearly choked on his words and had to take a breath. "Anyone in the palace is in great danger."

Piqued beyond subtlety, Lady Ashley turned again to Charles. "What the ambassador is trying to tell you, dear, is that it would be diplomatic suicide to suggest that Sultan Hasam is holding a British subject captive."

Charles burst to his feet. "But he *is*!" His face reddened. "How can we move so slowly when we know Jessica is being held prisoner in a political powder keg just waiting to blow?"

Silence dropped around them. Charles's words echoed in their minds.

"Randolph," the ambassador began slowly,

"perhaps you would care to take Lady Ashley to the gardens for some tea."

Taking her cue without pause and with some relief, Lady Ashley stood up and took the hand offered by the ambassador. "Ambassador Grant . . . Mr. Wyndon, I bid you good afternoon." She turned and took Randolph's arm and virtually pulled him from the room, murmuring, "It seems we've been dismissed."

Once alone with Charles, Grant groaned as he got out of his chair and moved to the window. "I realize you care a great deal for this girl, but you must realize that certain . . . things may have transpired by now. Certain things that will make Jessica's reentry into polite society impossible."

Charles swallowed the bad taste left by the ambassador's casual handing-down of Jessica's social "worth" and said, "She's the most resilient woman I've even known. Nothing could change my feelings toward her. Nothing."

"I see. Then we shall continue," Grant said, "with the tigers."

Diplomacy. Politics. Ambassador. For Charles the words abruptly lost all meaning and merely became jumbled sounds. He walked numbly from Grant's office, feeling spat upon, particularly grade-schoolish, and cruelly used. Every noble aspiration he'd ever possessed about working his way up to a position in the diplomatic corps that would let him make a difference, change the world for the better, feed a few hungry bellies and advance the unity of nations suddenly lay in puddles behind him, and he was walking away from them without a backward glance. At this moment those dreams were as much lies as Grant's "negotiations."

Lady Ashley was waiting for him in the garden.

"I'm so sorry," she said immediately, even before he dropped into the wrought-iron chair beside her on the lawn. "I had hoped you were right about the embassy. I'd hoped things had changed here."

"There's no use," Charles said in a flat, cold tone, "but I'm not giving up. There has to be a way to get her out of that palace."

"You love her very much, don't you?"

"I'd do anything."

Lady Ashley lowered her voice. "Even risk your position here at the embassy?"

He caught his breath on a mirthless chuckle. "Without hesitation. Right now I don't care if I never go back through those hypocritical doors."

She believed him. The substantiation shone clearly in his eyes as he turned them to her, a strength atypical of Charles Wyndon. Sympathy filled Lady Ashley's heart, and a pulse of excitement began there as well.

"Then I may be able to help you," she said. "I know of one man who is cunning enough to slip into and out of the harem. He is also a man with a cause, and I suspect that his cause is in great need of money. If you like, I might try to arrange a meeting."

If there was a moment's pause in Charles's

answer, it came only because the hope seemed so ethereal. "Arrange it," he said.

Some things come about faster than the speed with which dawn strikes the desert in its sudden, harsh light. By noon, Charles found himself in a grubby Turkish coffee shop, dressed in rather abominable clothing borrowed from the gardener. He waited at a secluded table in a dangerously dark corner for someone he had been told would "know him." As he sipped a poor imitation of English tea he marveled at Lady Ashley's courage and intuition. This meeting had been arranged hours ago, long before he and Lady Ashley approached the ambassador. She had known how things would go, and which oar to put in the water, even before this tipsy dory had gotten a good start. Her spirit and intelligence reminded him of Jessica, enhanced by the patina of age and experience. Not only could she handle situations at hand, but she beckoned the future.

The potential danger had been consumed entirely by a cold determination swelling within him until no room remained for misgivings. Despite the disreputable condition of the coffee shop, with its animal smells and measurable layers of filth, not to mention the suspicious eyes turning his way, Charles had no trouble ignoring his precarious position. His coloring and bearing marked him as a stranger, a foreigner, easily taken advantage of and probably with some wealth worth stealing. But he cared not at all what these scurvy creatures thought of him or saw in him. He would deal with the lowliest, most serpentine agent if it meant freeing Jessica. His own safety, his career, his reputation no longer held sway in his decisions, so he was ready. Ready to deal with whomever approached him. Meanwhile he sipped tea and waited.

People, dark people in dark robes, moved like ambulatory shadows in the dimness against the background of the bright noon sun out in the marketplace. The brightness prevented a good look at any face, turning humans into flat black silhouettes. No wonder the meeting was arranged to take place here. The coffee shop itself was a perfect cloak. And, judging from their food and tea, its primary means of income had nothing to do with eating.

"You are the man who is waiting?"

The voice startled him. Several seconds passed before Charles made sense of the question and answered, "Yes. I wait."

He did not turn around. His skin prickled, expecting the sharp slice of a blade or the blast of a pistol. After all, he was the enemy here, embodying the British government, which supported the Sultan.

Two men came from behind him, one from each side. Smoke moved around their heads as they sat at his table.

"Who sent you?" he asked, ignoring the examination he was getting from them.

"A certain lady," the one on the right said.

He had a compelling way of staring straight into the human soul.

Charles leaned forward immediately. "Good. How much did she tell you?"

"Your fiancée is being held against her will in the Imperial Harem and you want me to help her escape."

"I'm willing to pay a large sum of money."

The two natives glanced at each other, professional at reading the intentions of others behind their words.

Charles pressed on. "I want to know your names."

"Why?"

"A show of trust. I have to trust you. I want you under the same kind of obligation. It's only fair."

Another glance passed between the two, of much shorter duration. Evidently he had demonstrated the right kind of integrity, because the man on the right rested his elbow on the table and said, "I am Tarik Pasha. You have heard of me."

Charles sighed and leaned back. "Quite."

"My friend is called Salim. We are both wanted men. You know that."

"Yes. And I understand the danger you're in just by coming here. I also understand you are in need of funds to supply your army. I'm prepared to . . . contribute."

Tarik waved the scrawny waiter away and paused until the three of them were alone again. "Is this woman British?"

Charles nodded, then amended, "Her father was. Her name is Jessica Grey."

Salim choked on one of the figs he'd taken from a dish in the center of the table and started to get to his feet. Tarik dragged him down again and refused to meet his eyes, though he saw clearly in his peripheral vision what was going through Salim's mind.

"What's the matter with him?" Charles asked.

"The danger frightens him. You're asking the nearly impossible from a man who already has the highest price in the Empire sitting on his head."

"Or not as much to lose," Charles suggested.

"It depends upon how you look at it. And there is much to be gained." He drew the men's attention to the chair beside him, which he pulled out from under the tablecloth. A small jewelry chest sat upon it. Charles wordlessly tipped the lid back. Even in the dimness, the splendor within the box gleamed in testimony of its own worth. "I'm told this is enough to arm a thousand men." Charles no longer cared if his ignorance showed. "I need an answer."

Tarik and Salim immediately launched into a heated, though nearly whispered, argument in Turkish.

"You are crazy to do this," Salim told him, hoping the Englishman didn't understand enough of this nation's tongue to know what he was saying. "The woman is not worth risking your life, and there are other ways to get money."

"The challenge is incredible," Tarik told him.

"Tarik, only a madman tries to break into the seraglio. If they catch you, they'll do things to you that haven't even been invented. Can't you see that your life is more important right now than the money? And surely more than the woman's life. So why would you be going in there? Just tell me, eh?"

"It is a chance, Salim."

"Sure, a chance to discover new heights of agony."

"I'm going to do it."

Salim slumped as though exhausted, closed his eyes, regrouped his thoughts, and went in for another try. "She might already be dead by now. You told me yourself that she was not one to give in. How long do you think her stubbornness would have been tolerated?"

Tarik's eyes grew unexpectedly deep. "She's smarter than that."

"You're dreaming!"

"Yes," Tarik told him. "Of a chance to rectify the injustice. I've discovered I can no longer live with what I did to her."

Salim paused. Such a sonorous tone from his friend told him that Tarik had made up his mind to free Jessica Grey long before now, that he had thought of this adventure even before someone offered him money to try it. And Salim knew Tarik expected an argument, so that he could bounce his decision off the dissent and see how it held up. Salim provided the argument and saw in Tarik's eyes how well the conviction fared.

He slumped back in his chair and gazed at his friend for what he presumed would be one of the last times.

Tarik turned to Charles. In English he said, "I accept."

Charles swallowed a hard lump. "Excellent. You will receive payment when you bring Jessica to me."

"Impossible. Salim is to be paid as soon as I enter the palace."

"But what if your plan fails? I shall be left with no other recourse."

Tarik shrugged. "This plan cannot be explained in terms of success or failure. It will be a matter of freedom or death . . . for myself and for your lady. I'm willing to risk my life to arm my soldiers. But you must decide whether or not you are willing to risk *her* life." Tarik raised his chin slightly. "Call it a show of trust."

Charles's lips felt dry, his eyes hot. He considered and said, "In the palace she has no life."

"Then you agree to the terms?"

"I agree."

"I'll need something for bribes and something else to . . ." Tarik reached into the jewel chest and drew out a particularly unusual crescent-shaped brooch lined with tiny diamonds and centered with a cluster of opals. "Will your fiancée recognize this?"

"It belonged to her mother."

"Then I will take it with me," Tarik said, and stood up, "so she will know who I am."

* * *

"Know who you are." Salim's voice rumbled through sarcasm and right into irony. "Oh, she'll know who you are, all right." He wasn't smiling.

They strode together through the worst quarter of Constantinople, a squalid cluster of impoverished lodgings and dubious businesses, and fortified themselves as they rounded a corner and walked toward the doctor's shabby wooden house.

Salim had been mindlessly following Tarik, hardly noticing where they were going, so engrossed was he in the sudden foolhardiness his friend had espoused. Every block or so he would speak up, voicing some snide comment about Tarik's unexpected insanity and how it would affect the success of their cause, then lapse back into silence. He scanned the packed ground skimming by beneath his feet, and looked up only a few times and only to throw strength into his current comment.

Now, though, as they were swallowed by this deep and cavernous street, Salim was shaken out of his thoughts by a chorus of moans and screams coming from within the dirt-gray walls of the house just ahead. The shingle hanging from the roof slats proclaimed what went on inside the house and that for a few days of agony a man could obtain employment in a place where only certain men were allowed to work.

"Wait for me here," Tarik instructed, the first thing he'd said since leaving the coffee shop.

He strode onward, leaving Salim to stare after him.

Salim jolted out of his shock and burst forward, pulling Tarik hard by the arm and holding on to him. "Wait a minute . . . you can't be serious. Do you know what you're doing?"

Tarik looked at him with frightening passivity. "Inside that house is my passport into the seraglio."

"That house is a chamber of horrors! Can't you smell it? Can't you hear it?" His grip on Tarik's arm grew prohibitive. Risk was one thing; mutilation was another. "It's absurd. There must be another way." His eyes narrowed with concern. "Tarik—"

"How else is a man going to be admitted into the harem? Only eunuchs are allowed within the seraglio."

"But you can't seriously intend to . . ." Salim shuddered but failed to finish.

"Well, you're the one who's always pointing out how willing I am to make sacrifices to our goals, aren't you?"

"You *have* gone mad. . . ." Salim stepped back as though Tarik's insanity were contagious and looked for the yellow rings that appear around a horse's eyes when it goes mad once and for all.

Now Tarik smiled. "Of course not."

Salim stared at him, saw that he meant it, that he had something else in mind, and drooped with relief. Then, once recovered, he shook his head. "This could be one of your more challenging disguises."

The doctor's office was only slightly more filthy than the doctor himself. His clothing was in tatters, Tarik saw when the toil-worn surgeon joined him from the back rooms where the screaming and moaning came from. The laboratory smock draped on the bony frame was soaked with blood—fresh red blood over gradually darker layers of brown and dried, crusting blood. The doctor himself epitomized the Ottoman Empire in heritage, if not in splendor, for he seemed to be made up of traits from half a dozen cultures; a Greek nose, greasy black hair in waves like an Arab's, the sallow olive complexion of a Persian who had not eaten well recently. And his age was impossible to guess. Tarik wondered how incompetent a doctor he must be to have come to such a state.

Tarik shivered, wondering if perhaps the idea of submitting oneself to this mangling might not be almost as bad as actually doing it.

Without a word of ceremony in any form the doctor immediately recited, "Have you considered the consequences of becoming a eunuch?" When Tarik nodded, he went on by rote. "If you survive the operation, it is possible to enter the Sultan's service by the end of the month."

Another shudder stole up Tarik's spine. "I want to be in the walls of the palace by tomorrow morning."

"Impossible," the doctor said, his saggy eyes opening a little more. "There is no way you

could be recovered from the operation by then."
He wiped a gory stain from the back of his
hand and lit a cigarette for himself, not bothering to offer one to Tarik.

Tarik studied this human refuse with a cunning eye and waited until the doctor looked at
him again. With deep implication he said, "I
have no intention of having the operation."

The doctor's face screwed up into a grimace.
"Get out of here! Don't waste my time with
your games."

"I intend to waste none of your time," Tarik
said calmly. "I simply want you to lie for me.
Slip me in with the others and trust my wits
that I don't get caught."

The doctor stared, then laughed bitterly. "You
must take me for a fool."

"No," Tarik murmured, shaking his head
slowly. His hand stole into his coat pocket. It
came out dazzling with the links of a silver
necklace mounted with two strands of faceted
rubies, each surrounded by a trickle of diamonds.
"I take you," he said, "for a very rich man."

The jewels glowed in the eyes of a man who
had given up all hope of reentering the delicate
lace of social status above that of a scorpion.
One blood-caked hand trembled as it reached
for the necklace, and soon the rubies and the
blood were glowing upon each other.

The marble slab was moist and cool beneath
her naked body. She let her mind drift to the
sensation of the hands that massaged her limbs

and perfumed her shoulders, and she ignored the slight tug as her slave crimped her wet hair into fluid waves. Her eyes were closed. She had lost count of how many women were tending her. Her mind was empty except for the lulling recurrence of Usta's Delphic announcement this morning: "The Sultan will see you tonight."

Jessica tried not to hate Usta. No . . . she didn't hate Usta. She had admitted to herself that she alone would carry the burden of her own salvation. Neither Usta, nor the Kislar, nor anyone else could do it for her. She had neither the energy to spare, nor the time to waste, to hate Usta. She would need a clear head for what was to come—a clear head and all her strength.

Music began in the corner of the dressing area. A group of eunuch musicians plucked mandolins and beat drums and trilled flutes, and Jessica looked up.

Usta was leading in an entourage of dressers, each carrying a different element of wardrobe. Jessica rolled onto her side, practicing what she had seen the Kadin do, and propped herself up on one elbow. Wordlessly she watched as the dressers filed by her upon Usta's signals, one by one presenting her with parts of her attire for that evening's important tryst with the Sultan. Impassively she watched each item go by: the *dluma*, a caftan with pearl buttons and large, gold-threaded loop buttonholes; a silk chemise in rosy pink; an ornate pair of harem trousers—deep blue; a thick girdle entirely matted with diamonds; large tassles of pearls to tie around her waist; a headdress covered with bodkins of emeralds, diamonds, and opals; silver wristbands with miniature silver chains as thin as threads leading to an etched silver plate the size of a coin; then more chains leading to an ornate silver ring with tiny beads dangling from it. Her hands would sparkle. Her head would dazzle. Her breasts would inspire. Her legs would astonish. Her waist would amaze. Even her feet, housed in brightly embroidered slippers, would capture the imagination.

Of course, her face would be covered.

"Do you approve?" Usta asked from Jessica's right.

Jessica nodded. "Whatever you think is best."

"Then let us begin."

The slave girls moved in as Jessica rose and stood with her arms held slightly outward. She closed her eyes, knowing that when she opened them, she would resemble a harem Kadin more than the person she knew herself to be. And the transformation would have to be complete—within and without.

The music continued. She lost herself in it.

When she opened her eyes, Jessica Grey was gone. The woman who stood looking back at her in the mirror was no one she knew or remembered. This was a glorious creature, bejeweled and heavily veiled, light eyes artistically lined with black kohl, ivory forehead accented by tiny bangles hanging from gold circlets on her headpiece, each adorned with a

single crystal. She was radiant, exotic, Eastern—
an embodiment of mystery, especially to herself.

She took refuge in her own eyes as they looked
back from the mirror. Yes, she was in there
somewhere, still self-possessed and ready to do
what needed to be done. Freedom, she thought
purposefully, freedom . . . freedom . . . freedom.

"Thank you," she said to her slaves, surprised at the power in her own voice, "that's
all."

The ladies filed out without so much as a
backward glance. Usta remained. Jessica paused
for a moment before the mirror, then walked to
Usta, careful of the ankle bracelets and delicate
slippers and all the crafted hardware hanging
from her waist. Carefully she said, "I need some
time alone."

Usta merely smiled, kissed her unusual pupil
upon the cheek, and strode out of the dressing
chambers, lost in nostalgia.

Jessica moved back to the mirror. This time
she did not find the reflection disturbing. She
looked with a critical eye at each piece of jewelry, rope of pearls, chain, veil, and bauble.
Steadying herself with a deep breath, she reached
up and removed the headpiece, then looked
again.

In the courtyard, at the Gates of Felicity,
rows of eunuchs quivered at the bristling excitement. They lined up properly on either side of
the pathway to Sultan Hasam's quarters. They
resisted the urge to talk among themselves, lest
the Kislar hear of it, but they exchanged looks

of thirsty anticipation and entertained wild, hopeless imaginings about what would transpire in the Sultan's chambers this night.

Tarik tried to ignore the underlying mixture of tension and thrill, empathizing with these pathetic half men. The danger of his situation kept his nerves tingling. He couldn't be sure he was thinking clearly. Courage was one thing, but having to stand here in a line, overly aware of being one step from unspeakable torture, was beginning to tell on him. He tried to bury the doubts creeping into his head, ideas that perhaps Salim had been right—perhaps he was giving in to a pompous kind of challenge rather than doing this for the moral reasons he had been spouting. Yet Jessica had never once left his mind, not even as he stood on the balcony and watched the mindless slaughter of thousands of his supporters. In many ways she stood as an effigy of all those helpless people—another cog in the mechanism he himself had been forging. He owed it to himself, to all those people, and certainly to Jessica, to try to liberate her from this prison. He would go to his death with at least one less guilt, and Jessica Grey would have the freedom she deserved. If it meant his life, Tarik decided, she would have it.

Music . . . faint but definite. Tarik leaned slightly forward and dared to look down the lane toward the Gates of Felicity. A procession was coming.

One of the head eunuchs moved in behind him and, without hesitation, brought a stinging lash down on Tarik's shoulder. He winced but straightened up, having to rely on his peripheral vision for a look at what was coming.

Slowly, with great ceremony, a group of musicians walked toward Sultan Hasam's chambers, flowing within the long channel of eunuchs. Behind them came a line of slave girls, each carrying a tray of *şiş ketabi*, *revani* cakes, *türlü*, stuffed grape leaves, or *düğün çonbasi*—wedding soup. Behind the slave girl was a silk-covered divan mounted upon a platform draped with flowers and carried by six eunuchs matched for height, weight, and facial complexion. Beside the platform rode the Kislar Agha on a thickset black horse.

But no element of the procession was more brilliant than the being who rested upon the divan. Her eyes scanned the line of eunuchs without really seeing them. Her unveiled face had been washed to reveal its own naturally rose-tinted ivory glow, and there was no kohl around her eyes. She wore only the tiniest hint of makeup—a touch of eye shadow, a glistening of lip color applied sparingly and in European style. She wore only a thin muslin blouse with untied tassels and big draping sleeves, a pair of blue harem trousers, and simple bathing slippers. The only jewels she wore were upon the diamond-covered girdle showing off her narrow waist, which had grown even narrower since her arrival in the seraglio. Upon her head there was only a shimmer of yellow hair in deep curls to her shoulders. She was astonishing in her simplicity.

Tarik swallowed his heart. Jessica . . . going to Sultan Hasam.

His knees wobbled. He forced himself to stay on his feet but never expected the sight of her to affect him so profoundly, to see her committing herself to a fate for which she would pay all her life. Even if he freed her now, she would forever be haunted by what lay at the end of this corridor of eunuchs.

Suddenly he stiffened. She was looking at him. Salim had been quite right. She knew who he was.

Their exchange was sharp, short, and tumultuous. As the divan swayed past Tarik, Jessica gazed down at him coldly and with a depth of bitterness that he could not define. In the midst of it he felt the sting of how he had betrayed her, betrayed his own ideals—and how she knew it.

For an instant—a horrible instant—Tarik thought she was going to speak to him. Her lips, colored delicately and looking as though they had just tasted the most succulent of cherries, parted slightly. Tarik stopped breathing.

The shoulders of the black eunuchs moved with foreboding sensuality beneath the slats of the platform. Step by flowing step they did the job they had been trained and drilled to do, just as the eunuchs remained still and silent, as they also had been trained. And the woman they conveyed was not the same woman Tarik had thrown to the dogs.

Jessica reinforced his estimation of her as more than a foolishly emotional creature—an epithet only a barbarian would assign to women in general. He had pretended to be a barbarian, but he could not hide his true self from Jessica as they traveled across Syria and Turkey as captor and captive. She closed her mouth, raised her chin, and turned away from him, settling back on the divan and locking her eyes on the inlaid doors that would soon admit her to Sultan Hasam's audience.

For now her destiny lay only that far ahead.

PART TWO

PART TWO

CHAPTER TEN

Splendor knew no definition as articulate as that within the giant wooden doors of Sultan Hasam's palace. Even the gold-encrusted handles turned so carefully by the enunch guards gave no true hint as to the majesty within. Jessica was led gently from her divan by eunuchs who treated her as though she might break, and when the eunuchs turned those handles and pushed open the heavy doors, she who would have been the wife of a clerk was admitted into a place were only rare few women had ever walked. At this moment Jessica Grey was a potential queen. What future moments would bring, even she could not have foretold.

The great audience room of the Sultan's private chambers was aglow with fine wood, bordered by a funnel of deeply inlaid cupboards on either side of the long Oriental rug leading up to the Sultan's throne. And upon that throne the Sultan himself awaited her. His clothing outshined the brilliance of the throne itself only

by a small margin, and then only by the fact
that they were filled with a man who ruled an
empire. His collar was a ringlet of gold flakes
pressed into a pattern, his robe of the most
shimmering velvet, also gold. Thick red-and-
black brocades etched out the shapes of his
chest, arms, and waistline, and upon his fez
rode a single immense ostrich feather fastened
with a ring of pearls.

So . . . he had been preened for her viewing
even as she had been preened for his. Interesting.

Jessica moved a few steps into the room, unaffected by the show of wealth. As Usta had
taught her, she bowed her head and performed
the first salaam. In answer, Sultan Hasam
gestured her to come closer. She did, six steps
exactly, then another salaam. The Sultan's face
remained impassive. He beckoned her still
nearer. Six more steps . . . another salaam. This
was the third and final one, and she followed
her instructions to the letter by fixing her eyes
on the rug beneath her and crossing her hands
over her waistline.

Her breathing seemed as loud as the Bosporus.

Too long . . . then, "Are you going to watch
the floor the rest of the evening?"

His voice, even in this empty room, seemed
softer than when she had heard it before. Boldly
Jessica uncrossed her hands, stood regally, and
eyed him as thoroughly as he had looked at
her.

More than anything, more than the rich clothing or the jewelry or the feather, she was at-

tracted to his eyes—they were not like any she had ever seen before. Hasam's eyes were black but full of lights. It was as though someone had dropped two moist beads of oil into a squarish frame. Though his complexion had lost its youthful luster, those eyes still gleamed like polished hematite and struck Jessica even across the large room.

After a moment Sultan Hasam touched his own chest and asked, "And what do you think? No—even better—what did you think the first time you saw me?"

Jessica tipped her head slightly. "Truthfully?"

The ostrich feather bobbed. "Truthfully."

"You weren't as old as I thought you'd be."

Either her boldness was paying off or she was about to die.

Sultan Hasam's jewel-black eyes gleamed, and he began to laugh. He climbed down from his throne and joined her in the middle of the long carpet. He offered her his hand. She took it.

Thus began the tour of his own apartments—room upon room of mixed decor from a dozen cultures and time periods and finally to a balcony that ran the length of all three of the large rooms she had seen so far. There had been a formal parlor, then a vast room laden with sumptuous food spread on low tables, and the final room was his bedroom, complete with a massive four-poster bed, turned down and ready. While in the formal parlor the Sultan paused before a portrait of Theodore Roosevelt and turned to Jessica. "What do you think? Is it a good likeness?"

Jessica blinked. "Excuse me?"

Hasam pointed to the portrait. "Is this the way Mr. Theodore Roosevelt looks? You've seen him, have you not?"

"No . . . not in person."

"But you are an American."

"While my mother was alive we spent several years in Tallahassee," Jessica explained, wondering why her voice didn't quiver, "but we never saw the president."

"He doesn't go to Tallahassee?"

Tender ground. She could easily insult him with the wrong answer. "Not as a general rule, but from the photographs I've seen, I would have to say that this is a very good likeness."

Sultan Hasam smiled broadly at the answer he wanted to hear and led her into the second room.

Jessica looked admiringly at the endless sea of food, prepared so that every dish was an artwork, and wondered what she was supposed to do. Usta hadn't told her there would be a dinner involved. "Would you like me to serve you?" she asked.

She knew she'd made a fool of herself when the Sultan answered, "In a while, perhaps. Tell me. What is your Tallahassee like? Is it important?"

Damn! Tallahassee was the last thing she wanted to be remembering in light of what was to come. She sensed danger in memories of

times when this fate would have seemed ludicrous. In those days, not so very long ago, she
would have laughed at anyone relating such a
story as this. Why, Turkey was on the other
side of the universe! Who would ever happen
to end up there? She broke her own train of
thought and forced herself to answer clinically.
"Important? No. Not like New York or Washington or Chicago. But I thought it was beautiful," she admitted before realizing she might
lose control. "Lush, green hills . . . terribly hu-
mid in summer. We languished on front porches."

"Front porches?" Of course, he'd never seen
one. Not like a real veranda. He led her through
the great glass doors to the long balcony outside and asked for her approval with his eyes.

"Like a balcony," she allowed, "but on the
ground floor. In the evening everyone sat on
their front porches."

Hasam leaned on the railing. "Front porches. An interesting notion."

"You've never been to America?" Jessica asked,
damned well knowing the answer, yet she
couldn't resist the urge to put him in his place,
at least while she had the chance. When he
shook his head, she insisted, "Then you should
go."

The Sultan gazed out over his marble-and-
vine domain. "Impossible."

"I don't understand."

"I never leave the palace." He took her arm

and walked her across the balcony to a place with a better view.

"You've never been outside the palace?" Jessica asked.

He shrugged rather elegantly. "I went to Brusa once. Twenty years ago."

This stopped Jessica in her tracks, and she turned to him in unguarded shock. "You've never seen the very countries you rule?"

Another shrug—this one more noncommittal. "It is unnecessary. I have thousands of spies. They tell me everything."

A bolt of pity rammed through Jessica, more unexpected and unbidden than a sandstorm in the desert. "They can't tell you how the local wine tastes or bring back the sounds of the languages on the streets or the smells of the marketplace—" She stopped abruptly when he suddenly held one long finger straight up. Had she finally angered him?

"That," he began, "is what makes you more valuable to me than the other women. You can tell me about the front porches in Tallahassee."

He seemed more amused by her shock than intrigued by her front porches. So you are a prisoner here, too, she thought, and even your wealth and power can't buy you out of it. In fact, those are your prison bars, Sultan.

Oh, how she longed to tell him those things!

She was walking with him again, and before she knew it, they were standing near the huge four-poster bed. Hasam took off his outer robe, revealing only a silken nightshirt that glowed as deep as wine in the light of the sunset on the western horizon. His body was different from the stiff robes he wore at court. His shoulders were broad and slightly rounded. His chest still had shape in spite of his age, and his posture sang a song of grandeur from long ago. His physique was thick, like a tree, but not rounded like her father's. What the years had taken away, this man had retained in his personal prowess. He held himself proudly. He felt no shame that he no longer had the squared muscles and sharp sinews that had drawn attention in his youth. Jessica learned much from him in those moments, much about aging gracefully, just as she saw it in Usta and in the Kadin. When he took off his fez and turned to her, his eyes glowed like drops of fine oil in the candlelight, and the fine streaks of gray in his hair shimmered, not looking gray at all. She liked him very much in those moments, for this was no tyrant. This was a simple man caught in complexity. Just as she had left Damascus in search of an answer to an unknown question, Sultan Hasam also seemed to be searching.

Jessica felt that lace of pity entwine itself around her heart once again. She knew that no matter how well she could be trained, she wouldn't be his answer.

These apartments overlooked the magnificent Bosporus and had been designed to make the best use of the setting sun. The tapestries on the far wall came to life with the brilliance of their threads, and the tiles of the mosaics on the floors and walls moved in the deepening red-gold light. Around the room, tapers burned in platinum candlesticks, ready to light the room when the sun finally fell behind its evening cloak.

Hasam sat down on the bed, waiting.

And instantly Jessica knew herself beyond all unknowing. She stood on a precipice, ready for the high jump. Would it hurt her? Would it kill her? Would her pride survive at all? She was about to make love for the first time, and it would be to a man she did not love and certainly could find reasons to despise. *Daddy, I need to know what to do. Are you there? I need your advice. . . .*

There sat the Sultan, expecting what he had always received from women who were specially selected—a supreme honor, they all told her. *Guzdeh.*

She told herself over and over again that it would be all right, that it would get easier—if not this time, then the next—but would there *be* a next time? Even if she could force herself into this passionate pretense, wouldn't the Sultan know or sense the difference between a woman who was willing and a woman who was coerced? Jessica stared into the Sultan's deep black eyes and tried to know him, to see if he was the kind of man who couldn't tell the difference. And the answer came—he would know. He gazed at her with a wise sensitivity that went beyond his own gratification. This was not an ignorant despot. Jessica had looked into the eyes of intelligent men before, and this was one.

She closed her eyes for a long moment, went to the bedside, and knelt on the plush rug at Sultan Hasam's feet. She recited lines she never meant to say, lines that only her subconscious mind had dared memorize.

"I have studied the arts of how to please you. Everyone around me has taught me how to be the ultimate Eastern woman." She raised her eyes to him now. "But that doesn't change the way I was brought up. All my life I've imagined how it should be, and it's not like this. Not on demand."

Hasam raised his chin and eyebrows in the same movement. "Then how is it?"

Jessica swallowed hard and hoped she wasn't patronizing him. "In the West men seduce their women with time . . . with courtship . . . with marriage."

"Are you refusing me?"

Her blood turned to water. She bowed her head in submission. "I am yours, and I'll do whatever you want." Again she looked up. "But if I sleep with you tonight, it will be a lie. A practiced lie that will show you only what I've been taught. I've been trained to flatter you, to please you, to act flattered when you chose me. But you chose me by design. I'm not flattered by that. And how can I flatter you when I don't know you? Is that all you want? There's a palace brimming with women who are dying to lather you with empty flattery. Is that what you want from me too? I could do that. But it will show you nothing of my heart."

She'd been taught how to talk to a Sultan, and this was not one of the ways, yet the mild rebellion had come from something far deeper within her than merely the instinct to survive. It involved dignity, and it also involved the pity she suddenly felt for this man—not a monarch, not a king, not a divine being, but a *man*.

She knelt there, her life at risk, as Sultan Hasam considered.

"And what is so special," he began very slowly, "about a woman's heart that makes it worth waiting for?"

Sunrise over the Bosporus was a thing of lights. Lights in the sky, in the water, upon Sultan Hasam's marble palace. Within the palace, however, dark hatred ran as fluidly as the blue water outside, a hatred born of the kind of scandal of which the East had purged itself. Here such behavior was expected—a man who ruled a nation need not cleave honorably to one woman, even if only in appearances. Here other women could invade the domain of the first wife and thereby gain power, fame, perhaps even love.

Tarik understood these things, even if he no longer approved of many of his homeland's traditions. Because he understood, he also understood the rage cramping the Kadin's classic features when she yanked him out of the hallway with a snap of her fingers and ordered,

"Go to the palace and tell the astrologer to come here immediately!"

Thus Tarik experienced a rage of curiosity as potent as the rage he saw in the Kadin's face, and he hurried to bring together the Sultan's adviser and the Sultan's only wife. Of course, he was immediately dismissed, but in their pre-occupation, neither of the powerful figures noticed when he ducked behind a lattice enclosure and crouched down to listen.

"She's been with him all night," the Kadin said, snarling at the little man. "*All night.* She's still with him."

The astrologer's voice sounded at once soothing and patronizing. "And that might be the end of it."

"And what if it isn't?" The Kadin's tone shot upward.

"Why are you so worried?"

"I should have followed my instincts. I should have known she would please him. I should have trained her myself."

Tarik heard the astrologer's shrug clearly in the man's low-keyed voice. Obviously the astrologer meant to compensate for the Kadin's ire. "Even novelties become familiar."

The Kadin whirled. "What if she gives him a son?"

"You are the first Kadin. Your son is heir."

"If he lives," the Grecian said. "Hasam never asks about him, never sees him. . . ."

"Of course not. The boy is sequestered for his own protection."

"And who will protect my son from *her*?"

"Then it is your son you're worried about," the astrologer said slowly. "If she were to have a son, it is her son who would be in danger. You are far more powerful than she could ever become."

Tarik dipped farther back as the Kadin paced closer to his hiding place. She inhaled deeply, containing her intense anger, and the anxiety borne upon it. She said nothing, but her eyes combed the plush carpet.

"So that's not what frightens you," the astrologer deduced.

Desperation came to the surface as the Kadin turned. "What if she takes *him* away?"

"The Sultan? You lost him years ago."

"As long as I was in his presence, he was never lost to me."

"Then you will do," the astrologer said, pacing his words, "whatever is necessary."

"Yes, I will. But remember this, old man. If my influence with the Sultan goes to that woman, I shall see to it that yours is not far behind."

Tarik knew the true sense behind those words, a meaning the words themselves might not belie to one who did not know how to listen to them correctly. He knew that Jessica's life, even as she lay with the most powerful man in the Turkish Empire, was losing value.

He knew he would have to arrange to be closer to her, to protect her until the opportunity came for escape. Somehow he would have to convince those with the real power to put him in her company. With a polished stealth born of necessity Tarik stole away through the halls of the seraglio and headed toward the apartment of the Kislar Agha. As he walked, he thought of what he might say. He tried to remember back to his gypsy disguise when he had sold Jessica to the Kislar. Would the chief eunuch remember? Would he recognize him? Or had Tarik been dirty enough and heavily robed enough that the Kislar wouldn't know him as he looked now?

It didn't matter. The chance had to be taken.

His thoughts were interrupted only once, as he hurried through the arched gardens where he witnessed a sight that gave him a strange pain through the chest. Jessica being carried back to the seraglio upon her flower-draped litter, resting on the velvet divan with a vacuous kind of fatigue upon her face. Was she ashamed to have spent the night with Sultan Hasam, and so many more hours than night can account for? Could he be misreading her expression? Those pretty, angular features, those liquid eyes? Did she hate herself now? Did she hate him and the Sultan and all men, now that she had been betrayed and abused?

The pain grew more intense. Guilt, and other things, ate at Tarik as he watched Jessica step unceremoniously from the litter at the seraglio doors. She didn't seem arrogant as she walked through the flanks of women who parted for her as though she was special. Of course, she *was* special—now. Tarik read both respect and envy in the faces of the other women.

A regal woman of uncertain background walked elegantly to Jessica and embraced her. That would be the Hazinedar Usta. Tarik had heard of her in the idle talk among the eunuchs. An important woman. Another cog in the machinery of power.

Tarik's eyes clung to Jessica, then to the empty air where she had stood once she disappeared within the seraglio. Only after several long seconds did he compose himself and put his mind forward, to the Kislar Agha and the delicate bit of convincing he must pretend not to be doing.

Jessica and Usta walked the lengths of two corridors before speaking. Finally they were alone, and they sat together on a small couch in the middle of the corridor. Usta's eyes gleamed like those of a curious teenager, making Jessica smile. Jessica wondered if the victory she felt would seem as good to Usta, or if Usta would consider this a failure.

"We talked until dawn," she told her mentor.

"And then . . . ?"

"Then we talked all day long. He asks a lot of questions."

Usta's brow knitted slightly but not exactly in disappointment. "And he found you interesting?"

"He seemed to, yes."

Usta sat back. "Then this is a very good sign."

Jessica tried to read her teacher's restrained tone but couldn't. "It means he finds me different, doesn't it? Worth more than just a night of cavorting?"

Usta nodded hesitantly. "Yes . . . it means that."

"And that's good."

"Oh, yes, yes, very good."

Jessica leaned closer, the fire of anticipation underlying her whisper. "How long will it take to win my freedom?"

Having known this question would come, Usta had prepared an answer for it, but not for these circumstances. If Jessica had come back and told her of a consummation, she would have known better what to say. So she began slowly, feeding the lie gradually and hoping it sounded true. "First you must win him completely. Remember, Jessica . . . the real power comes *after* you make love to a man."

Jessica was aware of the gentle scolding behind Usta's advice. Still, she felt quite satisfied. A man interested in women only for their arrangement of breast and thigh had found her interesting in more cerebral ways—the ultimate flattery. Nothing Usta could say would discourage her. She would win Sultan Hasam, but she would win his mind.

"Well," she said, patting Usta's hand in a kind of dismissal that should have been the other way around, "right now I need nothing more than a good ten-hour sleep." She stood up and took both of Usta's hands in her own. "Thank you for everything. I know you've given me all your best secrets. I only hope you understand that I have to go at my own pace and do what's best for myself."

With a cloudy sadness Usta nodded and looked away from Jessica. "We all do that for ourselves," she murmured.

"Perhaps I can help you someday as much as you've helped me," Jessica said.

Usta managed a smile. "Rest well."

"What is *he* doing here?"

Jessica's voice rolled through her apartment with an authority she would never have dared before now. The Kislar Agha actually flinched at the intensity of it. He waved his large black hand at the eunuch, who stood like a manequin on display in the center of the carpet.

"He's yours."

"Mine?" Jessica glared at the eunuch.

"Yours."

"Why?"

"Because you've become very important. You need someone to protect you."

"Him?"

"He's very strong."

Jessica moved forward and circled the eunuch, totally enjoying the chance to belittle the man who had chiseled her life down to a value of nearly nothing when he had kidnapped and sold her.

Tarik tried to keep his eyes to the front and not meet hers as she moved around him, surveying him critically. He hoped she would go along with the ploy and not expose him. He hoped she did not yet hate him enough to wish him painfully killed, for that would seal her fate as well.

"He's loyal?" she asked.

The Kislar nodded.

"And he's mine," she repeated. "And he will do whatever I tell him?"

The Kislar had begun his escape, a sweeping stride toward the apartment doors. "Whatever you wish, he will do." And he was gone in a whisper of brocade.

Tarik stood alone in these plush quarters with the woman he had condemned to imprisonment. Condemned? All prisons should be so opulent. Obviously even he had underestimated her sense of survival. Not only had she gotten along well enough, but in a few truncated months—weeks, really—she had elevated herself to a perch where even the Kadin feared her.

Jessica stood back and folded her arms. Flatly she said, "This isn't one of your better disguises. I think I liked you better as a gypsy. You must realize it wouldn't be difficult to have you exposed. The evidence against you would be rather conclusive."

"You won't do that."

"I could have you killed."

"You won't do that, either."

"How can you be so sure? I'm not the same woman you dropped here."

"I've come to help you escape."

She nodded and pursed her lips. "Oh, really?

And after we escape who will you sell me to this time?"

Tarik buried the twinge of guilt that raced up his spine. "After we leave the palace I will see that you get back to the embassy."

"And you expect me to believe that?"

"I have proof that I'm telling you the truth."

Jessica's eyes narrowed dangerously. "Nothing you say would prove you want to help me."

Irritated, Tarik changed tack and dug for information. "Perhaps you don't want to escape."

She tightened her arms into a knot. "Perhaps I've found a way to survive."

Tarik felt his body grow as stiff as rope, anger building behind his eyes. "Then there's no reason for me to stay." He turned abruptly and headed for the open balcony.

"Where are you going?" she called, following him.

"It's difficult for a woman to leave the seraglio, but it's relatively easy for a eunuch to pass unnoticed." He swung one leg over the rail of the balcony.

Jessica heard the distinct ring of intent in his voice and dropped her indignance, rushing to the balcony. "Wait! Tarik—"

She stopped within inches of him. They stared at each other. Emotions of every kind electrified the space between them. From hatred to indignation to dependency and beyond, into an unexpected mutuality, each was a peculiar kind of prisoner. Tarik was imprisoned by his own ideals, and Jessica by these palace walls and by a blooming self-awareness that might have gone unnoticed had she not met the man before her.

Softly, severely, Jessica began to speak to him. It was as though he stood miles away instead of only inches. "What really brings you here? Guilt? Remorse? What?"

Tarik pressed his lips into a flat line. He felt a childish embarrassment that she read him so correctly and snapped back, "Money. Charles hired me with your father's money."

Stunned, she whispered, "How do you know Charles?"

"Lady Ashley arranged our meeting after she confirmed that you were in the harem."

Jessica faltered. Truth? Lies? She could barely tell the difference anymore. So many tunnels in this maze had turned out to be false. . . . "You could have heard those names anywhere," she said weakly. "I've been betrayed twice. Once by a man in the bazaar and once by you."

Instantly Tarik dipped a hand into his robe and pulled out the brooch Charles had said Jessica would recognize. The jewel winked in the bright daylight as he held it up to her, so close that its colors danced in her widened eyes. "Believe me now?"

Her answer was nothing more than a trembling tear in the corner of her eye.

The embassy was open for one of those annoying but necessary afternoon receptions for dignitaries and British subjects currently living in Constantinople. Charles was beginning to find such affairs less and less tolerable with each passing day, just as his front of diplomatic patience wore rapidly thinner. Each morning he awakened to thoughts of Jessica subjected to unthinkable humiliations, and each night he fell asleep imagining he heard her calling out to him in the depths of her troubled sleep. He had somehow betrayed her, even if he couldn't quite figure out how. He tried constantly to rationalize it, but the answer eluded him. He should never have brought her here—a true gentleman would never present a lady with this barbaric culture, least of all a spontaneous girl like Jessica. Had he been wiser, he would've introduced her to the world more gradually, taking her to more civilized places first—Paris, perhaps. Then Lisbon, Madrid, and Milan, in that order. But the Ottoman Empire, even in 1909, was still no place for a lady.

He experienced a totally vulgar thought when he got a full view of that Mrs. Somebody MacSomething pouring tea from a samovar and presiding over the elaborate table of scones and cakes near a group of Turkish officials who were chatting with Ambassador Grant. He could never remember that woman's name. Mrs. Teapot. Well, it certainly wasn't the first time someone acquired a name from his or her most obvious trait.

At least Lady Ashley was still in Constantinople, and thus here today. Charles needed her steadiness, her comprehension of his problem, and especially her very un-English boldness.

Charles tried to shake his attention back to the conversation going on in his own little group, which included several wives of British nationals and the Grand Vizer Bey from Sultan Hasam's court, who looked quite intercontinental in his English suit and Turkish fez. Bey was talking to the women with a particularly superficial flair, and Charles had to force his mind back to the people around him.

"I envy your husbands," Bey was saying, "who can show you off so freely—your beautiful dresses, your jewels—while I must spend a fortune on my harem. And for what? Dresses they wear only to please each other."

As if cued, Mrs. Teapot fluttered in. She had been listening quite artfully to two conversations at once, ready to pounce on the first juicy topic, and here she came. Charles braced himself.

"Sir, oh, sir—we have a question," the woman twittered.

Charles found it interesting how Mrs. Teapot suddenly became promoted to *we*.

"Madam," the Grand Vizer acknowledged.

"Something has puzzled us for quite a while."

"Yes?"

"Is it conceivable that a woman can be held in a harem against her will?"

Charles bristled. Teapot never liked him very much.

Bey shook his head. "That is not possible."

"Then what about Sultan Hasam's harem?"

Teapot twinkled on. "We've heard that women are kidnapped and forced into some kind of sexual slavery. . . ."

"Madam, this is the twentieth century."

Thrilled beyond words, Teapot crowded him. "So if a lady were in the harem, it would be of her own free will?"

She had pushed past Charles to shove this latest barb in, and now he began to feel the pinch. "Madam—" he began.

"Charles, don't." It was Ambassador Grant. A terse order, quietly issued from over his shoulder.

"Believe me, madam," Bey went on, "it is too difficult a proposition to keep a woman who does not want to be kept."

"Even for the Sultan?"

Charles knotted his fists. "Madam, if you have something to say, then bloody well say it." He felt Ambassador Grant grip his elbow in light warning, but this was not the first time Teapot had hedged insults regarding Jessica's predicament. This woman thrived upon the misfortune and infirmities of others, making use of them either in gossip or in other forms of social damage. He would've liked to see her strapped to a camel headed for Tibet.

She turned to him now, displaying a professional innocence that made use of her old-lady face and put him at an automatic disadvantage. "I'm sure I have no idea what you mean—"

"You know damned well what I mean!"

Ambassador Grant stepped in fully now. "Charles, that's quite enough."

But Lady Ashley also had sensed the trouble and appeared out of nowhere, carrying a large brandy snifter and smoking a long cigar. This quite effectively distracted Teapot from Charles's vulnerabilities.

"Why, Lady Ashley . . ."

"I find it goes very well with my brandy," Lady Ashley said, leaning toward the older woman and raising her eyebrows in perfect punctuation. "And it's gone out. Charles, would you mind?"

He inhaled deeply and cleared his head. "Not at all. Allow me." He struck a match and lit the cigar.

Teapot stared, amazed, as Lady Ashley indulged in a good long drag.

Rescued, Charles offered Lady Ashley his arm, and the two of them strode away from the others in a veil of stares.

"For a diplomat you're sadly lacking in subtlety and notions of propriety," she told Charles, amused.

"I'm getting sick of propriety," he said. "I think it's just another word for superficiality. Oh, I don't know"—he moaned then, his gaze dropping—"I'm beginning to wonder whether or not I'd be doing Jessica a favor by getting her out of the harem. I can't imagine bringing her back to people like that old vulture."

"Now, now, be polite."

"Well, it isn't fair. Jessica doesn't deserve to

spend the rest of her life being glared at and whispered about as though she's grown a second head or something. Every week, every day that passes, she sinks more deeply into ill repute. If only I could know what she wants . . ."

"You mustn't think that way," Lady Ashley said. "Do what you feel is right and it *will* be right. You and I both know Jessica isn't there willingly, and she's strong enough to stand up to petty gossip. The important thing isn't what other people feel but what you feel, Charles. Do you know what you feel?"

He was silent for a moment, and then sighed, the sigh betraying his inner doubts and worries, but most of those doubts had nothing to do with Jessica's captivity or what might be happening to her. "If she's still alive," he began slowly, "which we know she was when you saw her, at least, then she's obviously found a way to live within her circumstances. I knew she was resourceful, but I really never thought she was that pliant. I'm beginning to wonder if I'm worthy of her at all."

"Is that any way to think?" Lady Ashley said. "After all, few men possess the mettle to stick to an impossible situation as you have. Jessica hasn't given up, and I haven't noticed that you've given up, either. A lesser man would have by now."

"Thank you," he said, but the doubts remained.

Charles did not go back to the clutch of dignitaries. He felt he no longer belonged there. Perhaps he would again, eventually, but at this moment . . . no. For now he was a man caught between duty and devotion—a tricky precipice.

And this was a fine day for predicaments. That afternoon the Grand Vizer Bey went back to Sultan Hasam's palace to engage in another tier of careful discussion, but this time, rather than teetering on the line between social strata, he was teetering on the Sultan's capricious favor during a meeting at the Palace of Yildiz.

The audience room was filled with the usual advisers—the astrologer, the Grand Vizer Bey, the Kislar, and the Kadin, in her chair slightly behind Sultan Hasam's divan. However, today there was no special privilege involved for the Kadin, for there was an extra presence in the cupboard-lined room, a presence that insulted her. She turned her veiled face and heavily decorated eyes ever so slightly to her left, just enough to take in the form of that other woman, that American, sitting on the Sultan's left, robed in the finest brocades and delicate veils—as fine as the Kadin herself had ever worn. The Kadin tried to keep her inner fury from showing in her eyes but knew that the heavy kohl and colors on her eyes could not shield the pure anathema she felt. That woman. That woman would pay.

The proceedings went on—political problems and decisions—as the astrologer argued with Bey, who now wore his traditional Oriental robe.

"There has been rioting in both Syria and

Macedonia," Bey finally said directly to Sultan Hasam, tiring of the astrologer's attempts to understate the seriousness of what they were facing.

"What has the army done?"

"They can do very little. The officers are at a disadvantage. It's been three months since the soldiers have been paid, and we have reports from Syria that more and more soldiers are deserting every day."

The astrologer spoke blandly, without inflection. "Soldiers serve their Sultan for the honor, not for the money."

Bey risked his life with his next words, but the very honor the astrologer spoke of demanded the truth, for the sake of the Empire. "That may have been true once, but not anymore. The army must have funds."

"Maybe what the soldiers need," the astrologer guessed, "is a great battle. A victory."

"What they need is money to feed their families."

With a single gesture Sultan Hasam cut the discussion off. "I will consider the problem. You may both leave."

The two men did as they were told, but in two different directions.

Immediately the Sultan turned to his left, to Jessica. "This doesn't bore you?"

Jessica stiffened slightly beneath the folds of her elaborate robe. Carefully considering her answer, she said, "I find it fascinating. Mr. Bey seems a most reasonable man. He seems to weigh his decisions and opinions carefully. He is a man of conscience."

"This . . . conscience," Sultan Hasam began, "is something you value?"

"I value it very much," she told him with a nod.

"And what of my astrologer?"

So it was true. Sultan Hasam was bouncing his opinions off her. This added both danger and possibility to her presence here. "He seems loyal," she said after a moment, "but not very modern in his thinking."

"No conscience?"

Jessica only smiled, amused by his attitude. She hadn't expected to like him, but she did.

Hasam nodded slowly. "Modern. I see . . . Come, sit beside me."

Overly aware of the abject wrath prickling her from the Kadin's direction, Jessica rose and made her way the few short steps to the Sultan's divan and sat on the edge of it.

"I want to show you something," he said. He pressed a button hidden beneath the carved wooden frame of the divan.

Jessica flinched as every cupboard along the wall suddenly swung open, revealing a row of musket-length Gatling camel guns, mounted and aimed.

"To protect me from assassins," Sultan Hasam said proudly. He pressed another button. The room erupted into maching-gun fire.

Jessica clutched the velvet edge of the divan, noticing that some of the people in the room might easily have been cut down had they not been standing near the Sultan's audience platform. Evidently he meant to make his point, no matter the cost. He intended to impress her, and his intent was disturbing.

The Sultan beamed at her now. "Very twentieth-century," he said.

Her tongue stuck to the roof of her mouth as Jessica murmured, "Very."

Her hands took hours to warm up.

CHAPTER ELEVEN

The sun set over the courtyard. Its last rose-hued light spilled across the gleaming marble of the palace walls, turning them ruby where shadows lay, and pink where light still shone. A small group of young soldiers strode across the garden areas, laughing and talking idly. No one would have thought anything of it.

Unless, of course, one knew things.

Even as Sultan Hasam lay drowsily enjoying his wealth and what he believed to be security, Tarik gazed over the balcony rail of Jessica's apartments. He had awakened her hours ago, after slipping into her quarters unnoticed, and told her that it was nearly time. He realized that she had no true conception of what that meant— she believed he was speaking only of her escape. Together they had kept a silent vigil at the balcony rail, awaiting the signal to begin their escape. Had Jessica known more about military tactics, she might have figured out that the escape of two people need not be timed quite this carefully, and that other things were afoot, things that would shake the Empire from end to end.

Now Jessica sat near him on the balcony, watching for a signal she did not fully appreciate. She was thinking only of herself, Tarik supposed, while he had to think of everything *but* himself.

Even in the warmth of the summer night Tarik felt cold. And he felt other things, less tangible things—an awareness of what was happening outside the great wall and all around the nearby countryside, and he itched to be part of it, to know exactly what was happening, when and with whom.

All this time, he had tried to keep his eyes off Jessica, yet the sight of her sitting sideways on the balcony rail, diligently watching for some distinct sign that would mean freedom, disturbed Tarik down to the core of his being. She was beautiful in a sharp and defined way, not as the dark-skinned women of his people might be beautiful with their round faces and large eyes. Jessica's eyes were unlined, clear blue, and as quick as the eyes of a bird. Her face was once again the untainted ivory he remembered before he dragged her into the desert where the sun ruddied her cheeks. Her nose and chin were sharp, and her lips just right—not too thin, not too full. She looked most intercontinental, sitting there in her Eastern robes with the thin green veil around her neck, for she was

Western and did not feel the need to cover her face.

Part of Tarik was disgusted with her, even though she was resourceful enough to find her way to the top of this ladder of palace intrigue. How could she betray herself? Wouldn't an honorable death be better than prostituting herself to a despot?

His stomach turned over, then turned over again at the idea that Jessica might actually feel something for Sultan Hasam. Hadn't he seen a kind of pleasure on her face when she was borne back to the seraglio after spending more time with the Sultan than any woman had in a decade?

He clenched his fists to keep from touching her face, her hair, to see if she was real or just a legend he'd made up in his mind. From the beginning her courage had impressed him, and now he had to face the fact that she also was resourceful and determined to take care of herself, though she had no cause beyond herself. No purpose. No empire to conquer.

Tarik forced his eyes away from her, barely in time to see one of the soldiers in the group below lift his fez and wave it over his head as though to bid the sun good night.

He stood up. "That's it." When Jessica jumped slightly and came to her feet beside him, he clarified, "The signal. We must leave now."

Thoughts of anything but action flooded out of his mind, and he became a soldier again. He gathered up the few things Jessica had chosen to take with her, and together they hurried toward the door. Jessica never said a word, never argued, never looked back with a gleam of sentiment in her eyes. Tarik wasn't sure what to make of that.

"Hurry," he said. "Stay with me and do exactly as I—"

The apartment doors burst open seconds before they would have reached them, and the Kislar Agha flowed in rapidly, followed by a herd of slaves.

Jessica gasped. They'd been found out somehow!

But the slaves carried strange weapons. Musical instruments? Flowers? Food? Did they mean to capture her and Tarik or feed them to death?

"I'm only three footsteps ahead of the Sultan!" the Kislar said, in a near panic.

"He's coming here?" Jessica blurted. "Now?"

"A *very* great honor." The tall black man immediately began waving the slaves hither and yon, barking orders and waving directions. "Hurry with the *midye*. Make sure the olives are fresh. Be careful with those hydrangeas, you fool. Now, where's the music? You two, get Miss Jessica's blue robe and slippers."

Jessica stared desperately at Tarik. Tarik's face was limned with a painful, sinking despair as he silently communicated the hopelessness of trying to escape tonight. To her it meant loss of time—and the sudden fulfillment of a fate she had managed to put off. To him it meant possibly losing her altogether, for Tarik understood what was happening outside. There may not be a second chance.

They stood in this silent and disheartening exchange, each entertaining crazy thoughts of a sudden breakout, each measuring the distance between themselves and the door, but in seconds the room was twirling with even more slaves rushing to prepare things for Sultan Hasam's arrival.

Too late. Silence blanketed the entire room. With a clap of the Kislar's huge hands the slaves ceased their bustling and snapped to attention. The silence was unbearable. Nothing happened—until Hasam strode into the room. Even his slippers made no sound on the plush designs of the carpet. Behind him strolled several bodyguards and the astrologer.

The Kislar bowed immediately. "Everything you want shall be provided. Every whim shall be attended to. Every fantasy fulfilled."

Unceremoniously Sultan Hasam pointed at Jessica. How rude, she thought impulsively. "What I want," Hasam said, "is to be alone with this woman."

Again the Kislar clapped. The room emptied as quickly as it had filled. Only Tarik lingered, his face a mate of a dozen conflicting emotions. But he was helpless, as helpless as Jessica was, to alter the situation. His eyes burned with insane thoughts of murder—could he kill the Sultan and be gone with her before anyone realized? Could he slip to one side and hide in the room until Hasam really believed he was alone with her? Then he was stabbed with the realization that Jessica might wish to handle Sultan Hasam herself. After all, they were lovers now.

The idea of Jessica making love to the Sultan made Tarik ill, and for the first time he became aware that this wasn't the kind of feeling one gets about just any woman one is rescuing. And shouldn't the adventure of the rescue be more stirring than the woman herself?

Finally, driven to admit the inevitable, Tarik veered out of the room.

Jessica watched him leave, feeling as though she'd somehow become caught on a merry-go-round that was spinning out of control. A moment ago she'd been fortifying herself for a wild and deadly escape from the most heavily guarded compound in the Empire. Now, quite suddenly, she had to regroup her thoughts and devise some way to handle Sultan Hasam, who made no secret of the fact that his desires had come to a boil. Out of desperation she busied herself serving the *levrek buğulama* while trying to readjust her mind to this unforeseen situation—trying to accept the fact that she might indeed have to make love to the Sultan in order to get out of here. She had dismissed that idea . . . and here it was again, in full dress. Her hands shook. She kept her eyes averted.

Hasam never looked away from her. "They tell me you are not interested in jewels or dresses, that the treasury has nothing you want."

Having nothing better to tell him, Jessica handed him what she was really thinking. "They tell you the truth."

"If this is so, then how am I to court you? What is it you want?"

Freedom. The word rang in her mind. She closed her lips tightly, before it slipped out. She poured him coffee and smiled.

The Sultan settled down onto a pile of cushions and accepted the coffee, evidently satisfied with the quality of her smile, which told Jessica that the training had not been entirely in vain.

"I've been thinking," he said quietly, "of taking a second wife."

She straightened up, stunned.

Hasam noticed her reaction; in fact, he had looked for it. "What I'm saying is that you have the promise of marriage. You could be the second Kadin."

Jessica trembled with the combined honor and horror of the thought. "In America," she said with a slight quiver, "a man has only one wife."

Flatly he told her, "This is not America."

For him it was as simple as just that.

Suddenly Jessica felt steadier, as her own personal struggle for power flowed back into her veins. "And the first Kadin? Would she want a second around?"

"The first Kadin wants only what I want."

Aching to tell him the truth, to scream the death of Geisla right in his ignorant ears, Jessica allowed herself to be pulled down into his arms while she tried to think of the right words to get herself out of this and away from this man who knew so little about the nation he ruled.

"I would like the second to do the same," the Sultan whispered into her ear. He wanted her, and he wanted her now.

Calculatingly Jessica said, "If I were to be married, I would want to be a virgin on our wedding night." If English tradition couldn't get her out of this, maybe her own preferences would. The Sultan seemed interested in winning her over, in having her as a wife rather than just as a slave, yet he had no idea of how to go about it—the typical symptom of someone whose every whim had been satisfied all his life. She pitied him suddenly, even as she loathed him for his ignorance. His breath hummed in her ear, warming her skin with the scent of coffee and pilaf. She tried to hold herself back without actually pulling away.

"And I would want my wife to be experienced," he countered, showing clearly the difference between Eastern and Western men. He pulled her closer, tighter.

Jessica tried not to resist, but her natural revulsion and lack of love for Hasam rose to the surface unbidden. He was no longer a stranger to her, of course, but something within her remained a cold stone at the pit of her being as he drew her closer against his thick body and began to caress her with great experience.

"This Western courtship is beginning to bore me," he said. "You know, you really have no choice."

He was an intelligent man, if a spoiled one. Jessica knew quite well that he was correct. She had no choice. Her last bit of stolen time slipped away as Hasam's hand picked open the looped buttons of her robes and parted the front, baring one of her breasts. She closed her eyes and waited. Soon, some feeling, some sensation would come, and she would have to cling to it and hang on.

Her head started to pound. No—that wasn't her head. This sound came from outside, far beyond the palace wall. Metal drums and chanting—coming rapidly nearer.

Over her, Hasam froze and looked up. In seconds he dropped her and raced to the balcony.

Jessica caught herself on the edge of a thickly stuffed cushion and choked, "What is it?"

Before her words faded, the doors swung open and the astrologer hurried in with a dozen Imperial guards. "They move closer. Near the Treasury."

"Who?" Jessica demanded, forgetting her place. "What's going on?"

The Sultan turned to her, no longer a man of passion. Now something entirely different glared upon his face. "You'll be safe here. This has nothing to do with you." To the guards he ordered, "We must leave immediately."

The guards quickly moved to surround the Sultan, forming a grate of human armor, and the tight group turtled out of the room, leaving Jessica alone and confused.

*   *   *

Over a hundred soldiers stormed the doors of the Imperial Treasury, chanting and banging metal spoons against tin pots to ring out their discontent. It was a frightening sight to the armed men within the compound, for they had become accustomed to a life of military order and discipline. They might have better understood an angry mob of civilians than a mob of their own forces risen against them.

The revolutionaries continued their chant as another hundred soldiers added to the ranks of the chanting fury descending upon the outer wall of the Treasury. "Open the Treasury," they chanted, screamed, shouted, bellowed. "Give us our pay!"

Within the Treasury walls, scaffolding supported still more hundreds of armed men, protected from the revolutionaries by the wall itself. They stared out gun ports and over the top of the wall, wondering how to take action against men who otherwise might be standing beside them on this side. Each man knew the man next to him might turn at any moment and join the protest: soldiers against soldiers. Even the men within the Treasury wall understood the motivations outside, for they had not been paid very much more than the common soldiers of the field.

On the topmost scaffold the Imperial Chief Commander scowled at the mob below and spoke to his officers sharply. "It is too late for reason."

The officers couldn't tell if he was speaking a

genuine truth or if he had given in to the nagging tensions of the moment. Had he broken under the strain, or did he plan to use these men below as an example to the rest of the army? It seemed his decision had already been made—perhaps earlier than any of them realized.

The Chief Commander raised his hand, then brought it down abruptly in an unmistakable order to open fire.

Moonlight glimmered on hundreds of rifles. Dark silhouettes of men in uniform rose against the indigo night, coming up from the top of the wall like snakes rising from burrows. Given the order and trained to follow it, they opened fire on a mob they could just as easily have been part of. Not a man was spared that crawling awareness.

Gunfire lit the night. By scores the revolutionaries fell into a twisting mass of agony and spillage. The courtyard was riddled with bullets as the soldiers were mowed down. The revolutionaries scattered, wildly now, seeking protection from the unexpected violence. But there was no protection. In the openness of the Treasury grounds they continued to fall, picked off easily as their dark uniforms shone against the moonlit ground. The protest became a massacre. The death count climbed.

The Chief Commander watched with growing satisfaction. Yes, these men would learn their lesson. Those who survived—and he would make sure a precious few did survive—would spread the word of what comes when one protests against the supreme will of the Empire. They would learn that coins must never come before loyalty to their leaders, to their heritage. He stood boldly on the top of the Treasury scaffolding, hoping the soldiers below saw his broad form and realized who was in charge.

His only distraction came when he noticed that the young soldier beside him had stopped firing his rifle and was now gaping down into the courtyard with glazed eyes. The Chief Commander studied this young face for several seconds, wondering if the boy was out of ammunition and why he wasn't reloading his rifle. After a moment he perceived something else.

"Continue firing, soldier," he told him.

The young man nearly choked when he tried to speak. "But . . . they're unarmed!"

"They are traitors. Keep firing or you'll join them in their punishment."

The young man closed his eyes for a long pause, squeezing tears onto his cheeks, thinking back on his training and all the catchwords of glory he had been glutted with. Where was the grandeur in rifling down his brothers?

Helpless under the eye of his commander, he knew there was no choice. He lifted his rifle, aimed, pressed his quivering lips together, and fired.

In the courtyard a running man fell into the glowing blood of his comrades.

Order was eventually restored, but at the cost of hundreds of lives. To the Chief Commander, as he ordered a bonfire to burn the bodies, the cost was minimal. Without order there would be no Empire, and if soldiers clamored for money instead of going through the proper channels, there could be no order. The flames rose into the night sky, carrying the stench of searing flesh and crackling blood as it boiled. Body upon body was piled into the bonfire, and soon the stench poured out over the Bosporus, carried upon the sea wind—a great funereal warning to all who dared challenge the authority or wisdom of Sultan Hasam.

The Sultan, bracketed by flanks of bodyguards, surveyed the site personally, once it had been established that all danger was snuffed. He cruised the sea of bodies and watched with grim satisfaction as loyal men gathered the corpses of the disloyal and cast them into the hungry flames. Eventually he approached the Chief Commander, who told him, "We have found among the wounded some whom we suspect to be members of the Young Turks."

Sultan Hasam leaned over spontaneously and plucked the red fez from one of the bodies. "So," he murmured, "now they disguise themselves as soldiers. Where are these suspects?"

"In the dungeon, being questioned."

Even the Sultan couldn't escape a shiver at the thought of his Empire's effective methods of questioning. "I want to know where the revolutionaries hold their meetings."

"It will be done," the Commander said.

When the Sultan returned to his reception room, the Grand Vizer Bey was already waiting for him, holding a stack of pamphlets and papers. The Sultan glanced at them, putting down the expression of hungry curiosity he felt for those papers, suspecting their source and wanting to grab them from Bey and read them immediately. But he strode idly past the big man and lounged into his throne, measuring time carefully.

Bey did not wait. "Here is everything I have collected on the revolutionaries."

Hasam gestured casually. "Put them over there."

Bey dumped the pile on a mosaic table and said, "The revolutionaries may have been involved, but we can't pretend that all the problems have been caused by outsiders. Those were your soldiers who died tonight. Your men. They were striking out against you."

Sultan Hasam raised an eyebrow. "You exaggerate the situation with the army."

"Majesty, you must admit that the problems do exist," Bey said in a demanding tone, desperation driving him beyond propriety. The Sultan looked more like a bored child to him now than a fifty-year-old man. "They cannot be ignored any longer."

"A handful of greedy soldiers, greedy traitors, stage a foolish raid, and you would have me believe my entire army is ready to desert. There is no serious dissension."

"And what would you call tonight?" Bey shouted, his face reddening. "Without the army your power could be seriously threatened."

The Sultan froze him with a glare.

Bey returned the glare, just as coldly.

Hasam stood up, looming over his adviser as the old Byzantine Empire loomed like a ghost over all of Constantinople. "Even though our opinions differ on a great many subjects, I have always found your advice worthy of note. But perhaps you could be of greater value to me elsewhere."

Bey's mouth dropped open. He twitched in shock.

Sultan Hasam went on. "I believe the situation in Armenia needs some attending to. Mr. Bey, you may leave the palace tonight."

Bey stared, then shook himself. Exile. Plain and simple. With no other recourse, he stiffened, turned, and left the reception room. In a way, he was glad. . . .

Alone now with nothing but the past and an uncertain future, the Sultan went to the mosaic table and began studying the documents.

Jessica was finally asleep.

Once the gunfire stopped its hideous din and the bonfire began to grow slowly in the distant compounds, barely visible from her balcony except for the ominous glow it made on the clouds above, Tarik had insisted she try to sleep. It was no longer possible to predict how their escape would go. Certainly it would take more now than a few well-placed bribes.

But others were not asleep and took advantage of the moment to fulfill what they perceived their duty for the good of the Empire, its Kadin, and her son who was heir. They came out of the darkness, their blades glinting in the moonlight that streamed into the pale woman's apartments. She had no place here and was turning their Sultan's head, the Kadin had told them as she casually assigned them their orders.

They were dressed as dervishes, in the traditional turbans and skirts with floppy pants and boots underneath. Only their curved swords and the talcum smeared upon their faces set them apart from other dervishes. Their faces were mummified by the talcum, and their eyes were nothing but hollows in the dimness.

They plunged at her out of the shadows, a swift but casual movement because they never expected her to fight back. But Jessica had been only lightly asleep, kept from deep sleep by anticipation of the day to come. She bolted awake as a man's thick arm closed around her throat, and over her head she saw the flash of a blade in a stream of moonlight.

"No!" she screamed, terrified both by the blade and by the skeletal face of her attacker. She twisted out of reach. The sword plunged into her pillow. Feathers flew everywhere.

The other man climbed over the bed after her while the first attacker shook his blade loose from the snagging fabric. Jessica screamed again, but this scream was the platform from which she sent a fear-driven fist into the nose of the man who stumbled after her. He staggered back but caught her nightgown in one hand and yanked. Jessica went down hard, hearing the nightgown rip away from her shoulders. An arm came around her throat, choking off any more screams. The man struggled for a better grip on his sword while holding Jessica's twisting body against his own. She was young and strong, strong enough to throw him off-balance and stall his aim with that blade, but she couldn't break free. His arm on her throat tightened. She knew she would be easier to kill if he could weaken her by cutting off her air, and she clawed desperately at the arm. Tucking her chin to her chest, she tried to bite him, but his arm was like a band of ivory around her throat.

She kicked wildly. Out of the corner of her eye she saw the sword bob. She wondered about the other man. Soon he would free his sword from the brocaded pillow and come around to plunge it into her. A thousand thoughts ran through her mind. The arm at her throat grew even tighter. She couldn't breathe anymore. Her lungs burned for air. The strength of her kicks began to fade, and her field of vision was becoming a tunnel. Her ears rang now. She heard herself choking—a sound out of a nightmare. Her hands tingled as she clawed at the arm around her neck. Lights popped before her eyes.

Suddenly she was thrown, half strangled, to the floor. She sensed more than saw her attackers turn away from her and rush to meet someone at the door to her parlor. More killers. Her reprieve would be short—too short to recover herself and escape, even if it meant plunging off the balcony to another kind of death. She lay on the floor in a gasping heap. Her mind worked, but her arms and legs were like putty. Her chest hurt. Her head felt like a boulder. Maybe she was dead already. Maybe that's why they had dropped her.

Yes, she must be dead, because she heard Tarik's voice calling to her out of the dream of death. In a moment the darkness would close in completely and she would slip away.

In the abyss of her oxygen-starved mind Jessica heard the clang of swords against a single dagger.

"Jessica!"

Something stirred within her. Something reawakened. Could she still fight for life and win? That voice, as it called to her, was blooming with possibilities. But she was so tired . . .

The sight of Jessica lying crumpled upon the hard floor drove Tarik with an inhuman fury. He called to her twice, wasting breath that might better have been spent in his struggle with these two intruders who meant nothing less than to hack his limbs from his body. She never moved, no matter how loudly he shouted. He gritted his teeth and let the rage take hold.

It served him well, this unexpected rage of passions. He fought like two men instead of one and was a fair enough match for the assassins as their blades lunged around him, slicing his clothing and scoring his skin. He slashed at their robes, hungering to feel his dagger sink into flesh, and drove the fight from the bedchamber and into the baths. Against the cold white marble the battle scraped on. By now each man was gasping with each lunge. Tarik was spry and agile, but these men were trained murderers in an art as old as civilization itself. He managed to avoid their whirling swords but only barely, and the slippery floor beneath his feet did him no favors. He was driven backward onto the ridge of marble between two tubs and fought to keep his mind in order between the sound of water cascading into the tubs and the thought of Jessica lying dead only a room away.

The man nearest him followed him onto the ridge. Tarik took the moment of imbalance and turned it to his favor by grasping the man's wrist and twisting with all his might. The assassin howled in pain, then gasped as the breath gushed from his body. With a victorious slurp Tarik's dagger slid out of the man's stomach. Tarik pushed his opponent into the tub and kept the curved sword for himself. Water sloshed over his ankles as he spun to meet the second assassin.

Only reflex kept him from being beheaded. He arched backward as a *yatakan* blade whizzed under his nose.

Exhausted now, Tarik called upon every sense of survival left in him. He called upon the rage, and it answered.

He slashed out with the sword that moments ago had been aimed at him, hacking cleanly through the dervish robes and into the flesh beneath. Strength driven by bitterness pushed the sword through the assassin's body until it was stopped by his spine. Tarik dragged the weapon out, swept it around, and whacked it broadside into the man's head. Dead before it hit the ground, the assassin's body slid halfway across the marble floor, leaving a skid mark of blood and entrails.

Tarik's arms tingled at his sides, still poised in attack position. He turned slowly, knowing he had to face a horror worse than assassins when he went back into that bedroom. He hung there, exhausted, as though expecting the murderers to spring to life and attack him again.

Slowly the tingling faded from his arms as reflex handed control back to reason. He let his shoulders droop.

Turning on numb legs, he hardly realized the truth as the bedroom doorway came back into his field of vision. Someone was standing there. A ragged thing, bruised and ghostlike, as beautiful as dawn.

They took the few trembling steps necessary to reach each other and collapsed into an embrace. Tarik clutched her tightly against his heaving chest, burying his face in her hair. He smelled perfume mingling with the sweat of desperation. "I thought you were dead," he choked.

"I thought *you* were." Her words hung upon the threads of disbelief. She coiled her arms into his robes and found his body beneath them and held it as though it were her anchor to life.

Beside them, the bathwaters ran red with blood.

CHAPTER TWELVE

The Armenian quarter of Constantinople glowed with flame as the wooden house where Jessica had first been taken now burned to the ground. Sultan Hasam had been quite justified when he shuddered at thoughts of his executioner's methods of interrogation, for indeed they had proven effective in finding out where the revolutionaries had holed up. Now the house smoldered against the night sky. The streets were empty, but a thousand eyes watched as Imperial soldiers torched the house.

A caller hired by the Chief Commander moved through the streets near the burning building, voicing Sultan Hasam's decree.

"Anyone calling himself a revolutionary shall be executed in the worse possible manner. Any who distribute writings or voice ideas of the revolutionaries shall be hanged. This is the decree of your leader, His Majesty Sultan Hasam."

The decree was repeated with grating regularity all through the streets of the Armenian section.

266

Salim had already heard it too many times as he and Misha ran down the alley behind the burning house. They had barely escaped in time. The house was nearly surrounded now, and they hadn't gone unseen. A dozen Imperial soldiers chased them through the dark streets. But Salim knew the area well and led Misha through a maze of alleys and narrow streets, past windows where frightened Armenians watched them pass. He hesitated only when he heard the bangling Armenian music from a tavern as they passed it and clasped Misha's elbow to drag him back into the tavern doorway. "Come this way," he gasped. He pushed the door open, then slammed it shut behind himself and Misha. The two rebels leaned, panting against the wood. The music stopped.

They looked around. Armenians at bars and tables stared at the two breathless men. No one moved.

The soldiers clambered down the street outside, through puddles left by a recent rain, and when they realized the rebels were no longer in the street, they began searching houses and shops. They came into the tavern boldly and studied every face. The patrons in the tavern stopped their conversations and looked with mild curiosity at the soldiers as the Turks began searching behind the bars and under the tables. They found nothing. With careful aplomb they went back out the open door, not bothering to close it behind them. Their boots sounded dully on the cobblestones as they moved to the next building.

One of the Armenians quickly closed the door and bolted it. The tavern keeper then opened a heavy wooden door to the cellar. Salim and Misha emerged. Misha immediately went to the window and peered out suspiciously.

Salim took a deep breath. "You take great risk in hiding us," he said to the man beside him.

"How many of you are in the quarter?" the Armenian tavern owner asked.

Salim hated thinking about the numbers. Ever since the great massacre in the market square, numbers had little faces attached to them, and they gave him a headache. "Fifty, maybe a hundred."

The innkeeper turned to another Armenian man and asked, "Can we hide that many?"

The man shrugged, then nodded. Not very convincing, Salim felt.

Turning back to Salim, the innkeeper said, "We will hide you among our people. We will dress you as we are dressed and put you to work in our shops so no one will suspect you do not belong here. You will explain that to your men?"

Salim nodded. "You realize the risk," he pointed out, suddenly aware of how much his words sounded like something Tarik might say.

His lips in a bitter set, the Armenian went incautiously to the window where he stood beside Misha and stared out at the nearby church and the flames beyond it. "My daughter," he began, "was murdered in the streets by Sultan Hasam's soldiers. Her only crime was a desire to listen to the words of a man named Tarik." Now he turned again, his face shadowed, except for the faint orange glow of flames from the next street. "We will do what we have to do."

Salim wished he didn't understand, but he did.

On the other side of the universe, Sultan Hasam sat on his throne like a man sits on a weak horse. He looked older than Jessica remembered, even in so short a span of time. He looked gray and careworn, and she began to wonder if perhaps there was something beneath the spoiled despotic image.

She sat in her place at his left side, the Kadin across from her on his right, both women positioned slightly behind the monarch. Slightly in front of him to his left and right, respectively, sat the Kislar Agha and the court astrologer. Directly in front of all of them a small man, heavily cloaked, stood before Sultan Hasam and reported what he knew.

"The Armenians have given the revolutionaries refuge. They move from house to house in the Armenian section, never staying longer than a few days in one place. They are like ants in the desert."

The astrologer spoke up with, "The Armenians have always given us trouble."

Hasam inhaled deeply. He had not yet heard

what he wished to hear. "And what about Tarik Pasha?"

Jessica stiffened. The Kislar glanced at her, then said to Hasam, "It seems to me that men like this Pasha have the ability to die and resurrect at will—whenever it suits them."

Pleased, Sultan Hasam took the Kislar back into his favor with a smile. "Exactly."

"Which is why His Majesty must move quickly," the astrologer said, pouncing on an opportunity to steal approval back from the Kislar. He had been quite annoyed that Agha was back in favor with the Sultan since the night the Sultan spent with the American woman, and he meant to break that pattern.

"What would you suggest?" the Sultan asked.

"You should consider doing what your grandfather would have done."

"But the man was merciless," the Kislar pointed out.

The astrologer glared at him. "He was very effective." To Sultan Hasam he said, "He saved the Empire." You can do the same, his eyes added.

Now Jessica spoke up. If she was going to be allowed to view these sessions, then she would insist upon understanding what was happening. Perhaps then she could also affect what was happening. And why else would Sultan Hasam have her here if he didn't want to know what she was thinking? Maybe she didn't yet fully understand the proprieties of the Eastern court, but she would not sit back and decorate his reception room like just another cupboard. Of course . . . the cupboards were loaded, weren't they?

"What does he mean?" she demanded, gesturing at the astrologer. "What's he really suggesting?"

The Kadin came out of her own silence and snapped, "The Sultan has not asked your opinion."

"I'm not giving an opinion," Jessica said. "I'm asking a question."

The Kislar opened his mouth to rebuke her, but a wave of the Sultan's hand stopped him. "You have done well," he said to the Kislar. "She amuses me." Then, amazingly enough, he turned to Jessica and actually bothered to explain. "The astrologer is suggesting that the army move into the Armenian quarters to overwhelm the traitors."

Jessica's eyes widened in disbelief. "You mean murder them?" When his silence provided the answer, Jessica glared deeply into the Sultan's eyes and scored his mind with her thoughts as though they flowed directly from brain to brain. In a hushed tone she spoke only to him. "I can't believe you would allow innocent citizens to be butchered. I can't think it of you. . . ."

The astrologer, sensing interference, blurted, "The revolutionaries must be eliminated before they get any stronger!"

His words echoed along the ridge of cupboards. Then—silence.

Hasam rose slowly. He gazed at his advisers. At the Kadin. At Jessica.

He turned back and spoke to the astrologer. "There is one flaw in your plan," he said, "one problem we have not addressed."

The astrologer gaped, almost as though he preferred not to ask at all. Yet, with his manner, Sultan Hasam had just cued him to ask a question, and he must do so. "And that is?"

Hasam turned, put one foot up on the cross brace of his throne, and looked at Jessica. "My conscience."

Jessica swelled with pride.

The pride did not go away.

Even as she walked with Tarik through the seraglio gardens later that day, she couldn't bury a faint smile of victory, no matter how much Tarik told her of Sultan Hasam's corrupt monarchy. Tarik seemed afraid he might be losing her to a different way, that perhaps he had come here in vain.

"How can you defend him?" he demanded as they strolled in a pretense of casualness past the huge parrot cages. Women of the harem passed them from time to time, also strolling in the sunlight, and their argument had been pocked with periods of discreet silence.

"All I said," Jessica began patiently, "is that he can be a very compassionate man." In her way she was testing Tarik, intentionally irritating his stern hatred of everything the Sultan stood for. She knew he was loyal, very courageous, and willing to put his life on the life for his principles—and for her. But could he grow within himself enough to accept some good in the Sultan?

Tarik furrowed his brows at her, wondering if there was some hidden part of her that he might never understand—how could she speak well of a man who kept her imprisoned and used her sexually? Had she been brainwashed? He devised to shock her out of it, force her to realize the true mettle of Sultan Hasam. "Do you know why he had the parrot cages built?"

"No, and I don't want to know."

"You're *going* to. He built them so the shrieks of the parrots would cover the screams coming from the prisoners in the torture chamber just over this wall."

Angered, Jessica stopped short and faced him. "Why should I believe you? You have your own reasons for believing him to be evil, but he's not some horrible monster. I've seen him act otherwise."

Snidely Tarik countered, "What have you seen?"

"Even though he has proof that the Armenians are hiding the Young Turks, he refuses to allow the army to massacre them."

Tarik stood back, his dark eyes narrowing. "How do you know these things?"

"He talks to me." She shrugged to punctuate it.

"What do you mean he 'talks' to you?"

"He talks. Does it surprise you so much that

he might be interested in what I have to say? In what I think? You're more backward than I thought."

Tarik stared at her. For a woman he had clutched tightly to his heart in joy that she still lived, she seemed like a stranger now. He felt even more distant when she said, "Hasam has asked me to marry him."

His chest tightened. "I can't believe it."

Something in his tone, not intentionally, insulted her. "Is it so hard to believe that a man might find me desirable?"

No . . . not hard at all. "Sultan Hasam finds all women desirable," he grumbled.

Jessica's eyes flashed with rage, but Tarik's mind had turned to a second tier of possibilities and he dropped the conversation abruptly. He took her by the arm and led her under a canopy of wisteria, deep into the garden until he was sure they could not be overheard. Then he faced her, his expression as genuine and appealing as the integrity of a child. "Jessica," he began carefully, "if what you say is true . . . if you do have the ear of the Sultan, then what you learn could be very valuable. It might be weeks before we have another opportunity to escape. That time could be well spent."

Her lips dropped open slightly. "Are you asking me to be your spy?"

"I'm asking you to work with us."

"I'm sorry. I can't."

He gripped her shoulders. "Listen to me. I need not explain to you our ways of thinking.

You yourself are a victim of the old ways that Sultan Hasam is perpetuating. I think you've seen enough. There's going to be a revolution. That much is certain.''

"Nothing is certain," she said, fighting the idea.

"It is," he insisted. "You might help control the bloodshed. You could help thousands achieve the kind of freedom you've taken for granted all your life—"

"Stop. Don't give me a speech about making the world a better place to live, Tarik." Her blue eyes flashed violet with the wisteria flowers. "It's inappropriate coming from a man who so easily sold me into slavery. I'm not here because of the Sultan. I'm here because of you."

Tarik dropped his hands from her shoulders. They curved into fists. "And I find it hard to take blame when your life seems to have changed very little."

"Why? Because I don't share your capacity for abstract causes?"

His voice lowered, a smoldering sound now. "I expected more from you."

Jessica thought they knew each other, thought they had broken through the resentment and the bitterness and all the other things they'd felt for one another—she thought that pattern had been broken last night when they found such astonishing relief in knowing they were both still alive. During those horrible moments of attack she had unexpectedly found herself thinking more about Tarik's life than her own. And to find him alive . . . he saved her life too.

But to be a spy for a disjointed band of outlaw revolutionaries . . . She wished she knew better what she felt. Struggling with her thoughts, she whirled away from him and stalked off, taking refuge in insult. At the last moment she turned back and used a petty kind of ploy. "As Sultan Hasam's Kadin I would be very powerful, but I don't suppose you think a woman can handle that kind of power."

Stung to the core, Tarik glared emptily at her. "You're wrong. Many women could, but not you."

"Why not?"

He raised his head slightly. "Because," he said, "you don't have a woman's heart."

The Kislar burst into Jessica's apartment, interrupting Jessica and Usta as they shared breakfast.

"We leave immediately for Brusa," he said, and wasted no time collecting Jessica's apparel for the trip.

Jessica looked up from her cup of coffee. "Brusa?"

"The Sultan has decided to take an excursion."

With a surrendering sigh Jessica glanced at Usta and shrugged. What Hasam wants, Hasam gets. She got up unceremoniously and began gathering her things. "I'll have Lanie get my eunuch and—"

"No," the Kislar said. "Just you and me. And Sultan Hasam."

She straightened. "No entourage? No guards?"

Even Usta stared when she heard this, but she remained silent. Her silence told Jessica that this was most uncommon—well, the Sultan himself had told her he hadn't been out of the palace in years. But why now? And why with her?

"He's going in disguise," the Kislar explained as he packed several robes and chemises into a large case. "One of his nephews will take his place in the palace."

Suddenly Usta seemed to understand. She smiled, leaned over, and patted Jessica's hand. "This is a very important trip for him. For both of you. It's time for you to learn about *real* power. It's time for you to sleep with your Sultan."

Less than half an hour passed, and Jessica was riding in a motorcar beside Sultan Hasam. Gone were the royal robes, gone was the fez with the ostrich plume, gone was every sign of regality. In their place was a simple business suit and cravat. Jessica wore Turkish robes, but these were not so resplendent as the ones she had worn within the seraglio. She was veiled but with only a plain, thin pink veil without trimmings. She wore no jewelry at all. The Kislar drove the car. Beside him sat the astrologer, who somehow had finagled a way to be included on this trip.

"Why are we doing this?" she finally asked the Sultan in the privacy of a quiet tone.

"You have made me see my own blindness," he told her, turning his large liquid-black eyes to her. Today, in the dimness of the car's interior, those eyes were flecked with the silver of his sideburns and the memory of youth. "I will go out among my people to taste the local wines and hear the languages." The corners of his straight mouth curved up slightly.

Jessica studied him, feeling quite a bit more his equal than ever before. "And nothing else?"

His grin grew a little wider. "Perhaps there is something else."

"What is it?"

He looked forward again, seeing the streets of his Empire roll out between the Kislar and the astrologer in the front seat. "I want you to see the old ways. I want you to understand my nation's customs. And I want you to understand me."

Brusa was known as the city of a hundred mosques. Each mosque was a piece of heritage unto itself, a reminder and a testimonial, harkening back to the Old Empire that had forged the metal from which Turkey and the Ottoman Empire itself sprung. In the near distance black-and-green groves of olives trees grew in abundance, as though the twentieth century had made no entrance here. In the far distance—mountains.

The Sultan's motorcar moved sluggishly down narrow streets, past fine old Turkish homes mostly made of wood with overhanging balconies. No one bothered to explain what was going on to Jessica as the car stopped in front of one of the homes and she was escorted out by a servant who ushered her into the house. Shortly afterward more servants carried her luggage and the Sultan's into the supremely Oriental rooms. No Western decor interrupted the Eastern flavor here as in the palace in Constantinople. The walls were of carved wood. Divans lined them.

A second seraglio, she guessed. Bought or lent to Sultan Hasam, or something. It didn't matter. The Sultan got whatever he wanted.

The servants stopped unpacking suddenly, aware of something Jessica was not trained to notice, and sure enough, a moment later the Sultan and the astrologer entered the room.

". . . can't just go out like this," the astrologer was saying, "with just a few eunuchs for protection. What if you are recognized?"

Sultan Hasam turned to him but only with casual attention. "I want to see the marketplace." With that matter dismissed, he looked at Jessica. "Put on your plainest dress."

Wordlessly Jessica let the servants lead her into another room where she would change clothes. She took particular note of the fact that while the Sultan wished to update himself with her presence, he had no trouble speaking to her as though speaking to just another slave.

They walked the streets of Brusa beneath striped awnings, upon which the lowering sun played. The windows of the shops were framed with Persian and Kurd carpet, in squares of gold-and-silver embroidery. Sultan Hasam, in his plain gray business suit, followed Jessica, trailing behind her by several carefully measured paces. In her plain black *feridje* and *yashmac*, Jessica might have been just another Turkish wife on a shopping spree, except that six eunuchs walked with her. She wondered if that was quite as usual as the Sultan believed. She stopped at a display of Brusa brocade and flowing white Turkish towels, using the chance to drop back to where the Sultan stood.

"Why do you stay behind me?" she asked in a whisper, not wanting to break any local taboos.

He whispered back, "Because in Turkey the husband must walk behind his wife."

Serviceably he pushed her forward and they continued walking. So she hardly saw him all afternoon as they toured the marketplace in their disguises. Jessica walked in front of him, aware of his presence, but only able to see him from time to time. They inspected animal skins being sold from a wagon, and laughed when a shepherd came running through the crowded streets after a bleating lamb that had bolted from his flock on the way to the auction. Here in Brusa the marketplace was more primitive than those she had seen in the bigger arenas of Constantinople and Damascus. The smells were different too. Camels and donkeys were used as pack animals rather than horses, which had grown popular in the cities because of Western influence. Chickens nodded about between the legs of buyers, pecking at crumbs on the ground. And children—they ran freely here, for almost every business involved the entire family in the lesser economy of the small town.

Jessica hoped Sultan Hasam was noticing the faces of his people, the arguments going on, the bartering, the laughter of the children, the squawling of babies in their mothers' arms, the beauty of diversity here, which she had seen in every city square since Charles brought her to the East.

Guilt nudged her. She hadn't thought of Charles for days—how many days? Worse . . . while escape was still part of her plans, she could hardly imagine herself spending her lifetime at Charles's proper, sedate, extremely British side. Could she spend her life in an embassy, a little transplantation of England, and pretend she was happy serving tea and fending off pinches from weathered old diplomats? Could she ever again avoid bursting in on a political discussion when she heard the Sultan mentioned, or harems, or the revolutionaries, or insurrection, or—

"Come this way." The Sultan's elegant voice.

She turned at once. Towering above her were the spires of an ancient mosque, built upon the ruins of an old Byzantine church. Now the Sultan did approach her, took her arm, and led her into the long, elaborately tiled corridor. The tiles were Persian, formed and baked in every shade of green, from apple to viridian, from cypress to jade. Prayer niches added concave shadows to the gold-filigreed walls, and above, as she walked with the Sultan, Jessica saw a ceiling as high as the sky, etched and painted with glorious scenes of worship that must have taken a fortune to create. Their footsteps echoed in delicate throbs. In the center of the mosque was a massive marble fountain encrusted with porcelain. Its murmuring water trickled an endless hymn.

Jessica's senses were stolen by the ancient beauty. When she turned to Sultan Hasam, the effects shone plainly in her eyes. She had no words for the majesty of this place.

"I knew you would come to understand," the Sultan said when he saw her face. "I am beginning to understand things also."

"Are you?" she asked hopefully.

"Many things. Today I am nothing but a businessman touring the streets. Tonight I shall become the Sultan once again, but I shall be in charge of my Empire. I have hidden myself in the palace too long. It is time for me to truly govern my land once again."

Hasam's square face and straight lips held his eyes like an oyster holds it pearls, and Jessica believed she saw a different man than the spoiled, cloistered individual in the fancy clothes who had every whim adored by herds of slaves. She reveled in the idea that she might actually be having an effect upon his way of thinking, his way of perceiving his people. Was it possible that she, that Jessica Grey, could deflect a bloody revolution merely by changing the viewpoint of this important man? Could a single woman—a slave—gather to herself that much raw power? Oh, if only Tarik could be here to witness this. Then he would see what his little pawn had learned to do! And he would realize there were other ways than violence to turn the trail of history.

Jessica smiled.

Moonlight played across the grounds of the second seraglio in the heart of Brusa. Jessica was watching the moonlight, dreaming of her success with Sultan Hasam and lathering herself in compliments when a movement in the courtyard stole her attention.

Below, strangely dressed men began to mingle at the gates of the house. They moved hauntingly, as though rehearsing a dance. She gazed at them for a moment, then inhaled sharply. Dervishes—just like the men who had attacked her. Were they here to kill her? Or the Sultan? She gripped the windowsill when the dervishes began to file, one by one, into the house.

A touch on her shoulder made her jump. It was the Kislar.

"If you wish you may join the Sultan for a private ceremony."

"Oh . . . yes," she said. Her voice quivered.

The Kislar looked down onto the grounds and said, "Those men outside are dervishes. Real ones. They are holy men, here to advise His Majesty. Nothing to be afraid of."

Jessica knew well enough that the men who attacked her had been disguised as dervishes. When the bodies were removed from her apartments, it had been discovered that their outerwear was dervish clothing, but the clothes beneath were those of soldiers. With conditions in the ranks as they were, the assassins might have come from anywhere, anyone. Soldiers could be easily bought these days.

She went with the Kislar through the dim hallways of the seraglio, chilled by the eerie howls of jackals who wandered the outskirts of the town, scavenging for food in any form. Even in the palm of civilization the primitive past was never far behind in the East. She wondered what the Kislar meant when he said "private ceremony." Perhaps the Sultan was about to make Usta's prediction come true. Perhaps Jessica would no longer be able to evade a night of intercourse with the monarch. She began to prepare her mind, her soul, her consciousness for whatever might come. She'd had to do that so many times, she began to wish it could just happen and be over with. Then she could deal with it in the past tense, as a truth, instead of in the future tense, as a threat.

The corridor was long and dark. The faint sound of chanting voices and muted drumbeats filtered in between Jessica and the howling of the jackals. The mystic orchestration beckoned them deeper into the darkness.

The sounds grew louder. A small wooden door fell into the Kislar's reach, and he opened it for her. Immediately came a flood of long, inhuman wails and shrieks and the clatter of cymbals behind heartlike drumbeats. Jessica automatically brought the veil up around her face as they entered what appeared to be a kind of chapel.

The dervishes stood on a surprisingly large and solid platform in the center of the room, chanting drunkenly to the drumbeat. Jessica could not help but stare at them as the Kislar led her along the wall to a latticed chamber meant for the woman. On the other side of the room Sultan Hasam sat beside the astrologer. The Sultan saw her and gave her a slow nod just before she slipped into the latticed chamber.

There she sat alone.

The dervishes began to twirl, their skirts fanning out around their legs. They chanted muddled words to the cadence.

From outside her chamber the Kislar explained to her what was happening.

"They are saying a prayer for the great ones, for all who are in authority over them. Sultan Hasam is faced with grave decisions, and they pray he will find guidance."

Jessica pompously thought he had found guidance, but even as she thought it, she suddenly knew better. The Sultan had been faced with more influential people—men *and* women—over decades of his rule. She was abruptly aware of the Sultan's garb, once again the regal robes of a monarch, and wondered what else she had let slip away. "What decisions?" she demanded.

"Things that do not concern you. Things of a political nature."

Yet Hasam had asked her here for some reason. Jessica tried to think of what it might be. Was she here not for the ceremony itself but for afterward?

The Sultan left his chair and went to the platform where the dervishes danced around him in a gyrating circle. They frantically began to spread their own arms and faces with talcum while performing their crazed oscillations to the drumbeat. Their skirts, pleated like accordions and cut in immense widths, mushroomed outward from their legs. They were exciting, frightening, dazing.

Jessica slid forward on her seat, interlacing her fingers in the latticework, and whispered urgently, "What things? Tell me!"

But the Kislar remained silent. The dervishes spun and spun.

At their center Sultan Hasam's obsidian eyes grew vacant, as though the dervishes were sapping his strength with every twirl, drawing his power of decision right out of his body. The dancers inclined their heads slightly to their right shoulders, took on a kind of grace, and whirled even faster, until their inflated garments began to whistle like the wind.

Jessica felt cold. She drew her knees together and wished to be back in her own apartments if she couldn't be back in England. She felt acutely foreign and out of place.

She jolted as the drumbeat abruptly stopped. The dervishes dropped prostrate to the floor. Jessica dared not even breathe.

The Sultan hovered at the center of the prostrate dancers until every pleat, every fold, had deflated and lay flat upon the body of its wearer. He seemed entranced. Gazing upon the forms below him, he brought his sense of nationality back into himself and raised his eyes to no one but the helpless ears of his Empire.

He began to speak, his voice full and majestic, round words in Turkish.

The Kislar whispered, "He says it is time for the Sultan to rule, to take control of the Empire. There can be no more dissension . . . no more insurrections . . . He says the revolutionaries must be wiped out . . . the revolutionaries and all who support them."

The force of Mustapha's voice escalated—louder, stronger.

Jessica pressed hard against the lattice. "Tell me what he says. Everything!"

The Kislar nodded. There was no help now. She might as well know. "On the dawn of the Feast of the Flowers the army will march into the Armenian quarter against the revolutionaries. No one will be spared . . . none forgiven."

Jessica bolted to her feet, as though she meant to break through the screen and demand an explanation of His Imperial Majesty. On her first angry breath the Kislar cut her intentions down with a look and a simple truth. "Nothing you do or say will change anything."

She stared at the Sultan, who was still rambling on in Turkish like a giant among ants. In her mind she put everything together.

"You have to get me back to the palace."

The Kislar's eyes grew wide within his inkblack face. "That's impossible."

"You have to help me," Jessica begged, insisted, demanded. If she ever had any power as a *quzdeh* woman, she would have to use it now. "You have to get me back. Tell him I'm sick. Tell him whatever you have to tell him, but get me out of this place and back to the palace—now!"

CHAPTER THIRTEEN

The motorcar reentered the palace grounds with little ceremony. When it stopped, only Jessica and the Kislar emerged.

Jessica rushed immediately to her own apartments where her personal slave, Lanie, and several other slave girls were making small repairs on her lavish wardrobe. The only other figure in the room was a tall, disturbed form standing at the window, his back to her as she entered.

"You may all leave now," she said immediately to the stunned slaves.

"Do you want food or—" Lanie began.

"Nothing. Just leave me. Everybody"—when Tarik turned around, she met him with a multifaceted gaze—"except you."

The gaze became a stare, shared uneasily between them as the slaves filed quickly from the room. Jessica's eyes burned with anticipation, Tarik's with incense.

They were alone.

"Where," Tarik began, "have you been?"

"Brusa," she said.

"With Sultan Hasam?"

"Yes . . . of course. Why?"

"Why didn't you tell me?" In his voice came a quiver of anger, or concern, or a half dozen other undefinable disturbances. His eyes appeared glazed to Jessica as she looked at him from across the carpet.

For an instant she forgot why she was here, forgot herself entirely except for the reflection she saw in his face. "There wasn't time."

He lashed out with his deep, English-touched inflections. "How can I protect you if I don't know where you are?"

Jessica paused, trying to focus in on his anger. Her eyes narrowed a tiny bit, and she tipped her head. "Why are you acting like this?"

"Like what?"

For several moments she didn't know how to answer that, how to clarify what she read in his tone and his eyes, but when she spoke again, perhaps there was more hope working there than interpretation. Quietly she said, "As if you care for me."

Tarik closed his mouth, pressing his lips tight. He turned and moved away. After a moment he collected himself and turned back, sensing that her presence here was no casual whim of the Sultan's. He remembered now—now that his head had cleared—how she had come running into the apartment with need in her eyes and insisted upon speaking to him alone. Softly he asked, "What was it you wanted to tell me?"

She moved to him urgently now, crossing the carpet in three long steps. "Tarik, you were right about him . . . Hasam. About everything." At first she sounded desperate and realized it. Gathering her courage, she announced, "I want to help you. No, don't say anything. Just listen. In three weeks, as the harem prepares for the Feast of Flowers, the army will prepare for a massacre in the Armenian quarter."

Before her, Tarik Pasha turned to stone. At first she expected him to call her out for lying, for leading him on and making him believe that perhaps Sultan Hasam was affected by her presence and her words. A coldness covered his eyes as she watched, a horror beyond horrors, for they both knew the Armenian quarters were too large to be effectively evacuated without triggering the slaughter. Even Jessica, who felt so deeply for the people she thought Sultan Hasam had spared, had no real perception of what would happen until she saw the picture of it growing in Tarik's expression.

"Tarik . . ." she murmured, and reached for him.

But he was gone. Out—into the garden. She followed him without a moment's pause.

They sat in the garden for a long time. For a while all they did was stare at the lush foliage, feeling impotent against the menace lurking all around them, drenched in splendor. Jessica felt supremely foolish for having believed she could change the Sultan so completely that he would never revert to a way of life he had cherished for decades. She admitted all this to herself, knowing she was different from the woman who had stepped from the train in Damascus with her father and Charles. The world seemed clearer now—purposes, forces of will, the effects of simple decisions on people's very lives, all resounded in her head with new poignancy. The Sultan's effect on the lives of all his people, on any he felt might endanger his reign, would be felt with blade-keenness.

"I'm sorry for all this," she said to Tarik when only the crickets were speaking.

"It's not your fault," he said. He was unable to keep the dejection out of his words. "If anyone's, it's probably mine. I should've hidden the Young Turks away in a farther place." He sighed then. "But assigning blame does nothing to stop the slaughter. I only wish there was some way to at least get the children out, but that would cause a panic." He gazed up now, toward the starry sky and the pastel moon it held, wishing to be as peaceful as the moon and as ineffectual. "Many people have died because of me in recent weeks. I try not to think about it, but I always see the children's faces. Whenever there's trouble in the world, the children always pay the biggest price of pain and fear and sorrow . . . and children shouldn't have pain."

He stopped talking quite suddenly, so suddenly that Jessica looked up at him.

"This is more than just an ideal for you . . . this revolution," she said. "Isn't it?"

The moon fluttered in his eyes as he blinked. "Sometimes it seems to be all I think about . . . all I've ever thought about."

"It means that much to you?"

Before her very eyes there in the garden, Jessica saw a man reexamine himself. Tarik felt back through time to where it all began for him, the moment the urge to change things—the perception of the old order—first fused within his being. Such things seldom come gradually, nor with the impact he had felt when the revolutionary fervor first startled his mind and heart. It was a cruel way to get purpose in life.

Quietly, speaking only to himself at first, Tarik gave Jessica the gift of his past so that she, too, might understand without really feeling the pain for herself. It was a gift he had given only to Salim and a very few precious others. As he fell within himself he took her with him.

"There was a funeral pyre after a long siege. A battle that had no purpose . . . at least, I never knew the purpose. There weren't any burials that month . . . there were too many to bury." He stopped, cleared his throat, and labored on. Somehow the telling was harder this time. "The day before, my family had been hiding from the soldiers. We took refuge in a mosque—my father, my mother, my three sisters, and a hundred or so others. We didn't think we would be harmed in there. Even Imperial soldiers knew better than to desecrate a holy place with the blood of innocents. It was an unwritten law. The mosque provided sanctuary. We Turks are of many religions, but for the most part we fear each other's gods as much as our own." Here he shrugged, knowing it sounded silly but also knowing it was an inevitability where cultures meet head-on. As he continued, the words became tighter, more solemn. "But even the unwritten laws were broken that day."

Jessica's hands gripped the edge of the marble bench beneath her. She sensed, even knew, what was coming, and longed to touch Tarik, help him through it. But that would have been an invasion . And she had learned much about privacy since coming here.

Tarik now lowered his eyes, as though what he was about to say might be too sad for the moon to hear. "When the soldiers stormed the doors, my mother covered me with her own body and took the bullets meant for all of us. I remember little else . . . except for the funeral pyre. I remember that very well. My entire family had been killed, but I couldn't see their bodies through the flames, no matter how hard I looked. They became nothing. Indistinguishable. Lost with countless other dead."

"Oh, Tarik . . ." Jessica mourned with him, shared his hurt.

"Even though I was very young," he said decisively, "I knew that, at least in death, there should be some dignity. And as I grew older I began to believe there should be dignity in life

as well." Now he looked straight at her, strongly
and boldly, with the firmness of expression she
had come to recognize as uniquely his. He was
no longer afraid, no longer mournful. Something had replaced all that quite suddenly.

Jessica reached out, almost unknowingly, and
touched his cheek. She lay her palm against his
dark, smooth face with its shade of whiskers
and felt the life in this man who somehow was
spared death like the children he wished to
spare now.

Tarik moved to close the space between them.
He put his arms around her, and she lay,
drained, against his chest. They held each other
until the crickets grew tired of their own song
and the moon had risen high into the velvet
night's blackness.

His kiss, when it came slowly through the
mutual sadness, wasn't totally unexpected. Certainly it was well received. Jessica let herself
sink against him. The night now wrapped them
up in its warmest cloak, a cloak of impending
love that seldom had touched the seraglio.
Though a place of passion, the seraglio knew
precious little of real love, of a bonding of senses
and sensibilities, of intellects and ideals. Like
Sultan Hasam himself, the moon over Yildiz
was a stranger to love of the heart. Jessica clung
to Tarik in that kind of tender mutuality, hardly
aware of the change when he began absently
stroking her hair, her shoulders, her back
through the silk gown, her arms, and finally
even her outer thighs. Jessica discovered herself

swelling into Tarik's touch, barely aware of the dark lashes shuttering his eyes as she nestled against his ear and looked up into his face. Awash with moonlight, he no longer seemed the dusty Bedouin—or an Eastern type at all. Gray-blue in the night, his features seemed inanimate, frozen in peace for all time, and Jessica longed desperately to help him stay that way. If only he could forget. . . .

She raised her hand to his cheek and cupped it. Not really surprising, her skin had turned opaque also, and seemed unreal now. That made things easier, the idea of not being quite real at this strange and mystical moment. It was a bizarre kind of lovemaking, this entwining of the hearts with a mere fringe of physical joining. He never really invaded her, after all, and Jessica never knew exactly when the moment of change came—the moment when she started loving him with her whole heart. They touched and stroked and reassured each other without ever crossing the long bridge to consummation. But that enticing voyage was on their minds, to be sure, like a star just within reach.

Tarik's arms tightened around her in a loving tease of ownership, not the kind of ownership espoused by his culture from man to woman— not that kind of misuse. The chains of this kind of slavery were made of flowers, with warm little serpents coiling softly against, within, around each other. There was nothing predatory here. Jessica felt the generosity of his embrace, smelled the mannish scents of his body, felt the firmness of his jaw against the bridge of her nose, and pressed her face into the soft underside of his chin with a wonderful intimacy. It felt so good. Was it wrong?

He continued to stroke away her doubts, until her thighs had slid up onto his and she was sitting across his lap, curled against him like a kitten. Cherishing the trust she had in him then, Tarik closed his eyes and drew in a long breath, then sighed and started slowly rocking, back and forth, back and forth. He would sell his soul to own free and clear the peace he felt in these moments here with her. Crazy dreams filled his head, dreams of carrying her away from this place, far away, out of the desert and far from Turkey, far from the Ottoman Empire, until those words became meaningless. Never had he come closer to abandoning his cause and the people who depended on him. It wasn't fair, after all. Right was right. It shouldn't all be lying on his shoulders. He was human too . . . a man with needs, with cold places in need of spark. Sadly he caressed Jessica's head in the palm of his hand, losing his fingers in her hair. Maybe she was asleep. He hoped so.

When the night air became a chilly breath, he lifted her into his arms, cradling her, knowing he could not protect her much longer. Step by step, each movement a lingering wish, he carried her back into the gilded cage.

The Kadin looked into her mirror. There she saw lines around eyes which once had been

flawless. She saw brackets around her once perfect mouth. Her tresses were still long but now
had to be rinsed with henna to imitate the glow
they once possessed on their own. And all this
for a Sultan who rarely looked at her anymore.
Now she had to surround herself with teenage
bodies as bait for his attentions, when once her
own body would have been enough. She was
still beautiful, but she was no longer young.
The realm of the harem demanded youth—the
only thing she needed and could not possibly
buy.

With pearl-handled scissors she clipped a small
strand of hair from the braid lying over her
shoulder and placed it on a piece of glass. She
gazed at it for a moment, as though imbuing it
with her personal will, then carefully and slowly
began chopping it into fine bits, as a cook might
chop celery. Beside her, she heard the satisfying crunch of glass being ground up in a mortar. She needn't look to see that her slave girl
was grinding the glass correctly. This girl had
done it before.

Once the glass was ground and the hair was
finely chopped, the Kadin ceremoniously joined
the two ingredients into a small vial. Then she
went to have her bath.

Jessica awakened with a start. Beside her on
the divan, Tarik also jolted awake. Both were
aware of an extra presence in the room and
instantly sought it out—there. Lanie, standing

at the doorway, holding a tray of coffee. She was staring at them.

Slowly Jessica realized she had been curled up against Tarik and that she was still wearing her clothes from yesterday. His warmth beside her was a magnet. She wished to sink into it. But Lanie . . .

"This is not what it seems," she began feebly, smoothing her clothing.

Lanie took hold of herself with surprising aplomb and continued serving the coffee as she had intended to do. "Favored ladies have affairs— of sorts—with their eunuchs all the time," she said, though she no longer met Jessica's eyes. "What are your choices?" she went on, placing the silver coffeepot on the small inlaid table beside the divan and filling two cups. "You can have another woman or half a man. What can you do when Sultan Hasam can be so long between visits?"

Relieved that Tarik's integrity of manhood had not come into question, Jessica still felt a little embarrassed. So did Tarik, judging from his expression as he sat up.

"Thank you, Lanie," Jessica said, dismissing her with the tone of voice. "You may see to the baths."

Lanie straightened from the table, then nodded. "Also, the Kadin sends a message. She wishes that you join her for tea and sweets this afternoon. She will send Usta for you. With your permission I will prepare your frock for the affair."

But Jessica was looking at Tarik.

By the time her robes and veil were laid out, Jessica had almost completed writing out what very well could be a suicide note if it fell into the wrong hands. She sat at an ornate desk, hurriedly scribbling, while Tarik kept a lookout at the door. Finally she put down the pen. "Everything I saw, and what the Kislar told me," she recited, looking over the note. "The Young Turks will be attacked by the soldiers in a dawn raid in the Armenian quarters."

"It must go to Salim," Tarik said, thinking hard.

"But how do we get it out of here?" she asked, approaching him. "Since the attack on the Treasury, no one's been allowed in or out of the palace, not even the eunuchs."

"It can't go out through a bribe," Tarik told her in anticipation of her next suggestion. "It's much too volatile."

"Perhaps I can arrange a few moments of freedom for you—"

A knock at the door interrupted her. Jessica quickly slipped the note into the folds of her *feridje*.

Usta stepped in the door. "Ready?

"In just a few minutes," Jessica said, and went to dress, holding the precious note against her side.

Within that hour Jessica was riding with Usta and Tarik in one of a thousand caïques dotting the Bosporus. Tarik rowed laboriously over the surface of the rough water. The small skiffs

were perfect for the Bosporus—small yet steady
and seaworthy. Jessica and Usta had a fairly
unruffling ride. Finally Tarik rowed them into a
narrow estuary between two grassy banks and
maneuvered the caïque toward the shore. Upon
the green grass and against a background of
cypress groves and cemetery ruins, dozens of
veiled women laughed and talked and played
with their children. This was the place of women,
a place to come out into the sunlight with their
parasols and their veils and their tidbits of gossip, safe under the watchful eyes of eunuchs.
Itinerant vendors wandered among the chatting
groups, enticing the women with their trinkets
and paper kites and windmills and sweetmeats.

It was a beautiful pastorale, and Jessica might
have been happy to stay in the caïque forever,
eternally floating on the blue water, watching
peace unfold.

"There is an old saying," Usta said, rather
unexpectedly, "that once you taste the waters
of the Bosporus, you will never cease to long
for them. It's been true for me."

She looked at Jessica. Something had been
bothering her all morning. Jessica felt it bub-
bling to the surface and self-consciously looked
away from Tarik.

Usta opened her eyes wide, saying, "It's past
time for you to taste the waters. You know
what you have to do."

"I understand," Jessica said, hoping Usta did
not elaborate, but Usta was in a mood to tell
things as they must be told.

She squeezed Jessica's hand. "I hope the Sultan has not lost interest. You cannot put him off again."

Tarik suddenly stopped rowing. He looked at Jessica, and his gaze was magnetizing. Soon she felt compelled to return it.

His eyes were a mesh of insult and relief—she had lied to him with her silence, let him believe his suppositions. She had not yet slept with Sultan Hasam—somehow she had avoided it! The amazement in his heart and his mind showed clearly on the surface.

Jessica broke the stare. Why was she ashamed for *not* giving in? Had this revelation made her stronger, or weaker, in Tarik's eyes? She hardly knew how she felt about it anymore, much less what he was feeling.

Land grated under the caïque, jarring them out of their self-concern. Tarik set his lips in a line and went about docking up to the small private landing where the caïque fit in among a dozen others. He helped Usta out of the boat, then reached for Jessica's hand, but he did not meet her eyes anymore.

On the shore, bright yellow mats had been spread out for the ladies of the Imperial Harem. At their center, beneath the fronds of a cypress tree, sat the Kadin, merrily laughing and gossiping—with Lady Ashley.

Jessica tore her eyes away from the Englishwoman, forcing herself to appear casual and content. Now Tarik did look at her. They knew she would be their carrier pigeon: luck had taken a hand in a cause that somehow had become hers almost as much as it was his. Jessica thought fast. How to get Tarik and Lady Ashley together?

She flopped her hand delicately at him. "Bring me some sweetmeats and a few trinkets—anything you think might amuse an Englishwoman."

At first Tarik seemed confused, but then he nodded and slipped away into the crowd.

Jessica grinned to herself about how much she sounded like an Eastern woman. Amuse an Englishwoman indeed!

She and Usta approached the Kadin slowly. The Kadin watched them for some sign of recognition, keeping her eyes resolutely on Jessica's face, but there was nothing. Nothing at all.

"My dears," the Kadin greeted, "please join us. It's so hot in the sun."

"Yes," Jessica said, "it is. But I've always liked the sun."

A young girl came to sit on one of the nearby mats and began plucking a gypsy mandolin. After a few chords she entered with a song. Her voice was high-pitched and fluttering, exquisitely Oriental. For a long time the four women merely listened. Jessica was pointedly aware of the fact that the Kadin hadn't introduced them to Lady Ashley by name. Of course not—it would be the perfect way to initiate a slip on their parts, to cause them to accidentally show their knowledge of each other. Privately she vowed that any mistakes would not be hers. Her escape from the palace might be through the channel of death, but it would *not* be to the satisfaction of the Kadin.

While they listened to the song Tarik delivered a tray of trinkets and little gifts draped with a handkerchief. Jessica thanked him coldly—a calculated coldness, of course—and inspected the gifts, rearranging them, checking them for quality.

"How long have you been in the harem?" Lady Ashley asked her then, while Usta and the Kadin kept anxious watch over the conversation for two different reasons.

"I don't really know," Jessica said. "Time has lost all meaning."

"Then you've learned to endure the endless waiting?"

"There's nothing endless about it. It's a way of living."

Lady Ashley smiled. "I think that's what I admire most about harem women. They have learned to be content."

Jessica shrugged noncommittally and saw anger rise in the Kadin's face. "Women weave waiting songs. It's in our nature."

"How poetic!" Lady Ashley turned to the Kadin, playing the pretense for all it was worth. "She's quite lovely, my dear."

The Kadin's cheeks stiffened around gritted teeth. "Isn't she?"

The singer's voice rose as the song reached its reprise, and the four women turned back to the entertainment. Jessica immediately slipped the critical note from her *feridje* into the handkerchief on the tray and folded up the linen corners. Tarik was watching her—she could feel it—but she carefully avoided returning the look.

The song ended. The woman applauded with practiced delicacy. The Kadin accepted a silver coffeepot from a slave girl and, one by one, filled four china cups, each on its own tiny silver tray.

Jessica handed the folded hanky to Lady Ashley. "Thank you for the compliment. Please take this as a token of my regard."

Lady Ashley smiled. The instant her hand closed on the linen, she felt the substance within and nearly gave it away. Recovering almost instantly, she nodded an exaggerated nod at Jessica and tucked the gift into her handbag.

The Kadin clapped her hands. "Play us another song. And a dance—show us a dance!"

The girl with the mandolin hardly let a heartbeat pass before she was playing again. Several slave girls, dark flowers with veils for petals, began dancing a traditional Turkish dance.

Quite relieved now, Jessica relaxed and watched the dance without distraction.

Under cover of the entertainment, the Kadin's hand moved from within her *feridje* to the coffee cup nearest Jessica. The movement was graceful, fluid, unnoticeable.

The mandolin changed its tune, and the dancers began a strangely Oriental version of a Western dance, dancing together like boy and girl, even though no boys were available.

"The latest Paris rage right here on the

Bosporus!'' Lady Ashley laughed. ''They're delightful!''

The Kadin lifted the coffee cup and extended it to Jessica. ''Jessica, some coffee.''

''Thank you . . . perhaps later.''

''I insist.''

Jessica looked at her, then gestured to Lady Ashley. ''Our guest first.''

''But you are my honored guest,'' the Kadin said sternly.

''I'm honored to be considered your guest.''

''It becomes bitter when it gets cold, my dear.''

''I must confess, though,'' Jessica said, ''that one thing I've never grown accustomed to is the Turkish coffee. Hot or cold, it seems bitter to me. I wouldn't want you to waste your efforts on so unappreciative a palate.''

''But this is a new blend—'' the Kadin said struggling on.

Usta interrupted. ''A more appreciative palate than mine cannot be found.'' She took the cup from the Kadin's hand, lay back, and took a long sip of the coffee.

The Kadin held her breath, watching Usta swallow the coffee. Then she, too, leaned back against a pile of silk pillows.

''It's a lovely afternoon,'' Lady Ashley said.

The dancers kept on dancing.

Later that same evening Charles poured over Jessica's note again and again, absorbed in her handwriting, her words—terse as they were— and the overlying awareness of the experiences she must be having to know these things. Sultan Hasam—she knew what he was thinking. Had she climbed so high in the palace power structure? He tried to imagine the Jessica he knew and couldn't see her exercising the patience and steadiness such a feat would require. And this talk of the revolutionaries . . .

He frowned. "I can't believe she would involve herself in insurrection. I can't accept it."

"Then tell me who wrote this note?" Lady Ashley challenged.

"It's her handwriting," Charles acknowledged, "but what does that prove?"

"Perhaps Jessica *has* become involved. The woman I saw today was very much in control of herself."

"What if Tarik has no intention of helping her escape? What if he's using her as a political pawn—"

"Charles, don't you trust Jessica?"

"Of course. Always."

"Then *trust* Jessica." Lady Ashley folded the note and stood up.

"Where are you going?" Charles asked.

"I have a message to deliver," she told him with stern resolution.

"But if you take that message to the revolutionaries, you put Jessica's life in even greater danger!"

The older woman's steady eyes embarrassed him. She gazed at him for several long moments, then spoke. "Jessica knew that. The choice is hers. None of us can determine history."

Charles felt betrayed. His shoulders sagged. "Has this become a matter of politics for you too?"

"My dear Charles," she said, "for me nothing is ever as simple as politics."

Thus, the note was delivered. To stop it in its course, Lady Ashley believed, would be a much bigger betrayal than to stay it in favor of one person's safety, especially when Jessica made quite clear her willingness to lay her life on the line for the lives of so many others. Definitely not the same Jessica who thought of escaping to the towers of Palmyra when her only captors were an adoring fiancée and a doting father.

On the open countryside outside of Constantinople, deep within the green-cloaked hills, more than a hundred deserting soldiers had come to join the revolutionaries. New recruits rode into camp every day, but the rebel army still lacked the single cog that would set their machine to work: They had no leader.

"It's not enough," Salim said, taking the unwelcome role upon himself in Tarik's absence as he scanned the encampment.

"It's more than we expected," Misha said.

"We can't make a stand against Sultan Hasam's army with barely a hundred men."

"Then what do we do?"

Salim considered. What would Tarik think of? Almost instantly the answer came to him. More men, obviously. And where to get more men? "We need Murat and his troops. Without him we have no chance."

"But he's made no commitment to us."

"He's going to have to make a commitment," Salim decided, "one way or the other. And he's going to have to make it now. There is no more time."

Time, indeed, was running out all over the Empire, from the hills outside the city to the Palace of Yildiz on the cliffs of the Bosporus. From the gritty streets of the marketplaces to the plush Victorian apartments of the Hazinedar Usta.

As Jessica entered Usta's apartments she neither heard nor saw anything unusual at first. "Usta?" she called. Long hours had passed since her mentor had come to her, and Jessica had learned to be uneasy when things were out of place or time.

Usta wasn't home. Jessica turned to leave and was caught back by a strange sound from deep within the private baths. It was a muted sound, hard to distinguish from the bathwater trickling from the founts, but it was enough to call Jessica deeper into the apartments. Someone was sick. Retching.

Jessica moved slowly into the marble bath area, moving around the lattice partitions until she spied a bent form at one of the smooth pink tubs. She watched, frozen in horror, as Usta raised a bloodless hand and wiped a fine trickle of blood from her chin.

"Usta—dear God—"

The Kislar Agha summoned the court physician immediately once Jessica found him and told him of Usta's illness. A black curtain was strung across Usta's bed. On one side of it the Hazinedar lay nearly motionless, her face pale beyond recognition, while Jessica wiped her forehead with cool cloths. On the other side of the curtain the Kislar Agha stood, watching as the doctor examined Usta through carefully placed slits in the fabric. Usta's right arm drooped through one of the holes, and the doctor felt for her pulse. After a half hour of this kind of examination the physician shrugged and straightened up.

"This woman is very ill, but I cannot find the cause."

"Very well," the Kislar said, his expression dissolving into sorrow. "I thank you." Without further talk he escorted the doctor immediately from the private rooms.

Jessica sat helpless at Usta's side, watching as the illness grew steadily worse. Usta wrenched in pain frequently now, choked by an agony within her body that came in shuddering waves. Jessica held her hand through one of the waves, then implored, "Usta, please. Let me send for a real doctor."

"It will do no good."

"I'll arrange for a British doctor."

"He will find nothing." The older woman almost smiled through her pain at the confusion of Jessica's face. "Dear child . . . I've been poisoned."

The bolt of ice rammed through Jessica, chilling her hands as they held Usta's.

With some effort Usta nodded. "There can be no other explanation."

"But the doctor would have found something . . . some sign. . . ."

"There is one poison that is untraceable," Usta said, nearly choking on bloody bile. "An ancient mixture of chopped hair and ground glass served in sweet coffee. For hundreds of years it has been used in the harem to dispose of . . . rivals." The pain took her again. She stiffened upon the soft velvet coverlets, digging her fingernails into Jessica's skin.

Jessica was numb, staring. "The Kadin . . ."

"It doesn't matter. . . ."

"The coffee," Jessica whispered. "It was meant for me."

"The coffee was meant for all of us," Usta gushed in a single breath. "Go now. . . ."

Jessica shook her head. "I want to stay with you."

Somehow Usta managed one more smile, from mentor to pupil, and taught Jessica one thing more before the lesson must end. "Go. There will be many dreams," she struggled, "before the final one."

The corridor was cold, empty. The silent line of eunuchs had become little more to Jessica that fixtures on the walls. She moved past them, resolve growing with each quickening step, and the tears streaming down her cheeks became fountains of courage.

She found Tarik in her apartments and clung to him desperately, purging herself of every last sob before a great single thrust of courage could replace the grief. Tarik didn't understand, but he held her tightly, for this might be the last time—and still they hadn't even had a beginning.

"I want you to go," she said, drying her tears on his robe. "I want you to go back to your people. They need you more than I do. If you're not with them, it's my fault if they die."

"Jessica," he began, "I made a vow not to leave you here."

"You didn't make it to me. And I'm the only one who can decide. You don't understand." She lifted her head and found his inner self with her wet eyes. "It's changed for me. The Armenians and the Young Turks aren't nameless faces anymore. Their screams can't be covered by the shrieking parrots. I still hear the voices . . . Usta's voice . . . yours . . . my own."

Unsure, Tarik stroked the tears from her cheeks.

"You have to go to them, Tarik," she insisted. "You have to go to your men."

For the first time since she first laid eyes on him during the raid on the train, Jessica saw uncertainty flow behind his expression. "It's too dangerous to risk an escape. . . ."

"For both of us, yes. But you can escape alone."

"That's out of the question. I gave my word. I'm not leaving without you."

Angered by his devotion, Jessica gripped the front of his robe in both fists. "Tarik, you sold me for twenty men. You can leave me now for the lives of thousands. We both know that only you can make the revolution happen."

"If I go," Tarik began, struggling to keep his hands at his sides, "you put yourself at great risk. . . ."

"And if you don't, then all the deaths will be because of me. You can't make me live with that," she told him in a strong whisper.

"Jessica—"

She pushed him away and deepened the space between them with a few backward steps. "You'll come back for me."

The words were so simple, so rife with conviction and trust, that Tarik felt weakened by them. He ached to hold her, to finalize this strange bond between them with something physical, but if he touched her now, he might never be able to let go.

She wanted two worlds, he read in her eyes. Wanted him to stay, wanted him to go. Her heart wanted both. Her mind demanded only one.

Before the breaking point drove him into her arms, Tarik wrenched himself away and walked out of her life.

The transformation was almost instantaneous.

A day later Tarik Pasha became once again the dashing revolutionary in the noticeable frock coat of the Young Turks, riding astride his lean white desert horse with Salim riding at his side. He hardly remembered how he got out of the palace grounds—he hardly cared. He divorced himself from the past few weeks with a cold knife that sliced out Jessica and the Palace of Yildiz and his vow to free her, and left his heart bleeding. Never before had anyone convinced him to break a pledge. Resentment for Jessica roiled within his unexpected attraction to her—yes, attraction. They were the same species now, himself and her. Too much alike for safety. Her bravery had startled him all over again. Just when he expected her to think of herself, she surprised him by sacrificing herself. No less than sacrifice—if she was in the palace when the revolution came, she had little chance to survive. The Sultan's soldiers would cut down anyone moving in the area, and Jessica would surely use those moments of chaos to try to escape. Tarik would do no less, and she had somehow become like him.

Murat met them at the appointed place. Tarik and Salim approached him, and immediately Tarik slid from the saddle and crossed to the big man, speaking even before he got to him. "We are forced to make our move. But without your armies we cannot succeed. What is your answer?"

If Murat was vacillating up until now about joining the revolution, the directness and conviction in Tarik Pasha's demeanor made his decision for him. "We are prepared," he said hesitantly, "to join you in your quest for a better government. Have you a plan?"

"Not a plan, exactly," Tarik admitted. "But at least we know what must be done first. Please . . . sit with us."

They moved to a soft mound of grass where Salim had spread a dilapidated map of greater Constantinople. The men knelt there. Murat watched while Tarik pointed out critical areas.

"The Sultan has ordered his army to march on the Armenian quarter," Tarik said. "He plans to make examples of them for harboring the Young Turks. They are to be slaughtered like pigs."

Salim burst in with, "That's why we must strike first!"

"Strike?" Murat grunted. "How?"

"At the palace. With your men and our own we can ride against Sultan Hasam."

Murat laughed openly now. "Storm the palace? With your handful of motley troops and my men—against the Sultan's army?" His laughter rolled across the hills. "Even for a writer your imagination exceeds itself."

Behind him, ignored until now, Murat's men also laughed. Salim's tawny complexion went beet-red.

Tarik silenced him with a look, then turned to Murat. "Is there a better way, then?"

"Perhaps," the soldier said. "The palace is a fortress, which gives Sultan Hasam and his men every advantage. But, once outside its gates—" He stopped and exchanged a gaze with Tarik.

"We have a much fairer fight," Tarik finished for him.

Murat smiled. In spite of their differences, he and this legendary rebel could think alike when it mattered. "We shall entrench ourselves throughout the Armenian quarter."

Salim's brow creased. "What?"

"As Hasam plans to send the Imperial Army into the quarter on the Feast of the Flowers, we can be ready for them. We can strike before they even know we are there." He looked at Salim then, and it was impossible to tell if he was joking or not. "Then, should we succeed, we can think about taking the palace, which should be considerably easier without the troops to defend it."

Confused and desperate now, Salim turned to Tarik. "But a fight in the Armenian quarter . . . how are we to protect the women . . . the children?"

Murat waved his hand. "We cannot help the loss of lives."

"These people have hidden us! Protected us!"

"People die in revolutions, Salim—" Murat said.

"That's enough," Tarik cut in. The decision, not an easy one, had to be made. "We shall try to get word to as many of the Armenians as we can—without risking discovery. I see no other way."

By that he was giving credence to Murat's idea. Murat looked at him but said nothing, no signal of approval or disapproval.

"You are with us, then?" Tarik asked him.

Murat wagged his finger. "That . . . I have *not* yet said."

Tarik gazed at this complicated man, wondering what Murat wanted. But a decision had to be made. Perhaps Murat could be influenced by forward movement.

Tarik rose to his feet. "Then I bid you good-bye."

"And I bid you good luck," Murat responded. With a snap of his fingers his men mounted their horses. In moments the deserters and their leader were moving across the hilly horizon, and disappeared.

"I still don't like him," Salim said.

"We need him." Tarik walked away. He went to his horse and reached for the saddlebag. The stallion snorted and bolted a few strides. Still half wild, the beast didn't like to be touched. Tarik murmured to him in Turkish and drew the eunuch's robes from the bag. Without a word he began to change clothes.

Salim appeared beside him and stood silent for a few moments before saying, "Oh, you're *not*."

"I don't want trouble from you, Salim."

"Tarik, we've nearly lost you . . . how many times? If you go back there, what are the chances you'll ever come out alive? Wasn't it enough to escape one time? Do you have to do it twice?"

"Salim, please. I'm going back."

"But why?" Salim's face grew red again. "Why go back now? You've been with us only a few days."

"I promised to deliver the woman."

Salim's hand closed on Tarik's arm and wrenched him around. "Is this Tarik Pasha talking? Don't you know half the Empire is preparing to die because of what you've been telling them? What will they think when you're not here to lead them, after all your big talk? Tarik—"

"Let go of me."

"Tarik, is there nothing I can say?"

"No. Nothing. Laying siege to the palace was a decision I had to make. No one will be safe there. I have no choice, Salim." He said it as though he really didn't, as though there existed no other course. Either he had sold his soul or given it away—neither of the two men was sure.

Salim stepped back as Tarik, once again dressed as a eunuch, swung into the saddle and pulled up on the reins, casting his friend one final look.

What he saw in Salim's face was something grown older, something quite worldly wise. The idealism was entirely gone.

Salim took his hand away from Tarik's stirrup, which he had touched in a last moment of physical contact before the final rupture. "Then things have truly changed for you."

Only a short count of steps from the place where she had been poisoned, Usta lay buried beneath a newly carved gravestone. The cypress trees murmured above in the light breeze, insensible, as a slow procession moved. Women of the Imperial Harem filed past the grave, as did a few friends and acquaintances from the city. Paid mourners wailed for Usta's soul as the women moved past the site and walked back to their caïques. The only male present was the Kislar, who stood near the grave with Lady Ashley.

Jessica moved through the line, numb and despondent, knowing that from now on her life was as insignificant as the melancholy ruins of ageless graves she walked between. All her life people had done things for her, tended and catered to her, and she had been well aware of her privileged position as Arthur Grey's daughter. She had always been given things. But no one had ever given up life because of her.

She was hardly aware of Lady Ashley shifting discreetly from the Kislar's side to a place where she would meet Jessica as the line progressed.

The Englishwoman's voice stirred Jessica's dull sensibilities.

"He's with his men," came the truncated whisper, and that was the end of it. Lady Ashley moved back to the Kislar's side.

That was one good thing, at least. Jessica felt a tiny light restore itself deep within the darkness of her empty soul. She, too, had given. She had sold her need for Tarik to the needs of others. And to this moment she felt nary a glimmer of regret—only a mournful sadness for what might have been, what *could* have been had Tarik been less than the one critical force in the revolution. Had he been anyone but Tarik Pasha, then there could be time to discover—

No.

There would never be time.

Jessica moved without feeling or sensation back to her caïque and sat in it like a statue as the eunuch rowed her across the blue Bosporus toward waters more turbulent than those beneath the bulky hull. From now on the waiting game of the harem would be like the cold grave Usta lay in. Jessica was ready.

Her apartments were dim. Lanie had known better than to prepare a cheery environment for Jessica to walk back into. It would do no good to pretend. Time would be the only help, even if death came at the end of it.

And the apartment was empty. A pot of coffee had been left for her, but she was being given the gift of solitude. She stripped off her shawl and dropped it on the floor while walking through the rooms to her bedroom. She shrugged the plush robe from her shoulders. It fanned out onto the rug behind her, sighed, and lay still. She stopped only when the windowsill pressed her thighs. Moonlight spread thinly over the Bosporus, showing the outlines of her body—thinner than yesterday—through the gauzy chemise. The sea breeze lifted her hair from the sides of her neck; she wished to feel it but couldn't. She couldn't feel anything anymore. Perhaps it was that she dared not feel. Could she numb herself so thoroughly that even death, when it came, would go unfelt? She tried to tell herself it was just the nearness of Usta's sudden, violent murder, but she was the real target and the Kadin was unlikely to miss the mark a second time. She would delude herself no longer about that. She had lost her chance with the Sultan and wondered now if it would have been so bad to make love to him— for a cause.

Jessica shook her head slightly at herself. For a cause. What would Tarik think of her now if he knew she was seeing herself in light of him? But that didn't matter. Usta was gone. The Sultan was lost to her. Tarik was gone. The Kislar had little power anymore. There was no one left to protect her, and she was no longer *quzdeh*.

But she had done it, hadn't she? She had given herself to a bigger ideal; she had sacrificed herself to the lives of those helpless people and handed them back her only hope so that it might become theirs. For that, at least, she was relieved.

If she died here, it wouldn't be because she was too stubborn to hand over her body to the Sultan. At least it would be for higher things.

She heard a noise behind her. At first she assumed it was the breeze ruffling something. When it happened again, she turned and looked to see what was disturbing her solitude. "Lanie?"

In the archway, a form.

They heard each other stop breathing.

Her voice swept across the patterns of the carpet.

"*Tarik.*"

He met her at the window. Their arms coiled around each other as the Bosporus sweeps the shore, and they melted together into human harmony.

Through challenge and resentment and the memory that he was the one who brought her here, Jessica floated until she reached the single star of commitment. There could be no more denial, no more questions. What can be asked when there are only two people in the world?

Tarik lost himself in her courage, forgetting all the other Tarik Pashas dueling each other within his soul. Her body was too soft to push away, her kisses too taking. He could no longer be the Tarik Pasha his people wanted him to be if he must do it without Jessica's strength of spirit to buffet him from his anchors.

Like an ancient play on some distance threshing floor, the man and the woman made a new creation for themselves, moving in that human melody through Jessica's apartments and into the garden. The moonlight tasted their nakedness and smiled. The stars winked. The breeze grew envious because it could not stop and feel.

Jessica felt the surging of passion and gave to Tarik all the benefits of Usta's experience, things she had been saving for the Sultan, but this time she could give without barrier or necessity, without worrying about how to hide her unwillingness. She was willing indeed.

She slid her thigh across his. For those moments her leg was as long as a kite string drawing itself along the wind. Tarik kissed her, then drew back, changing the moment. He traced her cheek with one venturing finger, showing her there need be no hurry in passion. He became the Eastern man, the slow-handed lover Usta had promised. Lifting her into his arms, he carried her, gently rocking, through her apartments and into the warm moisture of the baths where he stepped into one of the rose-scented pools and eased both their bodies into the water. Jessica floated in his arms. Their hearts pounded against each other, breasts to chest. Tarik ran his kisses around her neck, turning her over in the water, then kissed the whole length of her spine—a long and beautiful journey, kisses like those from bee to flower. Jessica's chemise floated up around her arms until it no longer concealed buoyant breasts. She reached up to hold him, and her hair fell across his face—in itself, a kind of caress.

His arms became tight around her ribs in a kind of possession Sultan Hasam had never known, he who owned all the eye could see. The chains of this slavery were soft and good, transformed from iron to softly coiling serpents writhing against each other. As his body changed and sought her, Tarik melted into Jessica. Dark lashes shuttered his eyes.

This lovemaking, Jessica knew, was nothing wild or enflamed or cannibalistic. This was a flowing series of thick, contoured moves, like membranes flexing in a tide of blood and flesh. It was a human experience, entirely beautiful because it was so fleeting. Usta had told her everything but this—that joy had its own sadness. In each caress of Tarik's hands upon her body, Jessica felt the emptiness that would come when they could no longer ignore the outside world. Now she knew why night was a time for lovers.

She closed her eyes and drifted into these wonderful sexual things, these grown-up things that she might never have felt if her life had gone on as planned. She explored Tarik with hands that Usta had trained and found the movements natural to her. Soon she forgot her training and simply moved as passion willed her.

Love or passion, need or desperation—neither could say what drove them together. Neither dared say anything, or they might also have to say that this first time could easily become the last. Each had another life elsewhere, and neither flesh nor spirit could change that. Jessica's whole self opened to Tarik, to the man whose inner soul she had come to know through these past strifes. Now she came also to know his body. She saw her own opaque skin press up against his bronze chest and golden arms. She felt their hearts pound against each other as the water surged and sucked at them in their pumping motions. They bore down upon each other.

They loved triply hard that night, struggling to keep the future out, to keep life in. For Jessica the overture was cleansing. Finally she was a lover! Finally she had climbed the mountain that had seemed so big. And to love Tarik . . . she knew now that a false passion might have damaged her forever if she had given herself to

Sultan Hasam, for she had felt nothing with him as she felt now. Her body took over and she was glad to let it. Her legs and hips and arms and mouth gave of themselves to Tarik, and he returned the gifts until the water sloshed and he arched his back, threw his head up, and laughed—actually laughed!

Jessica had never seen so pure a smile nor heard Tarik laugh. She leaned back in the water, still welded to him beneath the shimmering surface, and she began to laugh too.

The long night continued.

Dawn poured its buttery light through the window and touched Jessica's lightly veiled body as she drifted in and out of sleep in Tarik's arms. Time could end here, for all that mattered to her.

The brass handles on the doors clicked downward. Jessica roused herself and blinked in the dawn light. "Lanie?"

This time it really was the young servant who stepped in. The girl's face was ominously blank.

"Lanie?" Jessica asked again. "What is it?"

Lanie stepped aside. The door opened wider. In walked the Kadin and her entire entourage of ladies and eunuchs.

Sultan Hasam's first wife flowed into the room, smiling. "What have we here? How cozy. How luscious." She snapped her fingers at her eunuchs. "Take them."

Tarik dove for his robes, for his dagger, but the eunuchs descended too quickly, pinioning his arms in their trained grips and hauling him from the bed, naked, for all to see.

One of the eunuchs looked with a kind of bitter, envious victory at Tarik's naked body and announced, "This man is not what he pretends to be."

"All the better," the Kadin said.

Two other eunuchs had dragged Jessica from the quilts and now held her firmly before the Kadin as the elegant older woman surveyed her. Jessica struggled at first, but there was no point.

The Kadin's lined lips twisted into a grim smile. "Stupid, stupid little girl."

CHAPTER FOURTEEN

Jessica thought about how incredible it was
that a dejected man could still look dejected
even when wearing the world's brightest robes.
Also incredible how a quickly a woman could
go from queen to peasant and how hope can be
dashed to despair in the time it takes to crack a
whip.

The Sultan presided over a crowded court,
the wounds of disappointment glazing the dark
pools of his eyes. Before him stood the young
man who had breached the sanctity of the Imperial Harem with his manhood intact, who
had tempted with his wholeness the woman
Sultan Hasam longed to possess in more than
the terms of ownership. This man wore nothing
but a pair of trousers. Even his feet were bare.
His hands were tied. Next to him—Jessica, wearing only her chemise, no robe, no veil. And
now the Kadin sat where Jessica had once been
privileged to sit—the Kadin's final message.

The men of the court turned their faces away

from the unveiled woman. Only the Sultan lay his eyes upon her and did not move them as he pondered this betrayal, this transgression that, more than anything, showed him that he was finally getting old. Monarch or not, he could not summon time.

He rose, maintaining control with practiced regality, and moved to Jessica, trying to find shame in her eyes. None . . .

"Jessica," he murmured softly, with a barely perceptible shake of his head. To the men of his court he said, "Do not turn your heads away. I want you to look at this face." His finger traced her jawline. Then the pain returned, the insult, and he pushed her forward. "Gaze at it. Remember it. You will forever know the face of a traitor."

Without missing a beat the astrologer asked, "What shall be done with her?" His calm question belied an undercurrent of anxious thrill.

"How can there be any question?" the Kadin said, her breath fluttering the veil across her face. "She should be drowned in the Bosporus."

The Kislar, now out of favor on this political merry-go-round, spoke up impulsively. "It's been years since a ritual death—"

"It's been years," the Kadin insisted, "since a Sultan has been betrayed by a woman."

In the background, like echoes rolling through a nightmare, a chorus of dervishes began chanting in Turkish: "Drown her in the Bosporus, drown her in the Bosporus . . . drown her. . . .

Sultan Hasam scanned his court, affected

by the chanting, then looked at the Kadin as
though remembering something that existed now
only deep within the entrancement, then looked
at Jessica. With a slicing gesture he silenced the
dervishes. He was still the Sultan! The decision
would be his!

"I want to know what happened. All of it."
He walked to Tarik. "And you will tell me."

Stony silence met him, as did a stony stare—
not fear at all but raw defiance.

At the Sultan's glance a short lash came down
upon Tarik's shoulder from the strong arm of
the guard standing behind him. More out of
surprise than courage, Tarik barely reacted. By
the time the pain registered in his mind, he was
in control of it.

Hasam's complexion grew gray with fury.
"Again."

The whip flashed, harder this time. The bronze
skin of Tarik's back flared into angry red welts.
He cried out in pain now. Jessica's eyes filled
with tears.

The Sultan nodded again. Again the whip
descended. Tarik dropped to his knees.

"Stop . . . I'll tell you . . . what you want to
know."

Jessica blinked in shock.

Tarik stared to talk. "I was sent into this
palace as a spy by your enemies. I have used
this woman for information. When she discovered who I was, I raped her. And I would have
killed her if—"

The Kadin bolted to her feet. "She was in his arms, clinging to him like a lover!"

The court billowed with murmurs.

"Quiet," Hasam ordered. "Are we to believe that you—some filthy barbarian off the street—are a messenger of our enemies? That you're a spy sent here to gather information? Why, you hardly look clever enough to read, much less fool some innocent girl—"

"My name is Tarik Pasha."

The murmuring became a gushing blast of astonishment. While the court rumbled behind him, Sultan Hasam stared hard and long at this man and his wild claim. Truth? Or a clever ruse to sacrifice himself and therefore protect the real Pasha?

Even as he weighed the possibilities, the Sultan decided that he believed this was Tarik Pasha himself. Such a man as Tarik, a man who craved the glory of revolution as much as the victory, would relish this chance to die as martyr after standing firm before his greatest enemy. Odysseys were written about such men. Perhaps Pasha wanted his own odyssey, one that would carry his people on in a rage of dedication once they found out he gave his life for them. Yes, this was the real Tarik. And for some reason he wanted Jessica to live—enough that he was willing to swallow his renowned pride for her and pretend to go down beneath the lash.

Still, Sultan Hasam was not so far past his

prime that he could pass up a good wrestling match.

He moved back to his throne and motioned to Jessica. "Come. Sit beside me." When she did, he added, "Bring the executioner."

Jessica stopped short, halfway into the chair, and stared at him.

The doors opened. The executioner entered, masked and robed, for he had been waiting outside. When he reached Tarik, he drew his magnificent blade from its sheath and awaited his ruler's command.

Sultan Hasam turned to Jessica and spoke to her with a frightening calmness, as though he asked what she preferred to have for dinner. "If this man is telling the truth, then you would want him dead as much as I." He turned to the headsman. "Prepare him for execution."

Jessica noticed that Sultan Hasam did not have to say that horrible word but had added it for a specific reason. And it was working—her hands were cold and sweaty to prove it.

With a grunt Tarik landed on his knees under the forceful grips of two eunuchs. They wrenched his head to one side and held firmly, providing the executioner a clean slice.

Once again Hasam turned to the woman he would never have. "Tarik Pasha is yours. The power of life and death is in your hands."

Jessica swallowed hard and silently begged Tarik to make the decision for her. When his expression begged her to save herself, she bit her lip and felt the keen glares of the Kadin and the court attendants. The Kislar also glared at her, begging the same silence that Tarik begged of her.

The Kadin seethed, begging for something entirely different. If Jessica was silent, there would be exoneration, and the threat of a second Kadin would resume.

The sword crawled slowly upward.

Jessica stiffened until she thought her body was nothing but bones—no flesh, no heart, no mind.

The tip of the sword slanted backward slightly over the executioner's head, signaling the descent—and it began its plunge downward toward Tarik's bare neck—

"No! Stop!"

The blade halted against Tarik's skin. A trickle of blood trailed down his neck to roll over his collarbone. His eyes had been closed in private preparation and now shot open. Jessica had spared his life with her scream and thus sealed both their fates. Tarik damned himself for not explaining more about his culture to her.

But nothing could pull back the past few seconds.

The Sultan turned away from Jessica in another rush of disappointment. She was lost to him. Lost forever now. "Take her," he rasped.

They took Jessica's and Tarik's arms and pulled them in two different directions. Never had a gaze been more substantial as that which held the two "traitors" together during those last moments when they could still see each other.

Jessica was taken from the room entirely. Tarik was made to stand to one side of the Sultan, in the bitterly wrenching grip of two eunuchs who knew their places and reveled in them at rare moments like this.

The Sultan's expression was carved from stone. For many deadly moments he became as unpredictable as the tigers in his garden zoo. When the hardness went away, the entire court blinked with surprise.

"I must congratulate you," he said to Tarik. "In the history of the Empire no other single man has managed to create such a stir."

Tarik was unmoved. "Your Majesty has provided me with many opportunities for complaint."

"So it would seem. But tell me . . . do you really think any of you stand a chance against the Empire? That any of you have the right to tell *me* how to rule?"

Tarik leaned as far forward as the eunuchs' grips would allow. "To a man," he said, enunciating each word.

The Sultan did not go unaffected, though he retained composure at the unnerving conviction his prisoner displayed. Trying to downplay the effect, he said, "It would seem this annoyance is to be with us for some time, then." He smiled at his courtiers and got smiles in return, which seemed to fortify him. He once again had their confidence. Only when he turned back to the eyes that knew him best at this moment did he flutter slightly and have to recover himself all over again. "You are a clever man," he said into those eyes. "I admire your skill and conviction, however misguided they might be. You are also an extremely dangerous man." He waved at the executioner. "Take him."

The rebel was pushed roughly from the room under heavy guard. The Sultan pressed his elbows to his sides, trying not to let the court see how difficult it was going to be to get through the rest of today's business at hand.

Through the richly gilded galleries of fresh tulips in the garden Jessica walked, flanked by eunuchs in a procession led by the Kislar. It was a death march. It felt and looked like one. As the ladies of the harem planted the new shipment of roses, trying not to stare at the condemned one, Jessica stared straight ahead and accepted the idea of death. Strange how accustomed one can get to such an idea. No so long ago she might have dissolved into panic. Now such a reaction seemed useless and embarrassing. She might not have been aware of her own dignity, as was the Kislar, but she knew that her last wordless statement in this life would be, by design, a grand one.

Some people just die. She, at least, would die to save other lives. Things could be worse. Tarik could be here too. Oh, yes, he was willing to die for her, but Jessica had promised herself that not one more person would die because of her mistakes or blindnesses. Dignity.

They reached the gates of the palace and

walked down to the docks where two caïques waited.

"I know you feel I've betrayed you too," she said to the Kislar, who had been staunchly silent.

Now he turned to her while the guards prepared the caïques. "You betrayed yourself," he told her, not without pain. "You will die quietly, and your lover will die in a public execution." He started to turn away.

She grabbed his thick arms and pulled him around, her face blanched with shock. "The Sultan gave me Tarik's life!"

"Only for the moment. Your life only buys him a few more days."

"Tell me when they'll kill him," she demanded. "Tell me how. I have to know!"

"Why?" he asked with a bitter sadness. "So you can dream about it in your last dream of this life? What can you do for him now? We are all betrayed by ourselves. Nothing can help us now." The big man forced her into the caïque, as disturbed by her death sentence as if it were his own. He had been ordered to snuff the one ray of hope and change that had ever found its way through the ashes of tradition to glow for a moment at Sultan Hasam's door. Now it would gutter in the silty waters, and he would go back as though nothing had happened and would live the pretense until he began to believe it.

The eunuchs lifted Jessica into a large sack that had been spread on the floorboards of the caïque. They tied her hands with silver cord—

another tidbit of ritual. One by one they placed large stones in the bottom of the sack, arranging them around Jessica's feet with a grim touch of artistry. They lifted the sides of the sack up around her.

Jessica drew a ragged breath, clasped her bound hands tightly together, raised her chin, and closed her eyes before the darkness of the bag closed them for her. Death, death—did these barbarians know nothing more? Did they really believe they could conquer anything just by killing it? Tarik . . .

The Kislar's voice, rough and impassioned, filtered through the thick fabric. "Let me do it."

There was a jostling in the caïque. She felt the big black hands close the bag over her head and secure the tie. In the throes of desolation, Jessica felt for him.

The eunuchs began to row the two caïques out to open water, farther and farther into the blue Bosporus, where its uncaring arms would do good work for their Sultan. They rowed past the jutting promontory upon which the seraglio rested. Ritual always. It was a comfort and a direction.

The Kislar stood in the bow of the lead caïque, staring forward, his mouth set hard. Sooner than the eunuchs thought he would, he gestured for them to stop. Without further order the eunuchs put down their oars and grasped the lines leading to Jessica's caïque. They neither watched nor cared as the figure inside the bag stood up straight and waited. They yanked hard on the ropes. The second caïque rocked nauseatingly, yawned to one side, sucked in water, and capsized. The stones in the sack did their job immediately and very well.

As the bag bubbled upon the water's surface and hung on to the last dribbles of air seeping through the fabric, the Kislar Agha closed his eyes tightly. His head drooped until his chin rested against his chest, then he gave the sign to begin rowing back to the palace—to where he belonged.

She was under water. It was an expression without meaning, without substance.

All it meant was that the air went away.

Tradition had given a second occupation to the swaying coastal grasses on the sea floor. The long weeds waved a slow dance to the rhythm of the currents in an area that had become, over time, a landless graveyard. The waters were murky—nothing like the picture of blue-green waves when the sun hit the surface of the Bosporus. Within the grasses lay the chewed remains of a half dozen other sacks, shapeless coffins for other victims of the Imperial court. Marine organisms had preyed upon Jessica's predecessors in the silent underworld, breaking down the thick sacks until some were barely substantial, hardly more than silty tatters. Between the decaying tufts lay a few inelegant human bones. The remains had become part of the economy of the sea—survival of the smallest.

The stones did their job well. The sack dragged Jessica down with it until the mushy sea floor stopped it, and it settled drunkenly down. Jessica floated upward against the fabric, and the weightlessness of the water environment made her nauseated. When the caïque had first capsized, she'd forced herself not to take a deep breath, assuming it would be foolish to prolong the inevitable, but when the cold water closed around her nose and mouth, she suddenly wished she had taken that breath. She was overcome with a sudden urge to fight. This was no way to die!

The water, cold on her skin, shocked her into action. She forced her eyes open, though she could see nothing in the darkness of the sack. But it helped her think. With her teeth she tore at the silver cords around her wrists. They held tight. If possible, they tightened even more, cutting off the circulation from her hands. The sack—she had to get out of the sack! She grabbed for a handful of the soaked fabric, but it was heavy and resisted her control. Her lungs began to burn.

Panic set in. Her swaying movements became frantic. Her mind became a blank canvas of explosions as her body cried for oxygen.

The sack fell away.

Jessica surged out of it, shocked by her unexpected freedom. Then she saw the rope that had bound the sack, floating away as though it had never been tied in the first place. She remembered the Kislar . . .

In her panic and desperate need for air, Jessica spun around, looking for "up." Under water it was impossible to tell which direction was right.

Something touched her, a gentle sign. She twisted around and cringed back from the skeletal human hand that drifted from one of the rotting sacks beside her. Her mind screamed. She opened her mouth and expelled most of her saved breath on an aborted yell. Her voice sounded like a fist striking soft flesh. Terrified, she batted the hand away and did not stop to see the bones fall apart and disintegrate into the grasses.

The skeleton had pointed the right way. Light . . . there was light . . . a shimmering blue-white plate over her right shoulder—the surface.

She clawed her way toward it. The sea pulled her down, hungering for her. Now her ears roared and whined. The harder she paddled, the farther away the surface retreated. Her mind no longer worked. She knew only delirium. Her arms pumped desperately downward, propelling her toward the light, but it was too far away, too far . . . too hard . . . so easy to float . . . why did her ears sing? The water felt warm now. Tarik?

Voices . . . Tarik's voice. And wasn't there someone else's? So hard to remember now, so hard . . . so tired . . .

"I won the bet, mate, fair 'n' square. *You* lost.

You stand wheel watch for me the next 'ole entire week."

"Donny, you're a cruel an' 'eartless an' vicious sort and no kinda shipmate."

"Maybe not, but I'm the one what's not standin' watch on the helm for a 'ole—hello, what's this? Thatch, you see that?"

"See what?"

"Just abeam."

"Christ wi' pants on! I don't believe it . . . sound the horn. Man overboard!"

"Well, you're 'alf right. . . ."

The British pilot cutter ordinarily didn't cruise so close to the shore, but they had just put into port at Constantinople for repairs and decided to prowl the coastline to avoid the storm brewing on the distant seascape. They never expected to go fishing for mermaids, yet that is precisely what they thought they found when they came upon Jessica's body.

She lay in a soaked heap on the deck as the astounded seamen bent over her. They rolled her onto her stomach and pushed the water from her lungs, but she just lay there like so much mutton.

"Damn near drowned, poor lass," Donny said for lack of any constructive suggestions. Other men crowded around too. They hadn't seen a woman—not a real one—since . . .

"I swore she was a mermaid for a sure shot," Seaman Thatcher commented.

"More likely a 'arem girl. Weren't no accident, wi' them bound 'ands."

"Whatever she is, I'll wager she's a beauty, all dried and pressed. . . ."

Donny nodded. "Could be our lady luck come to visit at last."

The men flinched in surprise when the woman coughed and began to stir. Seawater dribbled from the corner of her mouth. The coughing helped rouse her. She rolled over and squinted in the sunlight, coughing more violently until her lungs were clear. Her voice gurgled. "Where . . . where . . . who are you?"

Thatcher's mouth dropped open. "Gawd love us! She speaks English, this mermaid does!"

Donny straightened up immediately and barked an order at the nearest man. "Tell the Captain. We gotta notify the British embassy 'bout this. Go on, then, scamper!"

Things happened faster than Jessica believed possible. Snatched from the grip of death, she found herself having to force the reality into her befuddled brain: she was free. Saved. Free.

The sailors gave her clothes to wear, which did nothing for her figure or femininity but which looked more glorious to her than the richest robes she'd ever worn in the harem. They hurried her ashore in the city, and within a few short hours she was riding a carriage into the one place she thought she would never see again.

The embassy.

Through the small carriage window she saw a running figure. Dismay filled her—a surprise when she had expected to feel joy.

The carriage grated to a halt and the door swung open. Charles dragged her into his arms.

"Jessica, I hardly believed it when we got the message," he whispered into her ear. "I *can't* believe it. . . ."

"It's all right, Charles," she said. "It's over now. I'm back."

He pulled her away and looked at her. Jessica suddenly wondered if she looked very different. Thinner, perhaps, and perhaps a touch more sallow. Did she look green like the seawater that had nearly taken her? Did her eyes have new lines around them from the worrying and the panic and the horror and the passions?

If Charles saw anything new there, he hid it well. "Come into the house. You've had quite an experience. I want you to start forgetting it as soon as possible." He smiled then and wrapped his arm around her waist, ready to lead her in. An embassy page stood attentively nearby, and Charles told him, "Bring us tea and something to eat. We'll be in the study."

Only then did Jessica come to life. "And tell my father, Mr. Grey, to join us there as soon as he can."

The page frowned in confusion. "But—"

Charles silenced him with a glare. "Just do it."

Jessica had serious trouble divorcing herself from the harem, the Sultan, and all that had happened to her—and Tarik. A much harder time than she'd expected, in fact. Even as she sat here in the comfortable study, she felt the intrusion of civility preventing her and Charles from saying what they really felt. She had been telling her true feelings for weeks now—oh, not the same kinds of frivolous opinions she'd spouted before she came to Turkey but *true* feelings. She'd told them to Usta, to the Kislar, to Tarik, even to Sultan Hasam himself. Of course, she had had to learn her feelings in order to tell them; that had been the real miracle.

Even the furniture in the room separated them. Charles sat in a leather chair, Jessica on the couch. And her mind sat somewhere in the Palace of Yildiz, pondering unfinished business. There were things yet to be done. Her newfound freedom was, in itself, becoming a prison. Here she had no power at all. Not like the power she had tampered with in the harem.

"I don't even know where to begin," she said feebly, staring into her cup of tea. I'm not sure I can explain. I feel disoriented . . . as if I know two worlds and find myself in neither."

Now Charles came to sit beside her in an effort to bridge the intangible gap between them. "Take all the time you need. I never gave up hope, Jessica. I never stopped loving you."

Whether it was a tribute or an entreaty, Jessica couldn't tell. She knew only that she couldn't return it, not yet. "I've . . . always counted on your devotion . . ."

"Jessica, what's the matter?" Charles unconsciously let a slight whine slip into his voice.

This just wasn't working out like the reunion he'd imagined.

Jessica looked away from him, gathered within herself. "Your love frightens me. I've changed so much—"

"People don't change," he said quickly. "What's important changes, and people adapt." Then he added, "I can adapt."

Jessica broke away toward the mantel, her back to him. "I betrayed all the values we shared." *And lost everything else we shared. I may never get them back.*

"Listen to me, Jessica." He followed her to the mantel, but wisely didn't touch her. "I fell in love with a girl in England. I was captivated by her innocence. But . . . I'm prepared to love the woman."

Truly torn now, Jessica looked at him to see if he fully understood what he was saying. "You could forgive everything I've done?"

"I could forgive and never ask," he promised.

She turned away. "And what about what I'm about to do?"

"What, darling? I didn't hear—"

"Where's Daddy?" She twisted around and looked impatiently at the doorway. "I think it would help if I could see him. He's always good at helping me understand myself."

The moment had to come. Charles had hoped to put it off a little longer, but now that was impossible. He decided not to try.

"Jessica, your father . . . never made it to Constantinople."

"What? You mean he returned to England?" Charles's face lost its color.

Jessica pressed the space between them with a force Charles had never seen in her. "Charles, where is my father?"

Impotently he took her hand and lowered his eyes, unable to meet the stern adult glare she gave. "He had a stroke. He died in Damascus."

The disbelief came first and soon after it the collapse, both mental and physical.

Charles held her, shielded her in his arms as his brave girl finally gave up control. He stroked her hair. "I'll take care of you, Jessica. Of everything. We're going back to England as soon as possible. I'll make plans tomorrow. We can have a life there. There's a whole life there waiting to be resumed . . . all ours. All ours."

Much later, unbidden and unwanted, morning finally came.

Jessica resented the sun today. It meant the ticking of a merciless eternal time clock. Her father, dead one extra day. Tarik, one day closer to death.

Accustomed to the casual impropriety of the seraglio, Jessica took her disoriented mind for a long walk in the embassy garden, still wearing only her nightclothes. She didn't remember changing clothes last night; didn't remember anything, really, and didn't care. The past was done. Today was waiting.

She wandered through the garden, appearing benumbed and insensible to the gasps of shocked embassy personnel as she walked past them in her nightgown. Within her own mind, though, Jessica was quite aware, keenly aware that, while she had escaped, she was still not free.

"Jessica . . ."

She barely responded to Lady Ashley's voice and was not at all surprised to discover the generous Englishwoman approaching her. Of course, Lady Ashley would want to see her, talk to her, make sure she had emerged from the harem without too many burdens. "Jessica, are you all right, dear?" Lady Ashley's arm slipped into Jessica's and they walked together as though it were perfectly normal to take a stroll in one's bedwear.

"What are the guards for?" Jessica demanded instantly, leering with unshuttered contempt at the mounted guns and guards at the compound gates. "Why do we need guns here?"

Lady Ashley, assuming that the young woman was still in shock over her father's death, hesitated to tell Jessica of the state of turmoil, the impending revolution she thought Jessica had been unaware of while in the harem. "It's for our protection, I suppose," she evaded, selling it with her tone.

Jessica stared at the guns. "A different kind of cage."

Lady Ashley led her past the gates and turned her toward the rose garden. "You know, of course, that you should be resting in your room, not wandering about in your robes." She leaned inward and smiled. "It may be appropriate for the harem, but it's not very English."

Neither am I. Jessica looked down at her negligee. "No—not very English at all." The realization jolted her. She turned to Lady Ashley with a stunning resolution in her face. "Lady Ashley," said the powerful voice, a grown-up kind of voice, "there are things I have to know."

Taken aback by the sudden change, Lady Ashley paused to see if it would go away. "What things, dear?"

"How widespread is the rebellion? Do you think it's inevitable?"

"Why, Jessica—"

"If it is, then we've got to act now. You must get me in touch with the revolutionaries."

"Jessica, you don't know what you're saying."

"I'm getting in touch with them. Your help will make it easier, but I *am* doing it. And I'm going back to the palace."

"Back to the palace? But you just got out."

"True. But I'm not finished. Come with me while I change into my traveling clothes."

The decision was made, and Lady Ashley knew there was no changing it. She knew that ring of determination in Jessica's voice.

The petticoats felt strange as Jessica slid into them and rustled around her bedroom, gathering her most rugged traveling clothes. Her silence had broken completely, and a gush of explanation had filled Lady Ashley's ears since they left the gardens. Tarik this, Tarik that, the Sultan this and that, the Kadin, Geisla, the Kislar, execution, water, Bosporus, Usta, Tarik, and Tarik, and Tarik. Injustice, barbarians, primitivism—the rush of emotional words would no longer be dammed back. Strangely enough, Lady Ashley noticed, even though she might have been inclined to attribute this to shock and disorientation, Jessica's tirade was chillingly logical. She knew exactly what she was talking about, to the detail, and it all sounded quite solid. The longer Lady Ashley listened, the flimsier her arguments for staying became.

"So you see," Jessica finished as she pulled on her Serengeti skirt and buttoned the side plaquet, "you must help me find Salim."

Lady Ashley felt torn. "Jessica, you sould like you understand everything frighteningly well, but do you understand *why* you feel obligated to go?"

Jessica looked at her. "I have a debt to pay."

"To Tarik?" Lady Ashley intentionally forced the point.

"My future is with Charles," Jessica said, "but I can't leave Constantinople until I finish Constantinople."

"Have you considered how your leaving will affect Charles?"

"Of course I have. He'll understand. I'll make him understand—as soon as it's over."

"At least see him before you leave the embassy."

"There isn't time now." The young woman's chin tightened and tears welled in her eyes, as though to assure her friend that this was not a blind impulse. "Not even time to mourn my father. Will you help me?"

By getting dressed and ready to go during her explanation, Jessica had effectively backed Lady Ashley into a corner. Yet it really wasn't a trap—Lady Ashley was not easily impounded. They understood each other. Their legacies would mesh, just as their courage stood over and above actions any other woman might shy away from. In Jessica's eyes, sitting on top of the old need for adventure, which both women understood so well, was a newly kindled need to realize a bigger dream than idle challenge can ever be. It was a need to, as Jessica said, *finish*.

Lady Ashley stood up slowly. "My carriage is waiting."

Jessica and Salim walked through the campsite of the Young Turks and the other rebel factions—citizens with a wish for betterment of their lives and their children, soldiers who had brought with them their knowledge of military action, members of all the Empire's many cultures who wished to unify in a more tangible way than merely by the map. A rush of anticipation made the camp buzz. The rebellion was coming. Even the children played mock battles while groups of women hurriedly stitched uniforms to make the rebels at least appear to be a trained unit. Psychological advantage had decided many a skirmish through history.

"It's not too late to save Tarik's life," she was telling him as they walked.

"We have no men to spare," Salim said, grimacing with the pain those words brought him. "Right now I doubt we could stage a raid big enough to be noticed at all, much less take over the palace. Believe me, there is nothing I'd rather do than save Tarik, but even he would disapprove. I can't take—" He stopped. He looked toward the hillside.

Jessica shivered and looked too. There was nothing there, nothing but the crest of the hill, until a dozen riders appeared, dark shapes against the sunset.

Salim watched expectantly. He felt Misha appear beside him, and a few other men also. He shook his head. "A few more deserters. That's all."

But Jessica didn't look away from the ridge. Intuition wouldn't let her look away. As she watched, thirty more riders appeared. Then thirty behind them. Then fifty more.

Salim's expression changed from despair to hope and disbelief. "Murat . . ." he murmured. "The army!"

Even as he said it, Murat's face became distinguishable over the distance as he rode toward them on a bony desert horse. Behind him, the Third Corps covered the hill like bees on a beehive.

"Set up more tents!" Salim cried to his own men. The joy in his voice sent them scurrying.

Two hours passed, and the jubilation settled down to a serious time for planning—victory was now possible. Jessica felt their anticipation and couldn't resist it, even though something in the back of her mind kept insisting that this wasn't her battle. She ignored the little voice. It was a human battle and therefore hers to claim if she wished. She walked with Salim now through the new tent of the Third Corps, her expression set with determination and steadiness.

Salim stopped her a few paces before they would have entered Murat's tent. Clearly he had been thinking about something all the while and only now had decided to tell her. "Perhaps I should explain about Murat," he said quietly. "He can be a difficult man." His eyebrows bobbed up once.

"If we're going to save Tarik, we need his help," Jessica said. Did it really matter what kind of person this Murat was?

"There has been . . . strain," Salim went on, "between him and Tarik. Both are natural leaders, but Tarik is the one with the charisma to summon the people. Murat is the one with the hardness to do whatever is necessary. They clash but their goals chime."

"Do you think he'll help Tarik?"

Salim shrugged. "A moment of truth can seldom be pretold."

"Then let's go inside," Jessica said impatiently, "and find out."

Inside the tent, Murat was already poring over maps of parts of Constantinople. He stood up to greet the woman he had been told to expect. Salim introduced them, and Jessica immediately said, "We have little time, sir. Tarik may be executed at any moment. I'm here to help in any way I can."

The big commander gestured her and Salim into simple wooden chairs. "Tarik's capture provides us with a double problem," he said, relinquishing amenities to the matters at hand. "We also must infiltrate the Armenian quarter and prepare for battle there without letting the Imperial troops know we are there. Such urban stealth is not so easy. I already have that to plan."

"Then plan it," she said. "Let me arrange Tarik's rescue. I know something of military strategy."

The bushy brows rose. "Oh? And where do you get your knowledge of strategy?"

"What little I know, I've read in books."

Murat looked at Salim. "Of course. What else could I expect from a writer? You've found a woman who reads!"

Jessica quickly interrupted with, "I'm not saying I can plan a battle, but I do know how to save Tarik."

Hasam took a serious moment to consider, and Jessica felt that he was genuinely weighing the advantages and problems. She had seen enough false consideration while in the palace that she knew the real thing when she saw it. Murat said, "I cannot risk sending one of my best men into the palace."

"Then send me," she said. "All I need is a soldier's uniform and money for the bribe."

Even Salim stared open-eyed at her. She looked from one to the other. "Well, why not?"

she went on. "I know the palace. I know what needs to be done."

"And you know the harem . . ." Murat added.

"The sound of the parrots will lead me straight to Tarik."

Murat stared into the light of a gas lantern until his eyes watered. Then he looked at Salim. "You are strangely silent."

Salim shrugged and gave an answer he might never have considered ten minutes ago, especially with his best friend's life at stake. "It seems she can defend herself."

Not willing to let the doubt sink in, Jessica plowed forward. To Murat she said, "I know there has been rivalry between you and Tarik, But I don't believe you to be the sort of man who would let rivalry cost him his life." With her eyes she tacked on the forceful question: Are you?

For long moments Murat was silent, gazing at the tent floor and plainly weighing every possibility, every alternative, every consequence. Jessica and Salim waited, not daring even to glance at each other.

Finally Murat looked at her as though to surprise her and see how she would take it. But the question was a legitimate one: "How do you propose to get into the palace?"

Jessica grinned.

Early that evening, once the plans had been made and the actions were being put into movement, Murat approached Jessica with a soldier's uniform—a smallish one. He looked long at this fair-skinned girl, at her round hips and obvious bustline, and wondered what kind of idiot could actually mistake her for a man, even if she did wear a soldier's clothes. He couldn't imagine it. The uniform might cover her body—maybe—but what would cover those large feminine eyes and the ivory skin of her face and those succulent lips? But if she was half as much an actress and she was a daredevil, then the pretense might work.

"If you survive tomorrow," he told her bluntly, "then leave this place. Go back to England and to your own people. You and Tarik will not be able to live together. Not in the new Turkey."

Jessica gazed at him. A strange warning, indeed. "Why do you assume my motives are romantic? Like you, I've only been committed to the cause for a short time, but I need not explain myself to you. You've given me what I need. And that's enough." She buried her indignance in what Salim had told her about this man: that he was a bigot, that he didn't believe people could forget their differences of blood and culture in favor of bigger ideals.

Yet there was a sniggering truth in what he said. The old culture would give way to the new, but the change would not come overnight. The prejudices would tarry and dissipate only over long years—perhaps too long for her and Tarik.

It didn't matter. Charles was waiting and she would go back to him. When she was finished, of course. Tarik was part of something that didn't really exist for her.

The last shipment of tulips for the Feast of Flowers entered palace gates after sunset. Dressed in a cloak that covered her entire body and her head, Jessica rode on the lead wagon beside the driver. Of course, the real driver was tied up in the bushes several miles back and the merchant beside her was really one of the Turkish citizens from the rebel camp. He was a chubby man who didn't fight well and who volunteered for this honor rather than doing more harm than good in the street battle to come. Jessica had readily accepted him.

She huddled inside her cowled cloak, knowing that she could only pull this off because of the darkness. In full daylight she would be recognized as a woman instantly.

She watched as each of the palace buildings filed past her in the compound, until finally they were near the seraglio. Giving no visible signal to her compatriot, she hopped off the wagon. The driver never even blinked. The wagons filed steadily past her with their loads of flowers. She strolled down the line, inspecting each of the loads, until she reached the last wagon. She strolled around it and ducked into the shadows.

The steady *clop-clop-clop* of the horse's hooves faded. Jessica waited in the shadows until they were completely gone. Now she listened for anything else—anyone who might be out there. Convinced that she was alone, she shrugged the cloak from her shoulders, revealing an ill-fitting Imperial soldier's uniform. Her hair had been darkened with dirt, and now she twisted it up and tucked it inside a fez. Not perfect but it would do. She ditched the cloak in the shrubs and moved tentatively through the courtyards.

A terrible feeling of unsureness crept up her back. She must be insane to try such a wild rescue. She felt suddenly more alone than she really was; she told herself over and over that Salim and the others were with her in spirit and that Tarik would be pleased with her daring. He had tried no less for her.

She stiffened. A sound—parrots! Yes, it was . . . the squawking of parrots in the aviary next to the torture chambers. Fortified now, she followed the sound of the birds.

There it was: a stone building with bars on the windows, suspiciously looking just like any of the seraglio chambers. No doubt it had been intended to look like that, as though it fit in perfectly with the sleepy peace of the seraglio. Jessica stole along the side of the building to one of the barred windows, stood up on her tiptoes, and peeked inside. An empty cell. A pile of straw . . . a stone slab, a wooden stool.

She sank down and crept around the corner to another window, her stomach knotting. Had they already . . .

She peeked in again: straw, stone, and a semi-conscious form, blue with bruises, stripped bare except for a ragged pair of eunuch's pants. His body was glazed with sweat, but his chest still rose and fell with steady breathing.

Clutched by relief and empathy, wishing there had been some way to get here sooner, Jessica murmured, "Oh, Tarik . . ."

Then a hand landed hard on her shoulder. A rough run of Turkish words snarled into her ear and she was yanked around. With a gasp Jessica felt herself being hauled upward until the ground left her feet and hope fell away.

CHAPTER FIFTEEN

The revolutionaries' patchwork army crept silently into the Armenian quarter under cover of darkness. They took their positions in alleyways, on rooftops, under wagons, and in any other nook that would hide a man. As they crept in, hooded figures crept out of the area—women nervously herding their children away, leaving their men as sacrificial lambs to the impending massacre. The men joined the revolutionaries in the streets and at their windows, built walls of crates to hide behind, and dug themselves in for a long, tense wait.

In another part of the city, men in newly made uniforms meandered through the streets, converging slowly but deliberately upon the Palace of Yildiz. These numbered fewer than the infiltrators in the Armenian sector, but their goal was no less critical to the success of the rebellion. The enthusiasm of awakening chance, though potent in their minds and a major driving force, tuning their bodies high like stringed instruments, could not completely eradicate the one plaguing question: Were they strong enough? For while enthusiasm is crucial, it does not win battles.

"Who are you? I haven't seen you before." The drunken soldier had dropped Jessica from a wild spin on his shoulder, thinking she was someone he knew. He thought he recognized the small frame and thin shoulders, but the face, now that he squinted at it in the night darkness, didn't look familiar. A very pale man, this young fellow, his large eyes staring into the prison. Probably one of *those*, those who like to watch other men.

He rasped at her in Turkish, wobbling on thready legs. Around him four other soldiers, just as drunk, fought to clear unclearable eyes. "Have any of you seen him before?"

Jessica knew she was in trouble but caught a glimmer of hope. These men had been celebrating, probably something about the impending Feast of Flowers. The spin on the big one's shoulder had been a sign of camaraderie, not capture, and she could still get out of this. She didn't understand what he was asking her, for he spoke in Turkish, but she had a pretty good idea.

Moving her hands carefully, she mimed the act of having her tongue severed. The men watched, perplexed, so she did it again, more dramatically. Suddenly the big soldier rolled back and laughed. "He's a mute. He can't speak."

He cuffed his huge hand around Jessica's neck

and gathered her into the celebration, bellowing to the other men. She recognized the Turkish word for *wine* and assumed he was demanding more, to give to her. A new bottle was produced from the coat pocket of one of the soldiers, but luckily they were too drunk to get the cork out without a group effort. The soldiers gathered around the bottle, struggling with the cork and a short knife. The cork did not survive intact. Victory—the big soldier laughed his conquest to the night sky and raised the bottle, then turned to offer it to the young, mute soldier with the big eyes.

But there was no one there anymore.

In a small anteroom beside the cells of the Imperial torture chamber, the executioner snoozed pleasantly on his cot. Beside him lay the black, hooded mask and robes of his station—raiment that struck a cold chill down the backs of all who saw him wearing them. The stench of human sweat and excrement no longer kept him from his dreams as it had when he first got this job, nor did the clinging odor of blood and festering wounds and burned flesh, which at first had been so terrible that he nearly got himself executed for refusing to the bidding of his ruler. After so many years, though, fresh air tasted funny.

Accustomed also to being completely alone in his decrepit little room, the movement from near the door roused him to a light grogginess, and he rubbed his eyes to see if one of those big rats had gotten in again. He blinked at what he thought he saw, rubbed his eyes again, and started to sit up. In Turkish he asked, "Who are you?"

In Turkish the vision responded, "A dream."

Her hair flowed across bare shoulders. Her alabaster body gleamed in a single band of moonlight from the window, breasts rounder than he could ever imagine, for never in his life had he seen such a woman. A dream? She leaned toward him, her lips parting, warm and fleshy.

The executioner marveled at his luck and wondered if there could be sensation in a dream. He hoped so. He felt it already.

He felt the burning pain in his side and mistook it for arousal—until the warm gush of blood beneath his ribs proved him wrong. The dream's face changed. Lights exploded before his eyes. He gasped for breath, but the air in his lungs flowed out in a hot, red gurgle. He slid to one side and died with his face lying upon the black mask.

The procession began. Pre-dawn over the palace compound saw the flicker of thousands of little lamps scattered among the gilded galleries of tulips, like something out of a fairy story. From his balcony the Sultan oversaw the exodus of soldiers—hundreds of his loyal men, flanks so wide that they would fill the entire width of the streets in the Armenian quarter. He saw it in his mind as they marched past him. In the lead was the executioner, robed and masked, followed by six soldiers carrying the animal Pasha, who was bound and riding in a wooden cage, as befits all animals. The foot soldiers tramped after them, in a great long phalanx. Then came the Chief Commander and his officer upon their jewel-bridled horses. The Commander nodded and saluted his Sultan, fighting off a smug grin.

The Sultan nodded at the Commander and willed himself to ignore memories, still fresh and vibrant, of a marketplace similar to the one these men were marching to, a place where children had played and merchants had hawked their wares within paces of him. For twenty years his orders had been followed without question, least of all without question from within himself. Today was different, though, and Hasam fought an inner battle, remembering with some struggle that order must be maintained. He submerged the memories and the nagging guilts and truly believed that there could be no alternative. This was the only way to retain his power.

When the army had passed his balcony, the Sultan did not wait to see them trickle out the main gates. He turned, breathed deeply the air of his fathers, and walked back into his chambers. The die was cast and could never be drawn back. Dawn.

The first shimmering lights touched the mosaiced outer walls of the church. The light, turned colors now, reflected into the shadows and touched the backs of crouching men—revolutionaries. They watched with silent apprehension as Hasam's Imperial Army marched into the quarter in rigid formation, moved toward the center of the market square, then came to a grating halt. Tarik's cage was placed on the ground. The Chief Commander reined his horse leisurely through the ranks until he reached the front lines.

"All Armenians! Open your windows and listen. Open your windows! I bring you a message from your Sultan. Open your windows or the soldiers will open them for you!"

He waited, and finally cellar windows and balcony doors began to crack open. The people were afraid to show themselves, but just as afraid not to. He saw parts of faces peeking through the cracks and smiled as his audience grew. "We come to you in the name of reason. For too long you have been manipulated by traitors. The time has come to give up the revolutionaries among you. Who will be the first to serve their Sultan?"

There was no response—a thick silence only.

The Commander pranced his steed down the ranks in front of the Armenian homes and businesses. "Perhaps you don't understand. People are going to die today. But you have a choice! Will it be the traitors or your wives? Your children? Give us the revolutionaries."

When the silence throbbed still longer, the Commander waved his hand to his men. "Bring that man forward."

Tarik was hauled out of the cage and brought to the front, in plain view.

"Perhaps this man's death will change your

minds," the Commander announced to the rodentlike eyes watching him through cracked doors and parted curtains. "Watch very carefully. As his blood flows, so shall your children's. Executioner . . ."

Two soldiers forced Tarik to his knees, forcing his head forward. The executioner closed the space between life and death, standing over the condemned man and ceremonially raising the curved, burnished blade.

The Chief Commander chanted, "By order of His Imperial Majesty Sultan Hasam, Tarik Pasha is condemned to death for crimes against His Imperial Majesty and the Empire." He nodded to the executioner.

The sword sliced downward.

Tarik closed his eyes. He felt the swish of air behind his back and felt something cut, but it was not his head that fell away. Instead the ropes that bound his hands and ankles dropped away, leaving him free. The soldiers who held him were easily thrown off as he jumped to his feet.

The executioner swept off the black hood. Long golden hair spilled across the shoulders of the silver robe. Jessica stepped forward to stand beside Tarik and announced, "You are surrounded by soldiers." Her clear voice sounded across the stunned ranks.

Salim stepped out of a shadow. Behind him, another two. Behind them, six more. In a spontaneous flood the revolutionaries' makeshift army poured from every crevice.

The armies were identical—uniforms, weapons, nationalities. They held guns on each other, but it was like looking into a mirror. The Imperial men were shaken. Even though they held their guns up, quandary showed on their faces.

The Chief Commander rode frantically down his ranks. "Open fire! Fire, do you hear?"

"No!" Tarik shouted. "Stop."

Behind him, Murat gestured for the revolutionaries to hold their fire as well.

"These men are traitors!" The Chief Commander's eyes glowed like fire.

"These men are soldiers," Tarik countered. "Like you. What separates you? Blood? Ideology? No! All that separates you is a command to fire."

The Chief Commander howled in fury at his men. "Do it now!"

Tarik's voice became even steadier, rising in entreaty to his countrymen. "Your silent guns have the power to free our people."

"In the name of the Sultan—"

"Do nothing in his name," Tarik countered. "The time has come when conscience overrides orders."

The Commander unsheathed his sword and raised it high into the air. "I command you to fire!"

But the massacres of the past weeks had not been easily forgotten. Once planted, the seed of resentment had sprouted and spread. His men had not forgotten the anguish of having to clean up the bodies and blood and ashes left from the slaughter at the Treasury, where they were made to fire on their brothers once before. Now, standing between choice and solution, they remembered the stench, the pain, the moans, the guilt, and the endless nights of questioning that followed.

The young soldier who had laid down his gun upon the scaffolding of the Treasury now raised the muzzle with new conviction. He had been forced to fire on unarmed soldiers before. Since then, he had come to realize that, armed or unarmed, men were men.

He stepped from the ranks. The clack of his rifle bolt rang into the square, a gauge for the thunderous boom that followed.

The muzzle smoked.

The Chief Commander stared in disbelief, convulsed once, then tumbled from his horse. The cobbled street was a cold caress.

In a panoramic sweep the two armies merged into a wild roar of celebration. A thousand red fezzes filled the air above the balconies.

Tarik and Jessica looked at each other, not exactly smiling, but joined in something beyond the joy of the moment. They were still gazing at each other when the Chief Commander's officers rode forward and relinquished their horses to Tarik in acknowledgment of the new leadership.

Tarik accepted two of the horses, then gestured for Salim and Murat also to be given horses. He turned to Jessica. "There are no words to tell you how impressed I am with you," he said. "I can give you no bigger thanks than to ask you to join us in our final victory." He handed her the reins of a big bejeweled stallion. "You lead the way to the palace. You've earned that right."

Jessica smiled at him, even though it didn't completely convey her satisfaction. "No," she said, wondering where this unexpected nobility came from, "we lead together."

She slid into the saddle, her silver robe spreading over the stallion's rump. Beside her, Tarik mounted a skittish bay. They rode together to join Salim and Murat. Flanked side by side, the harem girl, the rebel leader, the military man, and the writer led their army out of the Armenian quarter toward the palace. The hopeless rebellion had become a revolution on the march.

The panorama of the blue Bosporus flowing like some living thing between the green shores of Europe and Asia no longer stunned Jessica. She steered her stallion up the steep road to the palace gates, the same road that had once brought her there as a prisoner. She wasn't entirely unaware of the striking figure she made—bright hair, silver robes, jewel-bedecked black horse—riding beside the three Turks with the army close behind, but she was less puffed up by it than she might have been weeks ago. Pride swelled within her—yes, pride in herself but also pride that she had somehow become lucky enough to see history in the making, even to be a part of it. To ride beside men of such unremitting courage was an honor bestowed to few, and forever after Jessica Grey would be one of the few. She no longer missed the strange power she'd gained in the harem, if she ever really missed it at all; she'd brought it with her. She'd never really lost it.

The seraglio courtyard was an animated floral centerpiece with its galleries of tulips and lights, baskets of flowers on feast tables and garlands dripping from trellises. The Sultan lounged upon a divan, vacantly watching as harem girls danced. Instead of veils, the girls wore light nets interlaced with flowers, which was quite erotic. The Sultan's disinterest plagued the Kadin and the astrologer, who watched from one side. Whether they liked it or not, they found themselves wondering the same thing: Would there ever be another woman who would please Hasam?

Turkish music twanged and whined in the background, nearly hypnotic in its rhythm as it motivated the dancing girls into deeper rotations and wider gestures. They twisted their young bodies in easy motions, following the throbbing beat to which they had danced since childhood. Everything was as it should be, as it had been for untold years.

Then . . . the sound of hoofbeats.

The people around Hasam heard it and looked around in question. Horses? In the seraglio?

Some of the musicians fumbled through their notes, then stopped playing altogether as the thrumming sound crescendoed to a dull hammer, an ominous fanfare for danger they all felt vibrating in the air. The music stopped. The dancers stumbled to a halt.

This curious sensation was more feeling than sound; could they trust their senses?

Upon his divan, Hasam straightened up, unwilling to let his court be disrupted, but there was no time for him to snap an order that would retrieve the festive mood.

The latticework fence at one end of the court-yard suddenly vibrated, shaking the vines dripping from it. The court turned en masse and looked—and drew a singular gasp as two huge horses dawned, stretched out in midair over the top of the fence. Their riders appeared in perfect symmetry upon burnished leather saddles, leaning back as their steeds plunged downward toward the garden. The horses landed with a crash into the flower beds while the lattice fence rattled behind them. Drawing their horses up caused a pandemonium of its own kind as the beasts pranced and snorted in anger. From astride the furious beasts Tarik and Jessica met the stares of the Sultan and his court. The astrologer gasped in panic and ran to hide among the lattice separations. Hasam jumped to his feet.

A beat of silence throbbed by. Conflicting powers of will rolled across the seraglio garden in all its splendor—Sultan, rebel, victim. Their eyes met and pooled into indignation.

But once again, no time. The throbbing sound from behind the lattice walls began again, but this time it came not from hoofbeats but from the feet of men walking straight out of tradition and into history. The Sultan's lips parted, almost as though he knew. He drew a short breath.

The lattice walls trembled and came crashing down. A wall of soldiers replaced the vined partitions, clearing the way with their relentless numbers. Screaming, the harem women tried to cover their faces as they ran away, but there was hardly anywhere to run, for the lattice fences were coming down all around the seraglio under the feet of flanks upon flanks of soldiers. As the army moved, the fences toppled, including the fence that had hidden the astrologer. He went down beneath unknowing feet and was crushed to death before anyone realized he was there. Jessica saw him go down, his arms and legs convulsing upward in a single jolt before his body went limp. An unkind end, she thought, but one that befitted that man's way of thinking. A sudden wish to spare him poked in between her thoughts, but it was already too late, and she wondered if he would have afforded the same wish to anyone else.

She turned her attentions to Hasam. Before any victory could be claimed, the Sultan would have to be taken—alive. Thinking that her presence might help things go more smoothly, she urged her horse forward through the sea of uniforms. Then she saw someone else—the Kadin—and something within her soul gripped her horse's reins and turned them in that direction instead.

Tarik rode toward Hasam, toward a wall of swords. Forming a human blockade, the Sultan's personal guards held off the soldiers and gave their ruler time to escape. Tarik slipped from the saddle and fell in beside Salim. Together the two idealists came sword-to-sword with history.

Jessica reached the Kadin without knowing what she intended to do when she got there. She hoped the Kadin would try to escape, which would provide the perfect opportunity to kill her. Jessica was only partially surprised at her sudden bloodlust. If there was any one person who deserved her total contempt, it was this woman who looked up at her now.

The two women glared at each other, one from the flower-strewn ground, one from the grandeur of horseback. Jessica knew she wouldn't have to kill the Kadin herself; there were a half dozen soldiers following her who awaited her next order. If only the woman would try to run . . .

The Kadin nodded once to Jessica. Not exactly surrender . . . more of a tribute. The Sultan's first wife would not move, would not injure her dignity by scrambling for her life. Die she might but not that way. Jessica saw that the Kadin, who had sent so many to their deaths, understood dying from both sides of the coin.

Jessica returned the nod. To her soldiers she said, "Take her."

The men behind her gaped at each other and at the stunning, regal woman before them, not quite sure what to do. Her steadiness befuddled them. They didn't know how to touch her.

The Kadin clasped her hands elegantly beneath her breasts and stepped forward on her own. The men formed a line around her, following her as much as leading her away.

Jessica watched, holding her horse still, as the Kadin strode away in dignity. A tiny smile of admiration touched her lips, and she understood. She watched the Kadin disappear into the crowd, her passivity growing with each passing moment, contentment surging within her. Geisla's pretty, young face filled Jessica's mind, and unmendable regrets gave way to deeds she had followed through on. That thought squared her shoulders for her. Abruptly she reined the horse into a spiral beneath her, asking much of the animal to find footing among trampled flowers and slippery stepping-stones, and she looked around until she found Tarik. Only one thing remained to be done, and she was suddenly seething to do it. She had only one more message to deliver: that Jessica Grey did not die so easily.

While the takeover unfolded outside, the Sultan rummaged through a gilded cabinet and came up with several sets of official papers, which he crammed into the Kislar's arms. His hands were trembling slightly but not noticeably, and when he spoke, his voice still held the steadiness of a lifetime's worth of planning.

"See that the callers make these proclamations in the streets immediately."

The Kislar glanced over the documents, his face puzzled; he took a second look, just to be sure of what he saw. Shocked, he stared into his Sultan's glossy black eyes. "How long have you known about the revolution?" he demanded.

"We never *know* about anything," the Sultan responded instantly, "but we must be prepared for anything. Hurry, before you can no longer get out of the palace."

For the last time the Kislar bowed fully to the man who had ruled him all his life.

When he was alone, Hasam smoothed his robes and donned the majestic ostrich-plumed fez, a mark of his kingship, then walked down the long audience chamber to his throne. He put his hand on the carved wooden arm, pausing a moment before stepping up onto the platform and easing onto the velvet cushion. Absently he fingered one of the silver tassels next to his leg, inhaled a long, steadying breath, and leaned back. He fixed his eyes upon the ornate double doors at the far end of the audience chamber. In his mind he saw his enemies walking the maze of darkened passageways to the lit corridor outside those doors. He felt them touch the gold-encrusted handles as though the handles were his own limbs, the doors his body.

The doors swung open. Murat and Salim pushed the heavy wood aside and stood back, allowing the man and the woman to come between them into the audience chamber.

Tarik and Jessica walked together into the chamber, side by side, with a measured space between them to show their individuality. The space was not consciously made, but its effect was devastating.

Hasam gazed at them blandly, with cool assuredness. His eyes swept from Tarik to Jessica and held there. "You could have been my Kadin," he said. In his voice there was genuine regret.

"That time was gone," she told him, "even before we met." With her words she showed him that he had been losing his grip for years.

He raised his graying eyebrows and nodded slowly, his lips pursing. "I've been waiting for you."

His hand slipped under the arm of the chair, his tendons constricting.

Jessica sucked in her breath and screamed, "No!"

She hurtled sideways onto Tarik, driving him to the floor under a barrage of machine-gun fire. Round after round discharged in great roars over their heads as the cupboards full of Gatling guns ravaged each other from two opposite sides of the chamber. The sound was deafening. Jessica clutched Tarik's robes and felt his fingers digging into her back.

The barrage ended only when the guns had blasted each other to splinters. Smoke and the hot odor of gunpowder clouded the room. The gunfire fell away in fading echoes.

Tarik clutched Jessica's arms and looked hard

at her, making sure she hadn't been hit. They rolled to their feet, shaken, and looked back to see Murat and Salim cautiously lean back into the chamber from the corridor entranceway. Tarik nodded at them, too stunned to smile. He turned to Jessica again. "You seem to make a habit of saving my life today."

Furious, Murat raged past them then, Salim right behind him. Murat converged upon the Sultan with blade drawn. He strong-armed Hasam into Salim's grasp and lay his blade along the ruler's throat. "And who will save your life, eh?"

Calmly the Sultan said, "That matter has already been decided."

"What? What do you mean?"

"You will keep me alive," Hasam said. "You will use me to make a peaceful transition between our governments. I shall become a constitutional monarch—with no real power, of course. That is with the people now."

The Imperial caller walked through the crowds of elated citizens, trying to appear impassive to the embracing going on between Kurds, Greeks, Bulgars, and Armenians, as he announced the turning of an age.

"Sultan Hasam has issued a call for a general election, for a parliament! The Sultan wishes to bring equality to the Empire." The crowd cheered, and he was pleased to go on. "Muslims, Christians, Jews—no longer divided but working together for the glory of the Empire!" There was more cheering, and the caller ran onward, to carry his message to another part of the street.

Jessica and Tarik rode together out of the crowd, their faces placid.

"Today they celebrate their similarities," Tarik said, unable to avoid a little sentimental mistiness. "They celebrate the human bond that links all nationalities. But in a few days they'll remember their differences." He looked from the crowd to Jessica. "That's when the real work will begin."

"Is that why Murat said there will be no place for me in the new Turkey?" she asked, hiding a smirk.

"He said that?"

"He said there would be no place for the two of us together."

The truth made a twinge of pain in Tarik's face. "Where do you want to be?"

Jessica always thought she'd be able to voice her feelings when this moment came; she knew it would come, of course. Now she felt timid, even afraid. She seemed to have too many feelings to fill just one heart.

"Charles wants to return to England." Her voice lowered then. "We never talked about him."

"We don't have to," Tarik said. "We know he waits for you."

Jessica gazed at the reins in her hands. "What about you?"

Tarik now turned his eyes back over the pandemonium that was his badge of success. "My place has always been here." In the greatest act of generosity Jessica had ever seen in her life, Tarik reached over the gap between their horses and cupped his hand over hers. "I was part of your adventure," he said, "not part of your life."

Softly she asked one more thing of him. "I want to know that you loved me—at least for a while."

Tarik lifted her hand and gripped it with his own. "You rode with me today," was his strange answer. "You were unveiled. You led a revolution. Wouldn't that be enough for most American girls?"

Though Jessica understood what he meant, the honor he had bestowed upon her in gratitude for her bravery, she couldn't resist letting out the first words that popped into her mind. "I'm not most American girls."

Tarik withdrew his hand. "No, you're not."

How had Constantinople become so small? Mere seconds ago they had emerged from the palace gates, and now they entered the compound of the British embassy. Jessica was startled when she saw Tarik get down from his horse and walk around to her. Here already? No . . .

He helped her down from her saddle, took her hand, and pressed her fingers to the palm that waited a stride away. Tension drew the air snug among the three people as they stood alone in the embassy yard.

"Thank you for bringing her back," Charles said.

Tarik looked at Jessica. "It was her decision." Without ceremony he swung back onto his horse, catching Jessica's gaze one more time.

Charles read the lines written in their faces as he held Jessica's arm and felt the pressure. She wanted to go toward the horse. Charles would never be sure whether he had stopped her or she had stopped herself.

Tarik reined back, turned his horse, and rode out of the gates.

Both Jessica and Charles watched him go but with different emotions flying.

"I thought your apologies were because of what happened with the Sultan," Charles admitted.

Shaken from her trance, Jessica took his arm and turned him toward the embassy. "You said you were never going to ask."

By noon the next day, Jessica stood upon the platform where she had stepped from the train with her father so many months ago. How could so little time see so many changes? She had been wearing a Parisian dress then, too, not so unlike the pale green frock she wore today. Its dark jade ruffles reminded her of Usta, and the undergarments felt strange after the loose robes and simple chemises of the harem. Lady Ashley stood beside her, watching Charles and Sheikh Medjuel make final accommodations for several trunks of luggage.

"I keep remembering the first time we met,"

Lady Ashley said, baiting Jessica to test for her reaction. "Your Charles . . . he was so gallant."

Numbly Jessica said, "We both owe you so very much. . . ."

Lady Ashley gathered the younger woman against her. "Oh, Jessica," she said, "you've learned to live an adventure. I hope you can learn to put it aside."

But Jessica wasn't in a mood to be philosophical. "Did you?"

"Not very effectively. And never for very long."

Jessica nodded. "I'm doing the right thing."

"Of course you are. There are so many times when I miss England dreadfully," Lady Ashley admitted, "but it's impossible for me to go back now. You must realize that in a way, going back to England means opening up your options. But if you stay here, outside forces would determine what would happen to you."

The idea of anything, anyone, forcing her to do anything she wasn't inclined to do made Jessica writhe. She took Lady Ashley's arm and said, "We should be getting on board." The two women walked back to the men. Jessica waited until Charles looked up. "Is everything ready?" she asked.

"Seems that way," he said, his face full of questions. But he wouldn't ask. He straightened up and took Lady Ashley's hand, trying to find appropriate words for this kind of good-bye.

Jessica gazed past them, down the long platform to the open desert. Far, far out, a tiny cloud of dust rose, spinning and gusting. Someone was riding a horse, the kind of horse that knew how to run in thick sand. The revelation was startling.

Driven by impulse, Jessica walked alone down the long platform to the end and gazed out over the sea of sand while the little dust cloud grew larger and larger. Sanity caught up with her at about the same time Charles did.

"You're making a fool of yourself," he said, taking her elbow.

Her eyes were glued to the horizon. "I don't care."

"It's not him."

"Of course not."

"It couldn't be."

"I know."

It was a Bedouin. Indigo robes flew wildly as the nomad rode *djerid* across the sands, reveling in the thrills his ancestors had passed down through generations of desert dwellers.

"If it was him . . ." Charles began.

"If . . ."

Jessica's heart stirred. The rider drew closer.

Charles's hand fell away from her elbow. "I won't wait for you again," he said. No contempt, just plain truth. And it was only fair.

Now Jessica looked at him. She no longer had to gaze wishfully at the rider, for some things are known more clearly by the heart than by the eyes. "Charles, I'm sorry. I know—"

His finger touched her lips. He bent down

and replaced it with his lips for a delicate moment. Gallantly he turned and left her alone at the end of the platform.

The Bedouin chieftain descended upon the platform and hauled up hard on the reins. Wild-eyed, his horse snorted its protest and reeled back on its haunches. Sand flew.

Jessica waited.

The horse stomped the ground furiously.

"What do I do?" the rider asked her. "How do I get you to stay?"

Her voice came across the space between them as softly as the brush of a feather. "You ask me."

He reached for her. She extended her hand and gripped the thick folds of his robes while his arm went around her waist and scooped her up into the saddle with him. His shapeless desert robes enveloped her European finery in a sealike stream of blues and greens. The horse surged beneath them. The desert rolled out.

The Bosporus would be jealous.

About the Author

Diane Carey is the granddaughter of Assyrian emigrants who left Persia (Iran) as refugees during World War One. Raised in a bilingual household, she grew up thinking that everyone lived with Persian rugs, samovars, food wrapped in grape leaves, and line dancing. Since the Assyrians emigrated in larger groups, they tended to cluster in small communities and Diane has had no trouble maintaining contact with the Assyrian way of life. "Writing *Harem*," she says, "was rather like going home. All the flavors, sounds, and sensations were familiar." She lives in Michigan with her husband and collaborator, Gregory Brodeur, and thier little daughter, Lydia Rose Brodeur.

Buy them at your local
bookstore or use coupon
on next page for ordering.